Promises
UNBROKEN

D1261887

JANN BRITTAIN GARNER

ISBN 978-1-63525-882-0 (Paperback)
ISBN 978-1-63525-883-7 (Digital)

Christian Faith Publishing, Inc.
296 Chestnut Street
Meadville, PA 16335
www.christianfaithpublishing.com

Printed in the United States of America

Foreword

"Promise me. Promise me."

The words kept ringing in my ears as they lowered my mother's coffin into the cold, hard ground. How could she leave me? I especially needed her now. I looked at my father, who was all alone and seemingly in another world. He was crying, despite his best efforts to be strong for me and my little brother. This was just too much. Though his sobbing was silent, the tears running down his face were louder than any storm I'd ever witnessed. I wondered if he was thinking of the last few words my mother had ever so softly spoken to him. I knew that no matter what happened in our lives, my mother's faith and love for us would always prevail.

I didn't know if I should scream or cry or just run away from the awful reality unfolding before my eyes. Maybe, just maybe, if I ran away, all of this would stop. Then our lives would return to normal. My only thoughts were, "Why, God? Why did you take her? I needed her more than you did." If God really loved me, he wouldn't have taken her from me. I was so angry at him, at my mother, at the world. It just wasn't fair that so much had happened in these last few months that were leading up to these next few weeks...or perhaps even the next few years.

Chapter One

It was spring break. I was looking forward to my time off from school and the chance to visit with my family. The first thing I saw as I was pulling into the driveway was my mother standing on the front porch, calling my name with her arms outstretched.

"Beth, hurry over here and give me a kiss! I just need to hold my little girl." Mom knew I would just cringe when she called me her "little girl." I was, after all, in my freshman year of college. I was an adult.

Suddenly, I heard the screen door creak open. My father stepped outside carrying my two-year-old brother, Jonathen, in his arms. "Hold me, hold me!" his little voice insisted, giggling and looking at me with his turned-up angelic face. I took him from my father's arms and held him. His tiny fingers played with the brightly colored ribbons I had woven through my long ponytail.

My little brother was a surprise pregnancy for my parents. At the time, I was getting ready to graduate high school, and my mother was getting ready to have a baby. I couldn't help but be embarrassed whenever my friends would tease me about finally becoming a "big sister."

My mother definitely wasn't like the other moms I knew. Sometimes I would wonder why she had to be so different. She never missed an opportunity to let me know how much she loved me, even going so far as to openly express her love for me to my friends. I always knew I could count on her. I could tell her anything, and if something was ever wrong, she always seemed to know how to make it right. She had this amazing ability to sense things about me, even things I chose not to tell her. Mom prayed a lot. It was as if she had a direct line of communication to God. I tried to be a good daughter and a good student, but sometimes I just got caught up in trying to be part of "the in crowd."

One morning, after I arrived home from school, is one that I will never forget. I was in my old bedroom, just lying on my bed. The breeze from the open window was gently blowing on my face as the aroma of fried apples wafted from the kitchen. I sure had missed mom's cooking since I had left home for my first year of college. As I lay there, I could hear my mother praying as she was preparing our breakfast. I knew she was asking God to somehow bring her family to him and to keep his hand of protection over us. Mom would always pray that our family would someday be in heaven together. I have many cards from my mom; and in each of them, she would ask me to promise her to meet her in heaven. It wasn't unusual for her to ask all of her loved ones to make that promise as well. I was raised in church, so I never thought too much about her words. I guess you could say that I had grown accustomed to hearing them. I knew the right way to go, but after I had left home, it just seemed easier to give that up in order to fit in with the rest of my so-called friends. If I didn't think about the things that my parents had taught me, if I pushed their words aside, everything would be okay…or so I thought.

My mother's voice broke through my thoughts. "Beth, come on down for breakfast! I made your favorites."

I couldn't wait to eat. I descended the stairs, my mouth watering all the way down to the kitchen. My family huddled around the table and, as usual, Mom said, "Let's all hold hands and thank God for our many blessings." Then she added, "And for allowing Beth to come home safely to us." We all joined hands and my father began to pray. With the same breath, he told my brother to quit squirming in his chair. I tried not to laugh, but I just couldn't help myself.

My mother glanced up at me with her big, beautiful blue eyes. She didn't say a word, but I it was obvious she didn't want me to laugh—though I could see a smile creeping across her face.

Just as my father was finishing the prayer, a knock came from the front door.

"Who could that be?" my father muttered.

I watched as he answered the door, then slipped outside and closed the door behind him. Mom wanted us to wait until my father returned to eat, so I tried to pass the time by twirling my fingers through my little brother's curly blonde hair. My father was gone for just a short time, but I sure was getting hungry for those fried apples and over-sized biscuits. Just then, Dad walked back into the kitchen. My back was facing away from the door, but heard him say, "Beth, you have a visitor on the front porch."

It wasn't like my father to not invite someone into our home. I silently asked myself, "Who could it be this early in the morning?" Without asking my father who the visitor was, I simply excused myself from the table and decided to see for myself. I couldn't believe my eyes. It was Brian, my high school sweetheart.

My parents didn't like Brian very much. He was a restless soul and was always living on the edge. He also hated to attend church, but he would go with my family every now and then to appease my parents. My mother knew I was in love with him, although she did not approve. She would frequently tell me she was praying for me to make the right decisions in life, and evidently she did not think Brian was one of them.

I hadn't seen or talked to Brian since I had left over a year ago. He didn't want me to go to college, but after a big fight, we broke up. As I looked at him standing on my front porch right then, I couldn't help but wonder, "Why is he here?" I couldn't imagine why he wanted to see me.

I said hello and he gave me a big hug. I knew my parents would be able to hear us talking, so I shut the front door and sat down on the porch steps with him.

"Beth," he said to me, "I heard you were coming home and couldn't wait to see you again. How are you? Are you doing okay? I've missed you so much, Beth. I've changed."

He then proceeded to tell me how sorry he was for how he acted before I left for college. His apologies seemed to go on for an eternity, and I couldn't get a word in edgewise. As soon his apologies ceased, he was asking me to go out with him for that evening. I didn't know what to do or say. I still loved him, but I definitely didn't want to get hurt again. I asked him to call me later that day, and I would give him my answer then. We exchanged goodbyes, and I walked back into the kitchen. My parents pretended nothing out of the ordinary was going on, but I could see the apprehension in their faces. I had seen those looks before.

We all had finished eating, but somehow the fried apples and over-sized biscuits had lost their appeal. Perhaps it was because my mind was on Brian and his offer to take me on a date that night. Dad took my little brother by the hand, excusing himself. I watched my father take him to play on the swing set that had been mine when I was Jonathen's age. My father had built that swing set for me, and now I was enjoying Jonathen playing on it.

I turned to my mother, who was at the kitchen sink, and offered to help with the dishes. I could sense that she wanted to talk to me. Even though she didn't say a word, I believe she knew what had happened on the front porch with Brian.

"Mom," I began, "Brian wants me to go out with him tonight. I need to know what I should do."

My mom, who was listening carefully, stopped doing the dishes, wiped her hands on the dishcloth, and took my hands in her own. "Sit down with me, Beth. We can finish the dishes later."

My mother always had time to listen to me. It seemed that no matter what I did, even if it wasn't what she wanted to hear, I knew that she loved me and would be there for me no matter what.

"Well, what do you think, Mom?" I prodded.

"Beth, pray and take a little time and ask God what he wants you to do," was her reply. Of course, this was Mom's answer for everything. "Be careful, Beth. Something just doesn't seem right."

As we finished the dishes, I kept asking myself if I should take Mom's advice. I knew that I should, but I needed to go for a walk and mull everything over first. I was so confused and homesick. I just wanted to rest and relax for a while. Home was my safe haven, and now I was faced with this decision.

As I began to walk down the street and around the block, the morning sun beamed upon my face. I asked the Lord what he wanted me to do. I told him I knew I hadn't talked to him for a long time and that I was sorry. I just really needed his help on this one. A part of me reiterated, "It won't hurt just to go out for one night with Brian."

I had really missed him. I missed his arms around me. Brian and I were very close while we were dating. I wanted to stay pure until I was married. Although Brian would protest my decision to do so, he still respected my wishes.

I wrestled in my mind whether or not I should go out with him again. I reached the conclusion that just one date would be okay. After all, I would be leaving soon to return to college.

When I returned home from my walk around the block, my mom was in the backyard, hanging her bed sheets on the line. I walked between the sheets that were blowing in the wind and caught my mother's eye.

"Have you made your decision yet?"

I bristled. "I'll be alright, Mom. I'm an adult, and besides, just one date won't hurt. I can handle Brian. I promise I'll spend more time at home before I leave."

She looked unsure. "I hope you've prayed about this, Beth. I can't make your decisions for you, but please promise me you'll be careful."

I promised I would and helped her hang the rest of the sheets. Afterwards, I went inside to wait for Brian's phone call. He told me he would be calling me at two o'clock that afternoon, and it was already noon. I was excited to inform Brian that I had decided to go out with him, after all.

The anticipation of his phone call was a little intimidating. I was convinced I had made the right decision, but a part of me wasn't so sure. The phone's shrill ring sliced through the rampage of thoughts threatening to consume me. It was Brian.

I hesitated to answer the phone. I didn't want Brian to know how nervous I was for his call, of course. The enthusiasm in his voice was all too apparent when I divulged my final decision to him, and he agreed to pick me up at seven that night.

I tried to stay busy until seven o'clock rolled around, but it was very difficult to do. The memories of the last time I had gone out with Brian were still fresh in my mind. I waited for what seemed like forever. That's when I heard the doorbell ring.

My parents were snuggled on the couch watching Andy Griffith, one of their favorites, so I knew my father would not answer the door. He wasn't about to miss this episode, especially since he could practically tell you what was going to happen next with Andy and Mayberry.

I bounded towards the door and ushered Brian inside. I notified my parents that we were leaving and would be back in a couple of hours. My mother would worry if we stayed out too late, and I knew she would stay awake until our date was over. It didn't matter how old I was—I was nonetheless Momma's little girl, and she would be waiting up for me until I was back home.

Brian still had his beautiful red Camaro, all shined up and ready to go. He opened the passenger door for me like a gentleman. He had never done that before, and I deliberated on the fact that maybe Brian really had changed.

We decided to eat at a local diner to talk and get reacquainted. I saw a lot of my old friends there. The group of us exchanged fond memories and laughs that brought a wave of nostalgia over me.

After all my old friends left, Brian suggested going to our favorite spot, down by the lake. I loved to watch the sunsets there. It was especially beautiful in the springtime, so I agreed to go with him for a little while.

We arrived at the lake just as the sun was beginning to set. As we watched the sun go down, Brian and I reminisced about old memories we shared together. He grew quiet after a few minutes, so I asked him if something was wrong. He assured me nothing was wrong, but that he needed to ask me a few things.

"Brian, what is it?" I said.

He paused a few moments before telling me what was on his mind. He asked me if I was seeing anyone and if I was still waiting for marriage before I had sex. I was hesitant to answer, but I knew I had to tell him the truth. I assured him I wasn't seeing anyone and that I was still going to wait until marriage before I had any relations with a man.

"That's good," was his response, but I noticed something in his voice and the way he was looking at me wasn't quite right. Something inside of me instinctively quivered with fear, and I knew right then that I had made the wrong decision to go out with him tonight.

Brian leaned over to kiss me. I pushed him away from me, but he was so much stronger than I was. He kept saying to me how much he loved me and that he knew I would return to him someday. He went on to mumble weird things, like saying what I had was his and always would be. The more I resisted him, the more he tore at my clothes. I was so devastated and scared. All I could do was pray and ask God for help. Before I could get away from Brian, he had taken the most precious thing I owned away from me: my virginity.

I was numb from what had just happened. I hastened to get dressed and demanded that Brian take me home. It was silent all the way back to my house. As we pulled into my driveway, Brian yelled out, "I love you, Beth! Remember that you're mine, and you always will be." I dashed into the house. All I cared about was getting home, where I would be safe.

I could hear the sound of running water in my mother's bathtub. I didn't want her to hear me come in, so I scrambled upstairs to my room and crawled into bed. As I lay there trying to somehow erase this horrible incident from my life, I heard voices and a knock on my door. I couldn't tell my parents about this. I swallowed hard and wiped the tears away. Then I sat up in bed clutching the quilt Mom had made me, attempting to plaster a smile on my face.

"Come in," I called out weakly.

My parents were smiling as they came into my room. They wanted to know how my date was. I lied and said it was just fine. When my parents hugged me goodnight, I somehow managed to keep my composure. It was all I could do not to scream and blurt out the truth.

The next few days were very hard for me. I just wanted to stay home forever with my family, but it was almost time to go back to school and forget what had happened.

The day before I was to leave, Brian called me. I held the phone close to my mouth and hissed, "Don't ever call me again, Brian, and please get out of my life." I hung up the phone and proceeded to get ready to leave home. The anger I felt for Brian was almost too much to handle, but I knew I had to keep silent in order to protect both myself and my family.

My departure day had finally come. I stood on the front porch with my family. I didn't want to leave them, but I needed to get away from this place. I had to try to forget what Brian had taken from me.

My baby brother wrapped his arms around my legs, begging me to stay and play with him. I affectionately pressed my cheek to his and promised I would return soon. My father tried to be gentle when he hugged me, but ended up squeezing so tightly that he almost lifted me off my feet. I hugged him back as he murmured, "I love you, Elizabeth. Don't ever forget that." I told him that I loved him, too. I could see my mother standing there with open arms, anxiously awaiting her hug.

As soon as my mother's arms folded around me, I felt as though I would collapse. All I wanted was for her to hold me and never let go. I wanted to let her know about what happened with Brian, but I knew I couldn't do that. I inhaled my mom's perfume as we embraced. She kissed my cheek and whispered into my ear, words that I would always remember.

"Promise me, Beth, that if you ever need me, just call and I'll be there. Please, Beth, promise me."

I promised her I would and stepped off the porch. I turned to see my family standing there, my mother wiping her eyes with her apron. My father's arms curled around her, and my little brother gazed through the slats of the banister. I dashed to my car and honked my horn to them. Then I drove away as fast as I could, waving to them as I disappeared out of sight. That's when the tears started flowing like a leak that couldn't be fixed. I just wanted this to be the end of my horrible ordeal, but what I didn't know was that this was just the beginning.

Chapter Two

I arrived back at college. After getting settled down, I focused on resuming my studies and pretending as though everything was okay with me. If I kept smiling and burying my nose in my textbooks, everything would be back to normal.

One day my mother called me, and I could tell by the sound of her voice that she wanted to discuss something serious.

"Beth, are you alright?" Her voice was tight and strained.

"I'm fine," I assured her. I hoped she couldn't tell that I was lying.

"I had a dream of you last night. In my dream, you were screaming for me and you were really scared."

I told her that it was only a dream, but she said that she was sure God had given the dream to her. I believed that God had indeed given her the dream, but saying I agreed would mean the dream was actually true. I longed to share my secret with her, but I knew she would be devastated, and I loved her too much to hurt her. We conversed for a while, and before we hung up, my mother once again reminded me to call her if I ever needed her.

"You're still my little girl, Beth, no matter how old you are," she continued.

"Mom, please! I'm not a little girl anymore," I protested.

She replied, "You'll always be a little girl to me, and never forget how much I love you."

"Okay, Mom," I muttered.

We both said goodbye, and the conversation came to an end.

In my heart, I knew God had given Mom that dream. I just couldn't worry her, so I pretended the dream would somehow go away. What my mother didn't know was that my father had written me a letter telling me Mom wasn't feeling well. He was trying to get her to go see the doctor, but she had refused. My mom didn't need to know what had happened to me, especially not since she was going through her own issues. Consequently, I kept my secret to myself.

A few weeks passed. Though I tried to stay busy with homework, I kept feeling really sick. A virus was going around my school, so I naturally assumed I was just feeling the effects of it. I felt better in a couple of days, and the virus went away—or so I thought.

The very next week, I started to feel ill again. I decided to go to the doctor because I needed to study, and I wouldn't be able to so long as I felt this way. The doctor examined me and took several blood tests.

"You're healthy as can be. Just go home and rest; I'll call you with the results of your test," the doctor confirmed.

I retreated to my dorm room, relief washing over me. There was no reason to feel worried now. The doctor said I was going to be okay.

Two days had elapsed since my doctor's visit. I was tangled up in a web of homework when my phone rang. I answered it, only to hear a voice I did not recognize. It was my doctor's nurse, and she explained that my doctor wanted me to come into his office so he could disclose the results of my blood tests. The assistant scheduled my appointment for the following day.

The morning of my doctor's appointment, my stomach coiled in knots over the results of my blood tests. I quickly dressed and went to the office. My doctor shuffled into the room, clutching my chart in his hands.

He sure is young-looking. Does he even know what he's doing? I thought.

I took the opportunity to ask him how old he was.

He laughed at my question. "I'm twenty-nine. I've only been in this practice for a short time." His facial expression changed when he looked down at my chart, and my heart began to hammer inside my chest. Something had to have been wrong. He was just too somber this time around—a vast difference from only two days before, when he confidently declared that nothing was wrong with me.

"Beth, we have your results back." There was a pause. "You're pregnant."

I sat there in a daze for a second, not really hearing what the doctor had said.

"Are you okay?" he asked gently. His words gradually started to sink in, and that's when I felt like screaming.

"No, I—I can't be!" I stammered. "You're wrong, the tests are wrong!"

The doctor calmly verified the tests were run twice and had come back positive both times—that I was pregnant. I said he must have picked up the wrong chart.

"No, Beth, I have the correct chart right here. You're pregnant, and I want you to see an obstetrician as soon as possible."

I left the office in a complete fog. I couldn't even recall the drive back to my dorm. As soon as I was back in my room, the events from the past few weeks swirled around in my head. I remember calling out to God and asking him to please help me. I was terrified. I had no idea what I was going to do now. Then the awful truth exploded in my mind. What about my parents? What was I going to tell them? What were people from my little hometown going to say about me? I could already hear their snarky voices gossiping about the "good girl" who got pregnant and by whom?

I was reminded of Mom telling me to call on Jesus when I needed him or anytime I was in trouble. My body was trembling, so much so that I couldn't even clasp my hands to pray.

I cried out to God, "Please help me, please help me! Oh, God, please just help me! I need to know what to do, and you're the only one who can help me now." Through choking sobs, I pleaded his forgiveness for not listening to his voice when he warned me of going to the lake with Brian that awful, horrible night.

The sky had begun to get dark before I could stop crying. I was exhausted after such a long day. I curled into bed and tried to sleep, but sleep would not come. A loud knock startled me out of my quiet state of rest.

Who could that be? I thought.

I dragged my weary body to the door. To my shock, it was the very person I needed most at that moment: my mother.

"Beth, God sent me here. He said you needed me, so I want to know what's wrong. I drove as fast as I could to get here." Her blue eyes flooded with worry.

My college was a four-hour drive from home. I had only been back from the doctor a few hours. How could she have known so quickly?

I perched on the edge of my bed and patted the spot next to me, motioning for her to sit down. My mom impulsively reached out to cradle me in her arms. God knows our futures before we do, and I knew at that moment he had sent her. I was awestruck of how the Lord knew I needed her to be with me during that dark hour. I silently sent up a prayer of gratitude to him.

The words fled my lips almost automatically. "Mom, I'm pregnant."

"You're what?" My mother recoiled; then she rattled off a series of questions. Who was the father? Did I love him? Was I okay?

"I'm alright," was my feeble reply. "I need to confess something else, though."

The words leapt out of her throat. "What is it?"

I blinked furiously to try to prevent the tears from giving way, but it was no use. My throat threatened to close up, and my vision started to blur.

"Mom, I was raped." My voice broke. That's when my body convulsed into choking, heart-wrenching sobs. Through my hazy vision, I saw tears streak my mother's face as well. I'm not sure who cried the hardest—me, or my mom.

My mother was beginning to get angry then, and demanded to know who did this to me.

"I will take care of him. I will do what has to be done." She spoke with a quiet fury, one that sent chills racing down my spine. The anger was not directed at me, but towards the man that had committed this appalling act against her daughter. I was her little girl, and no one was going to hurt me without hearing from my mother.

When I finally got her to calm down, I told her Brian was the one who had raped me the night I went out with him.

Mom breathed out a heavy sigh. "Well, that explains a lot of things."

What did she mean? What did she know that I didn't know? Was she going to explain to me what she meant?

"Beth, after you left for school, Brian suddenly moved away. He didn't even tell his parents he was leaving or where he was going. They haven't heard from him since."

There was a pause before she continued. "It's going to be okay. Your dad and I will always be here for you, and God will help us get through this."

Oh my gosh. I forgot about telling my father! Mom said I needed to return home with her, and we would tell him together. I sure needed God more than ever to help me tell my father the horrible truth and how it happened.

My mother's reassurance that everything would be alright was the answer to my prayers. I drifted off to sleep in her arms, the safest place I knew.

I awoke with a start the next morning, my mother's arms wound tight around me. I turned to see that Mom was sleeping with her coat and shoes still on. I guess we both had dozed off as a result of yesterday's exhausting events. I didn't want to disturb her, but she woke up when I stirred in her arms.

"Honey, are you okay? Did we fall asleep and stay here all night? What time is it?"

Her questions went unanswered, as I suddenly felt very queasy and light-headed. I ran for the bathroom, crying as I left the comfort of my mom's arms. I was so sick to my stomach: I was starting to have morning sickness. I felt two very warm hands wiping my brow and sweeping my long hair away from my face.

"It's alright, Beth," my mom consoled me. "Morning sickness will go away soon."

Now I knew for sure that I was pregnant. This was not a dream, but a reality.

My mother continuously wiped my forehead with a cool, damp cloth, repeating: "You will get through this and everything will work out. Just trust God, Beth. He holds your future in his hands."

I knew I would have to leave school and go home with my mom. Saying goodbye to my friends would be hard, but it had to be done. I sort of misled my friends and reassured them I would see them in the fall. That wasn't true, of course, but how could I tell them the real reason for leaving in the middle of the semester?

My mother assisted me in packing my clothes and personal items before our departure. She was so proud of me when I started college, so I knew this must have been breaking her heart.

Mom was awfully quiet most of the drive home. Occasionally, she would sing a song we both knew, but I was sure she was doing it just to try to keep our thoughts and feelings intact. Since it was the weekend, my father would be home when we arrived. I had to calm down and prepare to face my father.

I could see my little brother waving to us as we pulled into the driveway. He was ready for his "big sissy" to start playing with him.

My father, who assumed my mom and I would be hungry after our long drive home, had cooked us a big meal. The aroma of my favorite foods hit me as soon as I stepped foot into the house: pinto beans, fried potatoes, corn bread, and tall glasses of cold milk. Oh my word! The instant I smelled the food, I became nauseated and made a beeline for the bathroom. I heard my father ask my mom if I was alright.

"She'll be okay. She just isn't feeling well," my mom said.

Dad seemed to accept her explanation for the time being. "I didn't know my cooking was so bad that it would make my little girl sick," he joked.

Oh, no! Now he was calling me his little girl! I knew he would be devastated and furious once he learned the truth.

I made my way out onto the front porch and sat down on the steps. I inhaled slow, deep breaths to help sort out my feelings. The smell of the flowers my mom had planted last spring seemed to soothe my upset stomach. The screen door opened behind me, and I felt two big, warm hands on my shoulders. It was my father, and he had brought me a cold glass of Coke to settle my stomach. I accepted the drink and took small sips of it. Dad thought a cold Coke could heal most any ailment. It tasted good, and it did help—for a moment, anyway.

My father sat down beside me. I knew he wanted to talk.

"Elizabeth, I'm so glad you're home. The family misses you so much when you're gone."

My little brother, Jonathen, appeared at the front door. He kept staring at us through the screen and saying, "Daddy, Daddy."

I could sense something was the matter, so I asked him, "Where's Mommy?"

Before Jonathen could answer, Dad bolted inside the house.

I heard my father crying out, "Hannah! Hannah, are you alright? Answer me, Hannah! Are you alright?"

I jumped up from the steps and went to see what was going on. My mother was lying on the floor. She had passed out, and my father could not revive her.

"Call 9-1-1!" Dad screamed at me, and I rushed to do so.

The fire station was just around the corner from our house. It was only a few minutes before the medics arrived. I rocked my little brother in my arms as the medics tried to help my mother. I knew Jonathen was scared, and I didn't want him to start crying.

The EMTs said my mother's blood pressure was dropping too quickly. Although my mother was still breathing, I could see it was quite shallow. I prayed for God to please help her.

My father was relaying to the EMTs that my mother had been feeling ill, but she would not go to the doctor. My mom thought she would feel better in a few days. Her mantra was "things will get better tomorrow." How wrong she was this time.

Mom woke up and opened her eyes right then. She couldn't say very much, but at least she could still talk to me. My father insisted she go to the hospital and, to my surprise, my mother agreed to go.

I watched as they loaded Mom into the ambulance. My father said he would call me from the hospital as soon as he found out anything.

"Take care of Jonathen," Dad said.

I promised him I would. Then I leaned over my mother and told her I loved her. I'm not sure if she heard me.

The neighbors saw the ambulance at our house. They rushed over to see if everything was okay and if they could do anything to help. Those that didn't come over to see what was wrong called to offer their help. Everyone was so thoughtful and caring, and I knew I could call on them for any help I needed.

While Mom and Dad were at the hospital, I did my best to keep Jonathen entertained with his toys and favorite cartoons on the television. He was just two years old, but he could sense that something was not right. I tried to reassure him that Mommy would be okay, that she would be home soon.

The time ticked by at an agonizingly slow rate. It had been two hours since Mom had left for the hospital, and no one had called me. The doorbell's ring interrupted my anxiety, and I went to go answer it. It was Pastor Johnson and his wife. My father had called to notify them about my mom. Mrs. Johnson could tell that I was a bundle of nerves. A mother's instinct can always discern when a child is upset or in trouble. The pastor and his wife have five children of their own, so I knew Mrs. Johnson could perceive how scared I really was.

Pastor Johnson asked if we could have a time of prayer for my mom and my family. I eagerly accepted his suggestion, and we all joined hands to pray. I felt so much better afterwards. I trusted Pastor Johnson and his wife. I had known them all my life. My family could depend on them to be there for us anytime we needed them.

We all sat and waited for my father's phone call together. At long last, Dad called. He let me know that Mom was doing okay, but that he wanted me to come to the hospital.

"I need you to take my car. The car keys should be in my bedroom," he said.

I told him the Johnsons were at the house with me. Dad requested to speak to Pastor Johnson, so I handed the phone over.

Though I attempted to eavesdrop on their conversation, I could only catch certain words, like "yes" and "okay."

Then I heard Pastor Johnson tell my dad, "I'll come over to the hospital and bring Beth with me. My wife will take care of Jonathen."

There was no doubt in my mind that Jonathen would be just fine with the pastor's wife. Mrs. Johnson was my little brother's Sunday school teacher, and Jonathen loved her a lot.

I barreled to the car to go see my mother. I still wasn't feeling well, but I wanted to be with her. The hospital was only about twenty minutes away, so I forced myself to calm down until Pastor Johnson and I got there. It didn't take long to get there, but it felt like an eternity to me.

I sprinted to the front desk and inquired about my mother's room number. A young man—who looked to be about my age—directed us to the room. Pastor Johnson and I waited for the elevator in the lobby. It seemed like the elevator wasn't going to stop on our floor anytime soon, so we decided it would be quicker to take the stairs instead.

We located my mom's room. My father greeted me with a hug and Pastor Johnson, a handshake. When I turned to redirect my attention to my mom, she was smiling as though nothing was wrong. I leaned over to give her a kiss and tell her I loved her. She smiled and assured me she was fine, that the Lord had already been there and things would be alright. I wondered how Mom could be so calm when all of this was happening so suddenly. Somehow my mother always knew how to make others feel better, even if she wasn't okay herself.

I swiveled toward my dad to ask him about what the doctors had said in regards to Mom's health, but Pastor Johnson offered to lead us in prayer before I got the chance to speak. I gently took Mom's hand. She still managed to raise her hands and pray despite her I.V. The presence of God was truly in the room, and I knew my mom had been right when she said the Lord was there.

After our time of prayer, I noticed a dark-haired man had come in the room. He had been quietly waiting for us to finish. He introduced himself as Dr. Todd Daniels. He graciously shook our hands after we told him who we were. Then he proceeded to go to my mother's bedside.

My father asked the doctor if he had gotten the results back from the tests that they had run on Mom. I had no clue what type of tests were done, so I was on pins and needles to know what the results were. Dr. Daniels said most of the tests were fine, but that he was concerned with one of them.

"It's the CAT scan, isn't it?" my mom said.

His grave reply was, "Yes. There is a mass on your brain."

My father tried to appear strong and undaunted, but his face suddenly went ashen.

Dr. Daniels requested Mom to stay at the hospital a few more days so he could take a closer look at the mass. My mother consented—however, she made it crystal clear that she would stay a few days and that was all. She had a family to care for, she said, and no one else could take care of them like she could. That was my mother: resilient, determined, and devoted to her loved ones.

I watched the staff parade in and out of Mom's room as the day dragged on, taking blood tests and changing IVs. My mother was so patient with them, that sometimes I felt like she was Superwoman.

After hours had ticked by, Mom urged us to head home. She was getting tired and concerned that Jonathen would be restless and crying. Though I wanted to stay with her, I knew it was time to head home. I kissed her goodbye, told her I loved her, and promised to visit again tomorrow. My father lingered a few minutes after Pastor Johnson and I left. I'm sure he had some personal things to say to my mother. Pastor did his best to comfort me on the way back to the car, saying that it would be alright. I prayed silently and wanted to believe that my mother would make it through this.

When we got home, we were met at the door with the sound of Jonathen wailing, just as my mother had guessed. He was scared and wanted to see Mom. I picked him up and started to tickle him, which always seemed to help, but he saw Dad and jumped right into our father's arms. Jonathen started to cry again and asked for Mom, to which Dad said that she was okay.

My father led Jonathen into the kitchen for milk and cookies, and they offered me some as well. My little brother went crazy for Mom's cookies. Our mother always made sure to put M&M's in them, since that was Jonathen's favorite kind of candy. I still wasn't feeling too well, but I pretended to eat the cookies so my baby brother would be happy again.

It was getting very late. My dad and I were both exhausted. I got Jonathen ready for bed and started telling him stories. It didn't take long before a smile spread across his angelic face, and his little eyes were slowly starting to close. I waited at his bedside until I was sure he'd fallen asleep, and then softly closed his bedroom door. I passed my father's bedroom. The door was slightly open, and I could see Dad on his knees, praying and clutching my mother's favorite bathrobe. I tried to be very quiet as I rushed down the hallway to my room, not wanting my father to know I had seen him praying. I accidentally stumbled into a small table that was sitting by my bedroom door. A small vase fell from the table and broke into a million pieces.

My father heard the noise and ran up to where I was kneeling on the floor, trying to gather all the pieces of my mother's vase. "Beth, what happened? Are you okay?"

I felt horrible for breaking the vase, but my father knelt beside me and told me it was alright. He wanted me to go to bed, so I hugged him goodnight and told him I loved him. He returned the hug and reassured me that things would be better in the morning.

I hadn't taken the time to unpack my suitcase—it was still sitting on my bedroom floor. I usually took a hot shower before bed to help me sleep, but this night was different. I was just too tired and worried to bother with a shower. My mother had left my room just as it was before I left for college, so I knew I would have clean pajamas in my drawer. I changed into my cozy PJs and crawled into bed. It had been a very long day for all of us, so I don't even remember falling asleep.

Chapter Three

The following morning, I was awakened by Jonathen calling my name and tugging at the blankets on my bed.

He laughed and yelled, "Sissy, get up! I want to play."

My goodness, what time is it?

I glanced over at the clock and noted it was only seven o'clock in the morning. I attempted to roll over and go back to sleep. My lovable, energetic little brother would have no part in this, however, and so I reluctantly got out of bed.

Dad was already bustling about in the kitchen cooking breakfast. I could smell the bacon frying, and for once I didn't feel sick to my stomach. My father asked how I was feeling, and I returned with, "I'm doing okay." My father still had no clue about Brian or my pregnancy, and I wanted to keep it that way for as long as I could. Consequently, I prayed I wouldn't get sick and lose my breakfast.

I made it through our meal without any bouts of morning sickness, thank God. We all dressed and got ready to visit my mother at the hospital. Then my father and I waited until Mrs. Johnson arrived at our house to pick up Jonathen for the day.

Upon our arrival at the hospital, my father and I swiftly made our way up the elevator, down the hall, and into my mother's room. Panic struck our hearts as we entered her room: the bed was empty.

I ran down the hall to track down a nurse. The nurse told me my mother had been taken downstairs to have an X-ray and MRI. She said Mom would be back in her room shortly, so my dad and I nervously waited to see her. She was wheeled into her room about an hour later. As usual, she was smiling and ready to go home. I knew she would not be going home for a few more days, though, since the doctor wanted to do more tests. We sat and chatted with my mom while waiting for the doctor to come in.

The doctor showed up about an hour later. He talked with us for a few seconds. Then he politely asked if we could turn the TV down to discuss the results of mom's tests. The doctor called my mother by her first name—Hannah—and that worried me because I could see the concern etched on his face.

"Hannah, I want to do a biopsy on the mass, and I need your consent to do so. I would like to do it this afternoon, if that is at all possible," he was saying.

I was so distressed that I couldn't help but blurt out, "What's the hurry?"

The doctor looked at me curiously, then ignored my outburst and refocused his attention to my parents. "I'm here for the day, and the operating room is available for a few hours this afternoon. With your consent, we will go ahead and schedule the procedure."

Oh, boy. Do they usually have the tests and the surgery in one day? I thought.

After carefully pondering the doctor's words, my mother agreed to have the surgery done that day. My family had a short time of prayer before the surgical team came to transport my mother to the operating room. It seemed as though Mom was there for an eternity. I kept pestering my father: "How much longer? Do you think she's okay?" I noticed it was already eight in the evening The nurse finally came out to tell us that my mom was doing just fine and that the surgery was almost completed.

At long last, the nurse came out to take my father and me to the consultation room, where we would be meeting with the doctor. Dr. Daniels walked in and informed us my mom was resting and the surgery went well, but that he wouldn't have the results until tomorrow morning. He encouraged us to go home for the night because Mom would be asleep for quite a while. The doctor gave us permission to see her, but that we couldn't disturb her. Dad and I tiptoed into the room, where Mom was sound asleep. She looked so peaceful, and I remembered when she had said, "The Lord is here, so don't worry." I clung to those words as we whispered goodbye and headed home.

The last few days had been so stressful on my dad, as well as me. I felt like I was in a daze and had forgotten something. We had just pulled into the driveway when I remembered what we forgot.

"Oh my goodness! Jonathen!" I cried.

My father and I hopped back into the car, exchanging amused looks. How could we have forgotten my little brother? Mom would sure be mad at us if she knew. Dad and I just smiled and agreed not to tell her of our blunder.

The laughter seemed good for us. It helped to relieve our mind of the past few days. I could see Pastor Johnson's house from a distance. I knew Jonathen would be excited to see us and go home to see his mommy. He was too young to realize the seriousness of our mother's health.

Before we got to the pastor's house, we had to go past our little church, which sat directly in front of the Johnsons home. The night was pitch-black, but a small glimmer of light was shining through the clouds that covered the moon. I could see just a hint of light illuminate the stained glass windows of the church. I recalled as a child how beautiful and scary I thought it looked after dark. Somehow, in my childish imagination, I thought that God—as well as the angels—lived in that church. I could still hear the preacher tell us, "This is God's house. You children should be good, because God is watching and he sees everything you do."

My thoughts were interrupted as we parked the car and headed towards Pastor Johnson's house. Dad pressed the doorbell, and the shrill sound seemed to pierce the eerily quiet night.

Pastor came to the door with his index finger on his lips. "Shh, Jonathen is asleep," he whispered.

I peered over his shoulder at my little brother, who was curled up on the couch. It looked like he was wrapped in a huge black, furry blanket, but it was just the Johnsons' big black Sheepdog. It was a precious sight, seeing Jonathen and the dog cuddled up together. I wished I had a camera to capture the moment.

My father stepped over to Jonathen to pick him up and take him home with us, but Mrs. Johnson entered the room. Mrs. Johnson gushed about Jonathen's good behavior, and then told my father she had already fed Jonathen dinner before reading him a story. She mentioned how my baby brother had fallen asleep in her arms, and then she suggested that Jonathen spend the night at their house. My dad consented with some reluctance, offering to pick Jonathen up early the next morning. I reminded Dad that we had to be at the hospital early the following morning. He apologized for not remembering, and excused his forgetfulness on the huge strain of my mother's health condition. Mrs. Johnson insisted that we go to the hospital as planned, that she would continue to care for Jonathen at her home as long as necessary. My father thanked the Johnsons for their concern and all of their help with Jonathen. Then we quietly slipped back out to the car.

"Be as quiet as you can when you close the car door," my father advised. "We sure don't want to wake the little guy up now." As if to further his point, Dad made sure to slowly pull out of the driveway. I could hardly hear the crunching of gravel on the road.

Our conversation on the way home was mostly about how grateful we were for the Johnsons' concern and compassion for our family. Mrs. Johnson had been an angel. If it had not been for their generosity, I would have had to stay home and take care of Jonathen. I knew my father needed my company just as much as my mother did.

It was midnight by the time we got home. I could tell my father was as worn out as I was. I had still been feeling very sick, but I never said anything because I wasn't prepared to tell my father about my pregnancy just yet.

I didn't want to delay my father for tomorrow morning, since I knew he would want to leave early for the hospital. Both of us wanted to be there when the doctor presented the results of Mom's tests. I showered that night so that getting ready for the hospital would be a no-brainer. That way, the following morning would only consist of throwing on some sweats and tying my hair into a ponytail.

I peeked into my father's room to say goodnight, but he was already sound asleep in bed. I knew the days spent worrying about Mom had taken a toll on both his mind and body. I was also tired, but I just couldn't sleep. I settled on brewing some herbal tea, but it didn't really help much. The house was far too quiet, and I was really missing my mom and the talks we sometimes had at night. Loneliness started to tug at my heart. All I wanted at that moment was to talk to my best friend in the whole world: my mom.

Chapter Four

I was beginning to feel as though I was somehow to blame for my mother's illness. After all, she was the only person who knew I was pregnant, and I was sure that the news had devastated her.

The time had come for me to really start praying for my mom. I was alone in my room, and I knelt by the side of my bed to do so. I hadn't been attending church as I should, and my praying had become quite scarce as a result. I knew that before I could really pray for my mother, I would have to pray for myself. I asked God to forgive me for not being faithful to him and my prayer life. At first, I felt like God wasn't hearing my prayer, but I kept talking to him regardless. I continued to apologize to him, saying how much I truly did love him. I remembered how my mother told me when I was a child that Jesus loved me and would never leave me. By the time I finished apologizing to God, my eyes had started getting heavy. I got back in bed, just staring out my window at the moonlight. I felt like a burden was lifted from my chest after talking to God, and I fell asleep.

I was abruptly awakened by my mother's alarm clock. I didn't remember even setting the alarm. I quickly dressed and went downstairs. Dad was already up, sitting at the kitchen table drinking coffee.

Dad smiled. "How was your night, Elizabeth?"

"Okay," I said. "How about you?"

I don't remember his reply, as I rattled on about making him breakfast. He declined, but offered to fix me something instead. I told him I wasn't hungry, that I could get something to eat at the hospital if needed. I hugged him and asked him if he was ready to go to the hospital. It was raining, so my father advised me to wear a raincoat. I didn't have one, so I grabbed my mother's coat on the way out. It was way too big for me, but it made me feel warm and safe.

It was pouring buckets by the time my father and I reached the hospital. We tried to dodge the pellets as much as possible as we cut through the parking lot. I saw a cluster of nurses running nearby.

"When it rains real hard, there are more patients to care for," they were saying.

I wanted to continue eavesdropping, but my dad grabbed my hand and dragged me inside to the elevator. I felt my stomach get queasy while we ascended.

My thoughts were screaming. *Oh no! Please, God, not now! Please keep me from having morning sickness. My father doesn't need to worry about this right now!*

The elevator came to a halt, and I darted out of it. I could hear my father calling to me, trying to demand what was going on. Before I could answer, we had reached my mom's room. Thankfully, this was another time I was able to avoid telling my father about my situation. I wanted to cry with relief.

Mom was sitting up in bed, picking at her breakfast. As soon as she spotted us, she playfully asked if her two favorite people wanted to share her delicious "gourmet" breakfast, then chuckled.

Dad said, "No, thank you." After all, hospital food is far from gourmet.

I became serious and asked my mother how she was feeling.

"I feel fine. I sure could use a good hair brushing, though," she said.

I knew if I brushed her hair, I would have to be extremely careful. The scar from her surgery was still bandaged very heavily. Nevertheless, I retrieved Mom's comb from her purse and glided it gently through her hair. Mom had such long, beautiful hair. She'd always taken pride in caring for it. Now, I could see where her head had been shaved, and it was a tremendous effort for me to hold back my tears. I knew I had to stay strong for Mom's sake, so I refused to let my emotions get the best of me.

I saw the anguish flicker in my father's eyes, too, when he looked at her hair. Dad had always loved playing with Mom's hair. My father would joke that if he ever went bald, his wife would have enough hair for both of them. That never failed to make Mom laugh, and she would teasingly reply, "I *might* let you borrow a few strands."

Looking at my mother now, she appeared so pale and frail, but I could never tell her that.

My father must have sensed Mom's next question would be: "How do I look now, with my hair brushed?" because he blurted out, "Ooh, la, la, you're my hot mama!"

His remark embarrassed me, of course, but my dad just laughed at my discomfort. Then he changed the subject. Dad asked my mother if the doctor had been in to see her that morning. Mom said no, but that a nurse said the doctor would be in shortly. Tension hung in the air as we all waited for the doctor to show.

It seemed like a very long time—but in reality was only a half hour—before the doctor came in. I recognized the doctor as the one my father and I had met the night before, but we didn't know the other man that stood with him. Mom's doctor introduced his partner to us. My dad was sitting in the chair next to his wife, so I perched on the corner of Mom's bed. The doctor was commenting to my mother how he was pleased to see her sitting up in bed and eating.

I could tell that Mom did not want to beat around the bush. "Are the results in yet?" she asked without hesitation.

The doctor I had not recognized opened his mouth to speak. "Yes, the results are in."

He moved to Mom's bedside, and his next words seemed to be going in slow motion:

"Mrs. Reed, the test shows that you have cancer."

My mother just looked at him intently, not uttering a single word. I could not be silent. I had a bad habit of speaking before thinking. The word "cancer" was not coming from the doctor's mouth...or was it? In the midst of my yelling, my mother was saying, "Beth! Beth, it's going to be alright." My mother motioned for Dad to calm me down.

My father came over to where I was sitting, encircled me with his arms, and held me close to him. "Beth, now let's calm down and hear what the doctor has to tell us," he said quietly.

I tried my best to obey their wishes. I regained my composure and apologized for my emotional outburst.

My mother listened very closely as both doctors began to explain the cancer. Some of the words they used were so big, I couldn't even pronounce them. Mom fired a series of questions at the doctors, such as: "What's next? What's the alternative? What is the prognosis? What is the plan for treatment?" Her questions tumbled out so quickly that the doctors could hardly answer her. The family doctor told us that he wanted Mom to see his associate doctor in a few days to go over a plan for her treatment. My mother agreed to do so.

Mom was trying to persuade Dr. McKinney into letting her go home, but he wanted her to wait at least one more day. My mother swore to him that she was feeling good and was strong enough to go home, but the doctor insisted it was best to wait until tomorrow. Mom accepted the fact that Dr. McKinney knew best, so she said she would be patient and go home tomorrow morning.

"Now, Hannah, you take care of yourself, and I will see you tomorrow," the doctor said upon leaving.

My mother thanked the doctor with a smile as he left the room, wishing him a good day also.

How can we have a good day after the news we just received? How dare them! Is this doctor crazy or what? My mind was going a mile a minute, and I couldn't slow it down.

I watched the doctors as they went down the hall and into someone else's room. Were they going to tell that person the same thing they had told Mom?

I turned back toward my mother and saw that Dad had seated himself on the bed beside his wife, holding her face in his hands and gazing into her sky blue eyes. My father assured Mom she would be okay, that she wasn't going anywhere without him.

"I love you so much," she murmured.

My dad gently kissed her and held her close to him for a few moments.

"James, would you pray for me? I sure could use it right now," my mom said softly.

My parents were always praying for each other. It was a very normal thing for them to do. I bowed my head as if I was praying with them, but really I just wanted to listen to my dad pray.

"Oh, God, my Heavenly Father, I come to you in the name of your holy Son, Jesus. I know you hear me when I pray. I thank you for my beautiful family and all the things you have done for us. We thank you for our salvation and for always being there when we need you. Lord, I know you know all things, and I know you heard the news we just received. Please, God, help my precious wife. Please fix this for us. I pray you will help Hannah to rest in your arms, and please help me to help her. I ask all of this in the name of your Son, Jesus. Amen."

I looked at my mom as she lay there on her bed. She seemed so peaceful, as if she didn't have a care in the world. She motioned for me to come over to her bed.

"Beth, do you remember what I told you when we were driving home from college?"

I told her I didn't remember, just so she would tell me again.

"I told you that God is in control of all things, and that our future is in his hands."

I wanted to scream out, "What do you mean, 'God is in control'? If he is in control, why is this happening to us?" I bit back my harsh words and, for the sake of a new topic, told my mother I remembered now.

"James, how is our precious little boy doing?" Mom said brightly.

"He's doing real well with the pastor's wife, but he sure does miss his mommy."

"Well, I will be home soon, and things will be back to normal," Mom declared firmly.

Normal? Normal? I thought. *How can our lives ever be normal again?*

My mother did very well that night, and we arrived the next morning to help her pack her things to go home. Although Jonathen was a handful, we took him with us to get Mom. I stayed in the car with him because he was too young to go into Mom's room. I pulled the car up to the out-patient door, waiting for my mother to appear.

Jonathen saw Mom before I did and began screaming, "Mommy, Mommy!" He ran to jump into her arms. That's when he noticed the bandages on her head and began to cry.

"Is Mommy hurt?" his little voice trembled.

Mom cuddled him and told him she was okay. Jonathen seemed to be a little puzzled, but he listened to her and stopped crying.

I started to make lunch for all of us as soon as we got home. I had tried to fry some chicken before we left for the hospital, but I had burned it with Jonathen running through the kitchen pretending to be an airplane. I apologized to my mother about the burnt chicken, but she understood. She assured me she wasn't all that hungry anyway. Mom suggested we all just have bologna and cheese sandwiches instead. I fixed Mom's sandwich; Dad prepared his and Jonathen's sandwiches, along with some chips. I wasn't hungry, so I excused myself.

I went out to the front porch just to rest and relax in the beautiful red rocking chair my father had made for my mom. I overheard Mom tell Dad she was going to join me on the front porch for a little while. Dad was fine with that and told her he'd clean up the kitchen.

Mom came out and sat on the cushioned swing my father had put up just a year prior to my high school graduation. My mother wanted me to sit and join her. She was swinging too fast for my already upset stomach to handle, so I declined her offer.

"I know how you're feeling, Beth, but we need to talk about a few things," my mother said.

I knew what she was implying. I had not told my father I was pregnant, and I knew I would have to talk to him about what happened to me.

"Beth, you have got to tell your father," my mom said firmly.

"Tell me what?" a voice said.

My mother and I turned to see my father standing before us. Neither one of us had heard him come out onto the porch.

I peered at Mom, who gazed at me expectantly.

My hands began to shake as my mother said, "Beth, you cannot prolong this any longer. You have to talk to your father."

"Beth, what's up?" my father urged me.

I could hardly suck in a deep breath before he spoke again. "What is it, Beth? Come on, spit it out."

Before I realized what I was saying, I blurted, "I'm pregnant."

My father just glared at me. "Come on, Beth, that is not funny."

Dad knew I'd always planned on going to college and graduating before I even thought of marriage and starting a family. How could I expect him to believe what I had just said to him? He had to know the truth.

I said it again. "Dad, I'm pregnant."

By the time I finished the sentence completely, chaos broke loose. My father paced back and forth, staring at me in disbelief. He held his head in his hands, and perspiration started to sprinkle his forehead.

"Beth, tell your father the rest of the story," Mom said.

"I can't. Please, Mom, I can't!" I cried, and with that I ran into the house for the safety of my bedroom. I shut my bedroom door, knowing my parents had followed me. I just couldn't talk about it anymore—at least not tonight.

My parents were outside my bedroom door, begging me to talk to them. I put my hands over my ears, trying to drown out their voices. I hadn't locked my door, so I heard it slowly open.

"Come on, Elizabeth, you can talk to me and tell me whatever it is," my father encouraged in a calm tone, perching on the edge of my bed. "You know that I love you and that I'm here to listen to you."

I knew I had to tell him. With tears streaming down my face, I relayed the entire story—every horrible part of it.

My father could only keep his composure for a few minutes before he rocketed up to a standing position. "I'll be right back," he called.

My mother was hot on his heels. "James Carl Reed, what do you think you're doing?"

I knew something wasn't right—Mom never used my dad's full name unless she was upset.

I could hear my father unlocking his gun cabinet. He bellowed, "I will find the little coward that hurt my little girl and teach him a thing or two!"

I rushed to the front door. Dad was getting in the car with his shotgun accompanying him.

"Please, Daddy! Don't do this! I need you, Daddy, please don't do this!" I shrieked. I fell to my knees, sobbing uncontrollably.

My father saw me and came back into the house. He handed the gun to my mother and stooped down to me. Dad wrapped his big, safe arms around me, gently picking me up to cradle me like an infant.

"I'm not going anywhere, Elizabeth. I promise," he said softly.

Mom had put the gun away. She came into my bedroom to sit on my bed, where my dad had softly tucked me in.

Chapter Five

In the midst of all our confusion, the three of us had forgotten about Jonathen.

I jumped to my feet and began calling his name. I turned and saw his little blue tennis shoes sticking out from under the kitchen table. He had never witnessed this much drama in our house, and he was terrified.

Mom moved the kitchen chairs, where Jonathen had been hiding. All she had to do to calm my brother down was say, "Come on, little man, Mommy is here." I was my father's little girl as a child, but Jonathen was definitely a momma's boy.

"Let's just all take a deep breath and relax, and then we can discuss this later on," my mother concluded. We all made our way into the living room, where we sat down for a long conversation.

My mother started the discussion with a simple, matter-of-fact statement. "We are a family that believes in God, and we will trust him to tell us how to handle this situation. If we listen to him, I know he will help us. he loves this family, and he will be there when we need him the most."

In our haste, we had forgotten to call the doctor to schedule an appointment for Mom. I sure hoped the office wasn't closed for the day. My mom called the office, and I could tell the nurse's voice was on the other end. The nurse had been expecting my mother's call, so the conversation was brief.

"Thank you. I'll see you in the morning at 10:00 a.m.," my mother spoke into the phone. She hung up and met us in the living room. My dad and I were busy playing with Jonathen. My father was tickling him and tossing him in the air. I loved to listen to my brother's little giggle.

The next morning, Mom prepared to go see the doctor and go over his plans for her recovery. The doctor informed my mother she needed to have a few radiation treatments, which my mother agreed to do. Her treatments were to start the following Monday morning. Her prognosis seemed to be very favorable, and the doctor was hopeful that the treatments would shrink the tumor.

A couple of days had now passed since the blow-up at our house, and Mom was waiting for her treatments to begin. Today was Sunday, so we would be attending church and Sunday School. Mom had gotten up real early and fixed us a big breakfast with all our favorite foods. We prayed, ate, and then headed out for church. We were a few minutes late, so I took Jonathen to his class before joining my parents in the adult class.

My mind was so preoccupied with the happenings of the past few days that I could hardly follow the pastor's lesson. My brain raced back to the last time I was in church with my parents. The church was hosting a graduation service for all of the high school alumni, including myself. I recalled the pastor had all thirteen of us join him on the stage—seven boys, six girls. Pastor Johnson congratulated us and asked each of us to tell the congregation what our plans were for the future.

I was the fourth one to speak. I really wasn't nervous: my parents had raised us in this church, and we very seldom missed a service. The church was like a second home to me.

I gazed out at all the smiling faces. I tried to act grown-up and professional as I thanked them for all of their support throughout the years, as well as for being a great influence in my life. I admitted to them that I'd always wanted to be a teacher, and that was my plan for the future.

The thunderous applause that followed sure did make me feel good. After the service, I was hugged, congratulated, and patted on the head. I think everyone there shook my hand. I was beaming with pride, and I knew my parents were, too.

Suddenly, I felt my mom poking my side. I realized I had been daydreaming about the past and had missed part of the sermon.

"Beth, it has been requested that you sing a song this morning," she whispered. Mom asked me to sing her favorite song, but I didn't know if I could. I felt that everyone would surely know about my dilemma if I sang it.

I slowly rose to my feet and walked up to the pulpit. I looked at all of the smiling faces, and it seemed as though a thousand eyes were staring at me. I glanced in the direction of my mother, who mouthed, "I love you." I knew then that I could sing this for her.

I told the pianist that my mother wanted me to sing her favorite song. The pianist knew exactly what song I was talking about, since I'd often sung it for Mom in the past.

I started to sing, and most of the congregation chimed in to sing with me:

Just a closer walk with thee,
Grant it, Jesus, is my plea
Daily walking close to thee
Let it be, Dear Lord,
Let it be.

The congregation stood to their feet. We continued to sing all five verses of the song. I noticed that Jonathen had come into the service. Dad was holding him, and they were both singing. My precious little brother was clapping his hands.

The song finally came to a close. I started to step off the stage, but Pastor Johnson requested I stay there with him and dismiss the service. I did as he asked, and I bid goodbye to most of the congregation after we prayed.

I spotted some of my old friends in the parking lot as I went out to my car, but I just didn't feel like talking to them at that moment. I knew they could tell by the expression on my face that I was in a hurry, so they just waved and went to their cars. I buckled Jonathen into his car seat and waited for my parents to get in the car. I just wanted to get home, where I would be more comfortable and could absorb the issues I now had to face.

My father rattled off the usual question for Sunday mornings after church: "Hey, guys! Are you hungry?"

My family had a routine that we followed every Sunday after service. Most of the time, we ate dinner at a certain local restaurant, and then retreated home for a catnap. I had already mentioned to my mom that I just wasn't comfortable going to our usual diner. There were just too many old memories. Mom brought up the idea of going across town to the new pizza parlor.

"Pizza on Sunday?" My dad was incredulous.

Mom told my father they also had a buffet with lots of desserts. This changed his mind real fast, and he gladly agreed to go. Desserts were my father's description of a "good meal"—even if the main course was pizza.

The smell coming through the door as we entered the dining area was so wonderful. I was afraid that the aroma would make me sick, but thank God it didn't. All of us ate too much, and my family concurred that we needed more than just a catnap. I knew we would be going back to church for the evening service, so I was hoping for a long, relaxing snooze. I seemed to be so tired lately, but I told Mom to wake me up when it was time for church so I could go with them.

What seemed strange to me when I awoke was that the house was dark and very quiet. I snapped my bedside lamp on and hurriedly stumbled down the stairs. To my surprise, no one was home, but I found a note lying on the kitchen table. My mother had written that I was sleeping soundly, that she had decided to just let me rest until I awoke on my own. I was glad I had gotten some much-needed sleep. I had been so exhausted, I felt as though I could sleep forever.

I chose to take a long, warm bath in my mom's oversized tub. I knew she wouldn't mind. While soaking there in the tub, I noticed something light red in the water. I'd been having cramps in my lower stomach, but the pain would ease up. I had just assumed it was a normal part of pregnancy. The pain did not subside, so I knew I had to call my mother at church. I dialed my mother's cell phone number, and she automatically knew that something was wrong. I could sense Mom's concern—she knew I would never call her at church unless there was an emergency.

"Beth, honey, what is it? Are you okay? Is the house alright?"

I tried to answer all of her questions. I told her about the incident in the water and that I was scared. Mom told me to go lie down and that she was on her way home.

I made my way to the couch and started to rub my legs, which were cramping badly. I started to cry.

Just then, the door flew open, and my parents rushed over to me. Mom asked me a few more questions, and then insisted we go to see the doctor at the urgent care office. The urgent care was open on Sundays. I didn't want to go, but Mom told me I could possibly have a miscarriage and lose the baby. I couldn't let that happen.

I clutched my mother's arm. "Please, Mom, help me. I don't want anything to happen to my baby."

My mother tried to soothe me and say it was going to be okay, but that we needed to get to the urgent care as soon as possible. We arrived at the office, only to find it was packed with all sorts of sick folks. My mother immediately explained to the receptionist at the front desk what was going on. A nurse overheard Mom, quickly getting me into a wheelchair and into a room. Dad assured us he would fill out the paperwork and join us as soon as he could.

A young nurse came into my room to take my blood pressure and all of my vital signs. I told the nurse I was not sure how far along in my pregnancy I was. The nurse said she would relay my message to the doctor, and with that she left the room.

I was still alarmed and wanted my mother to tell me what was happening to me.

"Am I going to die? Am I going to lose the baby?" I stammered.

"Beth, you are not going to die, but you need to lay down for both the baby's sake and mine," my mom said. It was the first time I could actually hear panic creep in her voice. My mother had always been a calm, brave person

A lot of commotion was going on outside my door. People were talking, slamming doors, talking on the phone—some were even laughing. This only made me more anxious.

I wanted my father to be there with us right then, but he wasn't finished with the paperwork. I had forgotten that my dad also had

Jonathen with him. While I was trying to relax, an older lady entered the room.

"Ms. Reed," she said aloud.

Mom and I both answered her. After all, I wasn't married, so my last name was still Reed.

The doctor asked me how I had been feeling. I told her about the nausea, but that the cramping was a new symptom.

"How far along do you think you are, Ms. Reed?" the woman inquired.

"Probably about two months," I surmised.

The doctor wanted to do an ultrasound and sonogram to confirm my baby's condition. I gave them permission to do so. I only wanted the best for my child.

The bleeding had begun to slow down, and that brought some relief to us. When the doctor left the room, I interrogated my mom about whether or not she had problems with either Jonathen or me during her pregnancies. Mom was telling me her experiences with both pregnancies when the doctor returned.

The doctor needed to listen to the baby's heartbeat and confirm that everything else was fine. I lifted my shirt so she could listen intently for a heartbeat. It seemed as though it was taking a long time for my baby's heart to beat. I carefully searched Mom's expression, looking for some sort of sign.

"Come on, baby, tell me you're alright," I breathed.

Suddenly, I heard a swishing sound. The doctor told me to be quiet and listen closely. Sure enough, there it was: *lub-dub, lub-dub, lub-dub.* I could hear my baby's heartbeat.

The tears started to flow, and I welcomed Mom to listen. I had never known so much joy.

"It's beautiful, isn't it, Beth? That's your baby, honey," my mom said, crying softly with me.

We both were overjoyed and could not contain our tears. Thank God we could now have hope that the baby would be okay. The doctor and the technician explained to me that sometimes things like this happen, but that my baby's heart sounded regular and strong.

In the midst of our conversation, I heard someone page, "Dr. Lena, you are needed in the emergency room." I learned then that was this woman's name. Dr. Lena told me I would have to see my obstetrician soon. With hesitation, I told her I didn't have one.

Dr. Lena said sternly, "Young lady, we can't have that. You must see the OB, and if you don't know one, I'll help you get in touch with one I do know." She handed me her card and told me to call her office as soon as I got home. Dr. Lena also let me know that I should go home, get some rest, and call her if the bleeding started again.

"My phone number is on the card I gave you, little missy," the doctor said as she turned to go. Seeing I was caught off guard, the doctor commented, "I suppose you've never had another woman call you 'missy', have you?"

I replied, "No, ma'am, I haven't, but my name is Beth."

Dr. Lena just chuckled. She knew I wasn't used to being called anything but Beth. I could tell she had used the term "missy" a lot, since it was apparent she had been a doctor for many years—possibly even before I was born.

"The nurse will be in to give you some instructions before you leave, and I hope to see you soon in my office," Dr. Lena said as she walked out the door.

I listened as the nurse talked with Mom and me. I had several papers to sign, then Mom and I went out to the waiting room to join my dad and brother.

Jonathen was at the Coke machine, pointing to the pictures of the soft drinks. "Coke! Coke!"

My father was trying to explain to Jonathen that they must share the drink together. Dad had not noticed us approach them. Mom gently tapped him on the shoulder, which startled him.

"Elizabeth, are you okay?" he immediately asked.

I hugged him. "I'm fine, and so is the baby."

My mom told my dad everything was fine, but that we needed to go home so I could follow the doctor's orders. It was necessary for me to get plenty of rest, and the sooner the better.

On that note, we all headed home. Though my hospital visit had only been about two hours, it felt like an eternity. The ride home was a little too quiet to me, even though Mom was telling Dad about the doctor's advice, and how I need to take care of myself for the baby's sake.

My dad whirled around to look at me from the passenger seat. "Beth, we'll do what it takes to make sure you and our grandbaby will be fine." It was such a relief to hear those words from my father. I initially wasn't sure how my father would react to this situation, but I was so grateful for his understanding and that he was trying to help me through this ordeal. I thanked God silently for my parents and little Jonathen. It was truly a blessing to have them in my life.

Dad made a beeline for the answering machine. There was a message from Pastor Johnson, who said the church would be praying for our entire family. I could tell from the tone of his voice that my father had informed Pastor Johnson of my mother's condition.

Out of nowhere, I felt compelled to throw my arms around my mom. I hugged her. "I love you so much," I said.

My mom gave me a bewildered look. Usually she was the first to tell me, "I love you, baby girl." This time, she smiled at me in response to my display of affection. With love in her eyes, she suggested, "Hey, why don't we have some popcorn and watch a little TV before bed?"

Jonathen liked that idea. He was already stifling his yawns and rubbing his eyes, doing everything in his power to stay awake.

I finished popping the corn, and we all sat down for a few minutes before bedtime. My father was usually the one to read a bedtime story to Jonathen, but tonight my mom wanted to do it. My father consented because he knew his wife wanted to spend some time with her little boy. I also knew that Mom wanted my father and me to spend some time together, too.

I could hear my mom talking to Jonathen. Even though my baby brother could not speak very well, I could hear his tiny voice repeating after Mom, saying "Jesus" and "Amen" loudly. My father was also listening to them, and I could almost tell what he was thinking just by searching his eyes. My father, commenting about how stuffy it was in the living room, raised the windows real high. I agreed it was stuffy in the room, so I stepped out onto the front porch, where the cool air was gently blowing. My father trailed behind me and settled down next to me on the porch swing. Dad wrapped his big, gentle arms around me. Without him uttering a word, I knew what my father was thinking, and I knew it was going to be alright.

The night air must have made us both sleepy, because Dad started snoring. I must have fallen asleep also, because the next thing I knew, Mom was trying to wake me up. I stumbled from the swing and into the house to my room. I kicked off my shoes and grabbed a blanket before jumping into bed. I felt a gentle kiss being placed on my forehead.

"I love you. And so does Jesus," my mother's voice whispered.

She quietly exited my room, and I settled in for some much-needed rest.

Chapter Six

I've never had that many dreams in my life, but that night I had a very strange dream. I didn't know what it meant.

I was standing on a huge bridge. The fog was so thick that I couldn't see anything, but I could hear the water rushing beneath the old bridge. In the distance, a woman was calling out my name.

"Elizabeth, Elizabeth, come to me," the woman was saying.

I tried to find the voice, but I couldn't see anyone. "Where are you? Who are you?"

The woman replied, "Don't be afraid, Elizabeth. Just follow my voice. You are going to be okay. Just take a few steps and come across the bridge."

I was frightened, but slowly started to take a few steps. As I neared the middle of the bridge, I felt someone take me by the hand. I still could not see who it was, but the hand was so warm and gentle that my fear subsided. The water under the bridge seemed much louder now, but I knew that I must hold onto the hand and make it to the other side.

The fog was still very heavy and damp, but with the urging from the voice of the woman, I made it to the other side of the bridge.

The fog had lifted somewhat, and as I walked across the bridge, I could finally see the woman's face come into view. Her hair, a beautiful rich brown color, was wavy and pinned on top of her head. She looked like an angel to me.

The woman said softly, "See? I told you that you could make it."

I woke up. The night had vanished and it was a new morning. The birds were singing, and a small blue bird was prancing on my window sill. I watched it for a few seconds before it flitted away. I tried to go back to sleep but couldn't, so I just lay there, trying to recall the dream I just had.

My eyes focused on the chest that was across from my bed. I noticed one of the drawers was slightly open, so I got out of bed to close it. I tried to shut it, but each time I pushed on it, it just jammed even more. I pulled the drawer out as quietly as I could, so as to not wake anyone else up. I reached into the back of the drawer and felt something very hard and oddly shaped. I quickly pulled on the object. To my surprise, I saw something I had not seen in several years: my journal. I knew it had to have been at least eight years since I'd seen it or even thought about it.

When I was in junior high, my Sunday school teacher instructed all of the girls in our class to start keeping a journal. My teacher had passed away recently, but now I was even more curious to see what I had written about.

"Beth, you really do have good handwriting," I said to myself, after getting a glimpse of the first page. I had to laugh because there's nothing sillier than bragging to myself.

I could hear Ms. Young's instructions on how to keep a journal resonate in my mind. Our class had been quite small, so we didn't have to be embarrassed about what we wrote down. Ms. Young wanted us to write down all of our hopes and dreams for our futures. There were no boys in our class, so we felt free to be honest with whatever we decided to write. I loved this idea because I genuinely loved to write—it was a joy for me. I recalled how my mother used to come into my bedroom late at night, insisting that I stop writing for the night and go to bed already. I would even get up in the middle of the night just to write in my journal.

I began to read my journal. As I did, I just had to laugh at some of the things I had written down. After all, I was just a child when I began to jot down my personal hopes and dreams. I seemed to write a lot about some of the girls in my class and how I thought some of them were really prissy. I thought they were too girly because I was a tomboy and could climb a tree just as well as any of the boys I knew. At this time in my life, I didn't have crushes on any boys. I only wanted to let them know that I could do just as much as they could when it concerned climbing trees, riding bikes, or whatever the occasion called for.

Back then, all of my inhibitions about boys seemed to change when the new family moved in just a couple of houses down from where we lived. As soon as Mom learned that we had new neighbors, she started to make plans to pay them a visit to welcome them to the neighborhood. My mom's welcome gift was a huge, homemade cherry pie. Mom sure did know how to make great desserts. She loved to meet new neighbors and share her time and goodies with them.

Now my thoughts were beginning to recollect this very special summer. Mom asked me to go with her to introduce ourselves to the new neighbors. I agreed to tag along and welcome them to our community.

As we neared their yard, I noticed a boy tossing a football in the air. The boy had on jeans and a T-shirt that looked pretty dirty.

Maybe if he had someone out there with him to catch the football, he wouldn't look so funny! I giggled to myself.

I smiled at the boy, but we never spoke. Mom and I started up the sidewalk towards the house, and I noticed the boy was staring at me. I asked my mother what he was staring at, and she sternly told me to quit gawking at him. I politely protested that he had started looking at me first.

We delivered the pie to the front door and introduced ourselves to the lady who answered the door. After a brief conversation, we excused ourselves and returned home.

"Why was that boy staring at me?" I just had to ask my mom again.

With a slight smile, Mom replied, "Beth, I don't know why he was staring at you. Just be polite and be careful when you see him again."

Be careful? I wondered. *Be careful of what?*

With my thoughts beginning to drift off, I decided to just drop the subject entirely.

Suddenly, I was brought back from my reminiscing by the sound of commotion downstairs. I quickly jumped back into bed and hid my journal under my pillow. I had been so caught up in reading it that I had forgotten about my dream.

I pretended to be asleep when my mother came to my door and poked her head in. "Beth, are you asleep?"

I didn't answer her, so she repeated her question. I pulled the blanket away from my shoulders and motion my mom to come into my room, scooting over just enough for Mom to sit on the bed beside me.

"How are you feeling?" Mom said to me.

I told her I was okay but needed to tell her about the strange dream I had. My mom listened attentively as I told her about it. I couldn't help but notice how my mother's facial expressions grew more intense. I knew Mom was concerned about the dream, since she believed that sometimes God talks to us through them.

"Can you tell me about the woman in the dream?" she asked me.

I described the woman in my dream to her. My mother just replied that she would be praying and asking God to help us know what the dream was about, or if it had a specific meaning.

I picked up my journal again when my mom was out of sight. The things I had written down began to jog my memory now. I was anxious to continue and recall my old secrets.

The boy I had seen playing football by himself was named Brian. I snapped the journal shut right then, because his very name made me tremble. I thought this was strange, but I felt the urge to continue. Just from reading fragments of my journal, I gathered that Brian and I had become good friends. I had written down that Brian had challenged me to a game of basketball one time, and he enjoyed teasing me that I was better at the game than most of his friends. I had not jotted down very much else about Brian—I mostly focused on writing about my other friends and some of our antics we did most every day.

On one page, I had talked about my PE teacher and how I would love to be a teacher someday. I loved sports of all kinds, and I believed that I would be a very good example for my students.

I thumbed through to the final page of my journal. I had written to myself that I wanted God to help me with the decisions I would be making in the near future. I was so excited that I would be starting high school the following year. I closed the entry with a simple written prayer that I had learned in Sunday school. My eyes immediately were drawn to a cluster of words scrawled at the end: "So long, Journal. It has been nice knowing you. Remain your crazy self and be sure you keep all of my secrets a secret. Signed: Elizabeth Hannah Reed."

I erupted into laughter at myself. My childish nature was evident in this journal. I closed the book and returned it to the drawer in which it had been tucked away for the last eight years.

I dressed and descended the stairs to see what my family's plans for the day were. I didn't hear anyone talking. It was really quiet. I went to the kitchen, and I saw that my mom had scribbled a note. It said that she and my father were going out to the grocery store and to my mother's monthly check-up. I was relieved that Jonathen had gone with them. I wanted to go outside and sit under the dogwood tree in our front yard.

The warm August sun felt so good on my face. I got lost in my thoughts as I soaked up the warmth of the sunshine. I stayed there for a long time. I must have dozed off, because I suddenly realized it was four o'clock and my family had arrived home. I knew Mom would need help with unloading the groceries. I went over to the car and offered to help. My father handed me a couple of bags and asked me to start unpacking the car.

I didn't see Mom or Jonathen, but dad pointed to the bathroom just down the hall. I could hear Mom talking to my little brother.

"Hold on, baby. It will be okay," she was saying.

My mom—or, should I say, all of us—were trying to potty train Jonathen. It really just depended on who got to him first, because my brother had his own way of letting us know that he "had to go."

"You're such a big boy!" my mother praised him. "Now let's wash your hands real well, and then Mommy has a big surprise for you."

Jonathen got so excited that I could hear his jumping and laughing. My mom and little brother came out of the bathroom, and Mom was surprised to see me standing right outside the door.

I laughed. "I heard everything. I wonder how much longer it'll be before he gets the hang of his new adventure."

Mom smiled. "It won't be much longer." Then she made a face and added, "I hope."

Little Jonathen was eagerly waiting to see the big surprise Mom had promised him. I watched as he picked up each of the grocery bags. He began to shake every single one of them.

"What is he searching for?" I said.

Mom explained to me that Dad had promised Jonathen a big surprise if he behaved himself while my mom was in the doctor's office. The excitement of seeing my little brother so happy made me want to join in the fun and help Jonathen find his surprise. Of course, we all let my little brother find the bag with the surprise in it.

My dad had bought my little brother a small yellow duck that quacked and walked just like a real baby duck. As soon as Jonathen discovered his new friend, he begged Mom to wind it up so he could see what the duck could do. My mother wound up the toy for him and placed it on the bare kitchen floor. The duck took off quacking and waddling. Jonathen was right behind it, clapping his little hands and trying to quack like a duck. It was so funny to see him act that way. I sometimes got frustrated with my brother—mainly because of our age difference, I suppose—but seeing him so happy and his big blue eyes lighting up made me forget all the times he had made me upset with his whining.

Mom and I finally got all the groceries put away. I turned to say something to my father, but he had left the room. I asked Mom where he was, and she told me that she thought he was out on the front porch. I peeked out the screen door, but he wasn't there. I went to the backyard to see if I could find him, but he was nowhere in sight. Then I heard a noise coming from Dad's workshop.

My father enjoyed making woodwork projects, and he often made them for people in our community. I was sure that Dad needed a place to go and relax; his shop was the ideal place to be alone. I could hear hammering and a saw buzzing as I got closer to the shop. I knocked on the shop door.

"The door is open. Come on in!" my father shouted.

"Hey, Dad…what are you making?" I said, closing the door behind me.

"I'm just putting away some things and cutting some boards for my next project," he said.

Chapter Seven

A few minutes had passed, and Dad had finished putting his tools away. He asked me if I had eaten yet.

I smiled. "Sure did. I heated the pizza—we had leftovers from last night."

"Boy, that doesn't sound very appetizing to me!" Dad said. "How about just the two of us go to the diner for some *real* food?"

I quickly agreed to go, since the pizza had not curbed my appetite and I was still hungry. The morning sickness had gotten better, but my cravings for a lot of strange foods had gotten pretty weird. The doctor had told me this could happen, so I wasn't too worried about what kind of food I had. I just wanted to make sure my baby would be healthy. I knew that I would have to watch my diet. Even though I loved junk food, I would need to let some of it vanish from my diet and stick with eating healthy. I just loved French fries and mustard. Dipping my fries in the mustard and then washing them down with a big, thick, homemade peanut butter milkshake was my idea of the perfect meal. Just the thought of having to quit eating all these unhealthy foods made me a little sad, but I knew I could do it for my baby.

I went back to the house to let Mom know that Dad and I were going back to the diner for some supper. I did ask her and Jonathen to go, but my mom wanted to stay home and rest. Jonathen was beginning to get sleepy, and he would be too cranky to go to the diner anyway. I kissed Mom on her forehead and told her we would be back as soon as Dad and I finished dinner.

My dad came to the front door and informed me that the car was running and waiting for me.

"Come on, Beth!" he called. "I'll race you to the car!"

When Mom heard that, she cautioned both of us not to be racing. She knew I could fall and possibly hurt the baby, and told her husband he was "too old to be running."

Dad and I exchanged looks. We knew we'd have to listen to Mom. Both of us walked swiftly to the car instead. As we glanced back towards the house, we knew Mom was smiling and making sure we weren't running.

Dad challenged me to a future race, after my baby was born.

I accepted his challenge and assured him I could beat him in the race.

He laughed. "We'll see who's the winner, little girl!"

With that statement, we headed for the diner and the healthy food I would have to order. I chuckled to myself as I knew what Dad was thinking—he liked junk food as much as I did, but I knew he would be eating healthy with me today to make me feel better.

The diner was crowded with people. The waitress seated us and handed us both our menus. The special of the day was meatloaf and mashed potatoes. Dad ordered the special, but I just had to have one more order of French fries and mustard before starting my "healthy food" diet.

Our food soon arrived, and boy, was it ever delicious! I enjoyed spending time with my dad and listening to his corny jokes. Time seemed to fly as we chattered to one another nonstop.

We hadn't noticed the folks behind us, but somehow I recognized the voices without turning around. It was our pastor and his wife. Sitting with them was a woman and a blonde-haired young man, both of whom I did not know. Pastor Johnson glanced over in our direction and excused himself from his table to approach my Dad and me.

Pastor Johnson wanted to know how we were doing. He asked how my mom was doing as well. School was almost ready to start back up again, so Pastor was curious to know if I was ready and anxious to go.

I didn't answer him, but I knew Dad sensed I was uncomfortable with Pastor's continuous questions. Pastor Johnson was not aware of my pregnancy, and I wanted to keep it that way for just a little while longer.

Dad invited Pastor Johnson to sit down with us, but Pastor explained he was with friends and that he wanted us to meet them. Dad and I finished our meal, and then went over to their booth to introduce ourselves. We said hello to the Johnsons, and then Pastor introduced us to Mrs. Turner and her son, Jacob. The Turners had just moved into town and lived close to the hospital, where Mom would be taking her treatments. Tragedy had brought them to our side of town. Their home by the hospital had been destroyed by fire. My father and I gave our condolences and said we'd keep them in our prayers. During our conversation, the blonde-haired young man kept staring at me. I thought he was cute, but I sure didn't want anything to do with boys ever again. I only smiled at him. Then Dad and I said our goodbyes and headed home.

On the way home, Dad expressed to me how he was afraid Mom would be worried about us. Neither of us had realized it was already eight o'clock. To our surprise when we arrived home, Mom was sitting on the front porch in her pajamas, wrapped in a blanket.

"How was dinner? Did you guys have a good time?" she said.

"Yes, we sure did," Dad answered with a big smile, "but we missed you and Jonathen being with us."

Since Mom had a blanket wrapped around her, I inquired if she was feeling alright. The temperature in Brookville, Georgia, sometimes gets a little cool at night. Mom said she was fine, just a little chilly was all.

We all retreated inside the house for the night because we had to get up early in the morning for Sunday school. Mom told us that Pastor Johnson had a surprise for us in the morning service. I wondered what it was, since Pastor had not mentioned a word about this at the diner. I kissed my parents goodnight and settled into bed. I was worn out and needed to get a good night's rest.

The warm morning sun awakened me the next morning. I loved surprises, at least good ones, so I hurriedly dressed for church. I really wanted to hear what the preacher had to tell us.

Both the parking lot and the inside of the church swarmed with people. Nothing draws a crowd more than something special going on at church on a Sunday.

Pastor Johnson came to the pulpit, and everyone took a seat. The preacher said a sweet prayer, thanking the Lord for his many blessings and for giving us another day to enjoy with our families. Afterwards, he asked all the young people to linger in the sanctuary for just a few minutes longer, so Pastor Johnson could introduce someone to them. The surprise was for us.

Who could it be? There's no one on stage with him, I thought.

Everyone knew that our youth pastor had moved away with his wife to take care of his father, whose health was beginning to deteriorate. Our youth pastor had also taken on another position at a new church. Our church had been praying and asking God for another youth leader.

Pastor Johnson continued speaking for a few moments before making his grand announcement.

"I want us to stand and give our new pastor and his mother a round of applause!"

I was in shock when I saw the young man and his mother come onto the stage. It was Mrs. Turner and Jacob.

I poked my dad in the side. "Hey, that's the family we met at the diner last night!" I whispered loudly.

My dad smiled in response, but Mom reprimanded me.

"Shh! Beth, we are in church!" she admonished.

I shrunk back in my seat and didn't make a sound after that.

Jacob confidently strode to the front of the pulpit and introduced the congregation to his mother. I was waiting for Jacob's father to be introduced. I just knew that Jacob's father was going to be our new youth pastor. That never happened. Jacob took the microphone and began telling us a brief overview of his life before he had come to our town.

Everyone listened closely as Jacob spoke of how he'd always had the desire to work with youth, and believed God had chosen him to do so. Jacob couldn't have been that much older than me, so it was a hard pill to swallow deeming him the new youth pastor. He thanked the church for their attention and that he was anticipating the opportunity to meet the youth.

Pastor Johnson took over again. He announced that there would be a "good old-fashioned Georgia barbeque" following the morning worship service to welcome our newest pastor and his mother into our church family.

Our service that morning was very inspiring. Mrs. Turner was still on the pulpit with Jacob, so Pastor Johnson invited her to sing a special song before he continued with the service. While she sang, several people came forward and gave their hearts to Christ. It was a great service, and the spirit of God truly was miraculous. The service was dismissed with everyone shaking hands and greeting the Turners into our congregation.

Everyone made a beeline for the recreation area in the back of the church. We were all looking forward to the great food. The ladies in our church certainly knew how to fix a meal fit for a king. I will never understand how my mother made potato salad, had it in our car, and I had no idea it was in there. I should have smelled it, but I didn't. Mom had been notified of the surprise, so she must have made the salad while Dad and I were at the diner the night before. My mother was always good at keeping secrets.

I was in church of keeping an eye on Jonathen and some of the other smaller children. We had to scoot some of them away from the dessert table, as they were anxious to get into the pies that were piled high with whipped cream. The men were in charge of the grills, busy fixing hot dogs. Some of us young adults decided to play games with the kids.

I sat down on the ground with the children in a big circle. I wasn't very tall, so it was easy for me to sit down and pretend to be a child. They giggled at me as we rolled around and tossed a ball to each other. The moms were so glad that we were taking care of their little ones, since they were preoccupied with preparing the food and placing it on the tables.

The pastor called us all together and asked Jacob to say the blessing for us.

Jacob bowed his head. "Dear God, I thank you for all things. I thank you for all your blessings on all of us. Lord, please bless and keep all of these wonderful people in your loving care. Bless this food and the women that prepared it for us. I ask all of this in the name of your son, Jesus."

In unison, everyone said amen.

"Oh, yes," Jacob added quickly, "and please take the calories from this food and help it to not hurt our bellies. Amen." Then he laughed. The rest of the congregation chuckled with him, and it was so good to hear a little humor from our new youth pastor. Pastor Johnson patted Jacob on the back and commented about how refreshing it was to hear the laughter.

Everyone flocked around the tables, and we all ate until we were stuffed. I sat at the table with some of the girls that were close to my age. We told funny stories and giggled with one another. The tone of our conversation changed when one of the girls started asking me a question concerning my plans for the future.

Chapter Eight

I was concerned about the direction of our conversation. My friend Sarah wanted to know if I had plans to return to school in the fall. I explained that I didn't have any definite plans yet, but that I probably wouldn't return in the fall like she'd asked.

"I can hardly wait for the semester to begin!" Sarah said gleefully. She turned towards the other girls at our table, who did have plans for college.

Maggie, another friend of mine from college, plopped next to me at the table. I knew she was going to ask me about Brian—after all, he and I had been great friends and almost inseparable in high school. Maggie inquired about how Brian and I were doing; I tried to tell her Brian and I had some problems, and we were no longer together. She couldn't understand why we had drifted apart. I was starting to feel uncomfortable, because I didn't want Maggie to know anything else about Brian.

Thank God for small blessings. I say that because before Maggie could ask any more questions, it started to drizzle. Someone said we were supposed to have a little shower. This gave me a reason to stop my conversation with Maggie and excuse myself from the group. I jumped up and began helping the ladies clear the food from the tables.

Thunder resounded in the distance. The light shower soon turned into rain. Everyone scrambled to get things put away before the heavy downpour began. It had been a beautiful day, so no one really believed it was going to be a bad storm.

The little kids were having a ball. Each of them held their little heads in the air and had their mouths wide open, trying to catch the raindrops. I wanted to join them, but I didn't want my friends to think I was immature. I really was a child at heart, but I thought maybe I should act my age in front of some of the older girls.

The rain started to come down in sheets, accompanied by crashes of thunder and lightning.

Someone yelled, "Everyone go back into the church!"

We all ran like a herd of cattle. It was sorta funny to see some of the older folks sprinting along. Though we all were basically soaking wet by the time we ducked into the church, we all sat down and waited for the storm to subside.

Pastor Johnson called the evening service off, so none of us were in a hurry to get home. I touched my hair, trying to do something with it. I had to smile, because I know how my hair looks when it is wet. I just knew it was a lovely sight to behold.

I was digging through my purse for a comb when I heard someone say, "Lose something, Becky?"

Becky? Who is Becky?

I looked up and saw that it was Jacob.

"My name isn't Becky. It's Beth, Beth Reed," I said.

I could tell Jacob was embarrassed, but he kept smiling. "I'm not very good at remembering names," he admitted.

Jacob wanted to help me find whatever it was that I was looking for, but I told him I was only looking for a rubber band to put my hair in a ponytail. I wished someone would come over and rescue me from this awkward conversation, and sure enough, someone did.

One of the ladies opened the door and began yelling for all of us to come and look at the sky. She was so excited that everyone ran to see what she was talking about. The rain had stopped, and a beautiful rainbow seemed to be suspended across the entire town.

I overheard one of the young kids say to his mommy as he gazed up at the sky, "We learned in Sunday School that a rainbow was a promise from God. God kept his promise, didn't he, Mommy?"

As the rainbow faded away, each of us once again said our good-byes and made our way to our cars. I didn't see Jacob anywhere, but that was okay because as I had noted earlier, I was still uncomfortable around men. Our new pastor was nice, but that was all I wanted to know at the present time.

On our way home, Mom and I discussed going shopping. Both of us had doctor appointments in a few days, and we needed to get a few things beforehand. My clothes were beginning to get a tad bit snug; Mom, on the other hand, had lost a little weight. I was feeling well physically, but I knew Mom wasn't because she would complain that she was getting a little chilly. Dad thought maybe she was getting a cold. He cautioned her to be sure to tell her doctor how she was feeling. Mom promised Dad she would tell her doctor everything.

The day for our appointments came too soon for me. The nurse came and got me, since my appointment was first. I was so excited to know that I would be able to hear my baby's heartbeat. Mom wanted to come in with me, because she wanted to hear her grandbaby's heartbeat, too. My mother's huge smile reassured me that she was happy. Despite the circumstances of my pregnancy, she wanted to be a part of all of my life and future.

Everything was great with the baby. The doctor talked with me and handed me some pamphlets concerning childbirth. I stuffed them in my purse and told the doctor I would look at them later. My mother's appointment was just across the hall from my doctor's office, so I told Mom I would be out in the waiting room. I found a magazine to read while I waited for Mom to finish with her appointment. It seemed like she was staying in that office just a little too long, and I began to worry.

The door of the office flew open, and Mom walked across the waiting room to where I was seated.

"Beth, honey, the doctor wants me to have a blood test taken. She thinks it's just a virus, or maybe just a cold."

"Did you ask the doctor about the chills?" I reminded her.

"Yes, I did. I'll be okay. Don't you start worrying just because I have a cold," Mom said.

I drove Mom to the lab, and they performed several blood tests. When she came out of the lab, she really looked pale. The nurse told me that I should take Mom home and let her rest. I darted out to the parking lot and to the front of the office to pick my mother up.

"I think we should postpone our shopping trip for today," my mother said quietly.

I heartily agreed with her and drove home. All the way home, my mother kept assuring me she was fine and that she just needed to lay down for a few minutes. Upon pulling into the driveway, Mom quickly got out of the car and went straight into her bedroom. That wasn't like my mom at all. She would normally go into the kitchen and start preparing my father's dinner. This day was different, and I was beginning to get scared.

I made a phone call to my father, careful to keep my voice low so my mom wouldn't hear our conversation. I explained to my father what was going on, and he promised he would be home as soon as he finished a few things at work. He told me to stay home with Mom and that he'd pick up Jonathen at the babysitter's house on his way home.

"Don't worry about fixing dinner," Dad said. "I'll pick up something as soon as I leave work. Just take care of your mom until I get there."

I assured him I wouldn't leave Mom by herself.

I peeked in Mom's room and could see her shivering under her blankets. I could see she was getting sleepy, so I covered her with an extra blanket and slipped out of her bedroom.

My father immediately went to their bedroom to check on Mom as soon as he got home. She was already asleep, so he didn't say anything to her.

Dad had brought Jonathen's favorite food home. My little brother loved chicken nuggets and fries. I tried to get Jonathen to dip his fries in mustard like I did, but he refused. I wanted to laugh at the funny little faces he was making, but I found it hard to concentrate because I was bothered over my mother's health. We finished eating, and I encouraged Jonathen to go play in his room. I heard the sounds of him playing and laughing at his new little duck toy.

I tried to stay busy doing laundry and keeping an eye on Jonathen, but my mind was playing all sorts of tricks on me. I couldn't stop imagining all sorts of bad things happening to my mother. I had to force myself to calm down and believe that Mom was going to be alright. My thoughts were interrupted by the phone ringing.

Who could possibly be calling at six o'clock in the evening?

My father picked up the phone. I heard him say, "Thank you, doctor. We will see you first thing in the morning."

What was that all about? I thought.

Dad said that Dr. Daniels wanted to see Mom in the doctor's office in the morning. It wasn't time for her next appointment, and that concerned me. My father was also very nervous, but pretended as though he was okay. Jonathen and Mom were asleep, so Dad and I followed their lead so we wouldn't sleep through my mother's appointment. I checked on my brother one last time. He was sleeping soundly. I tiptoed back to my room.

Morning dawned with the sound of Mom calling for my father. She had been awakened with a severe headache and an upset stomach. My dad helped her to get dressed. Then he gave her some Tylenol for her headache and just a small glass of ginger-ale for her stomach. It was nearly eight o'clock and Mom's appointment was at nine, so we needed to leave soon. I had already gotten ready, dressed my little brother, and fed Jonathen breakfast.

What is this day going to bring to our family? I pondered, as we piled into the car.

We arrived at the doctor's office right as the nurse opened the door. My mother had the first appointment of the morning, so we didn't have to wait long before her name was called. My dad asked the nurse if Jonathen and I could accompany my parents. The nurse said we could and that she would find my little brother some toys to keep him occupied. How wonderful it is to have the mind of a little child, with no worries or fear. At the moment, I wanted to be Jonathen's age again so I wouldn't have to deal with any problems my family possibly would be facing.

The nurse ushered my family into a very attractive room. The only way I could tell it was an examining room was all the certificates and diplomas displayed on the walls. Other than that, it really looked more like a business meeting room. I gazed at the things on the walls, questions still nagging at my mind.

It seemed like ages before the doctor came in, but it couldn't have been longer than a few minutes. I glanced at Mom and noticed she still wasn't feeling very well. I asked Mom if she needed anything and she tried to smile.

"Maybe I could drink some water," was her weak reply.

I walked down the hallway to the water fountain to fill up a cold cup of water for my mother. The doctor and I reached the room at almost the same time.

Dr. Daniels greeted us with a friendly smile and handshake. He proceeded to tell us he had some films that he wanted to show us. He stood up and faced a small screen that was on the wall in front of him. The doctor placed the film on the screen. I couldn't tell what I was looking at, but I did notice some different-shaped blotches on the film.

Dr. Daniels began interpreting what we were looking at. He turned towards Mom. "Mrs. Reed, I am so sorry that I must tell you these results. The cancer has returned, and it has spread very rapidly."

I could not grasp what he was saying because I thought Mom was doing fine. I was paralyzed and could not utter a word. The silence that filled the room was overbearing.

"I don't understand what you're saying, Dr. Daniels," my father sputtered. "Hannah has been feeling fine…except for this cold she's had for the past few days."

Mom reached over to rub my father's arm ever so sweetly. "It will be okay, James," she said as she turned to look at Jonathen. Even my little brother sensed something was not quite right, because he had gotten strangely quiet. He had even lost interest in the toys the nurse had given him.

My mother told the doctor she had been doing fine but would consider more treatments if he thought it would help. Dr. Daniels replied that everything is in God's hands now.

"How long is my life expectancy?" my mother said bluntly.

The doctor hesitated. "Maybe six months or so," he answered. "Hannah, it's really up to God now. He is the only one that knows."

I had to cut in. "God can do all things. Right, Mom?"

"Yes, Beth, but if he has other plans, we have to accept what he wants for us," Mom said calmly.

"Please don't say that, Mom," I said. "I'll ask God and I know he'll listen. Please, God, listen to our prayer."

The doctor started to speak again. "I'm sorry I had to tell you this, Hannah, but that's part of my job. I only want to do what's best for all of my patients. I'll write you a prescription for pain medication, and I want you to schedule an appointment to see me in the next two weeks. We'll see how you're doing and then make plans for any further treatments." He shook Mom's hand and left.

Mom wanted me to watch Jonathen while she made her appointment. I suddenly felt an extremely queasy feeling in the pit of my stomach. I ran outside to the bushes next to the parking lot. I was so sick to my stomach that I had not noticed Jonathen. I guess I had grabbed his arm as I dashed out of the office.

"Ooh, ooh, stinky, Sissy!" Jonathen made a face and looked up at me with those huge eyes of his.

I would have laughed at him, but I was too sick. My throat felt like it was on fire.

My parents stepped outside and were concerned that I was sick to my stomach, despite the fact that they had just heard much more devastating news. I took Jonathen by the hand and strapped him into his car seat.

My mother had Dad call Pastor Johnson as soon as we got home. Mom said she needed to talk with the preacher and suggested that Dad and I fix some sandwiches. She wanted to invite the Johnsons over for lunch. My father did as she requested.

Mom settled into her recliner while Dad and I prepared lunch. Jonathen had fallen asleep in the car, so I tucked him into bed and returned to the kitchen to help my father. Not too much later, the Johnsons arrived. I couldn't hold back my tears as soon as I saw them. Pastor Johnson handed me his handkerchief, and his wife wrapped her arms around me in a big hug.

"Come on in!" my father called to the Johnsons from the kitchen.

The pastor and his wife had eaten at our house many times before, so they strolled into the kitchen and made themselves right at home. I followed closely behind them, and both of our families settled at the table for a simple meal. Pastor Johnson began to pray. Our preacher had a booming voice, so it was no surprise to me that Jonathen woke up right then. I went to go fetch my little brother, secured him into his highchair, and served him his food.

My mother's walls of strength seemed to collapse around her. "James, I am so scared," she suddenly whimpered, clinging to my father.

My father responded by tightening his arms around her. By this time, everyone at the table was crying.

Pastor Johnson took both of my parents' hands in his. "Hannah, James—we all know that the Lord is omniscient. Whatever Hhe has planned for this family, he will see you through it."

He placed his hands upon my mother's head and began to pray again. "God, I know you are a miracle-working God, and I know your Word is true. Lord, I know that you see my precious friends need you. I am asking that your mighty hand will come down and touch this family. This problem is in your hands. Please help us to lean on you and listen for your voice while we are in this storm. Dear Lord, if it be thy will, please bring healing to Hannah's body. We thank you, God, and we trust you in all things. Amen."

I couldn't help but take notice of Pastor Johnson's hands. He was an older man, but when he laid his hands upon you, they radiated strength.

When the prayer came to a close, my parents seemed to appear consoled, but I hadn't. I just had to ask the pastor one question.

"What did you mean when you said 'if it be thy will' that God heal my mother?" I demanded.

Though taken aback by my question, Pastor Johnson said, "Elizabeth, we don't know what God's will is or what our futures are going to hold. We just have to trust him. I have seen many miracles in my life, but I am only a servant. God's Word tells us that he will never leave nor forsake us. I trust the Lord to do what is best for all of us."

I felt anger bubble up inside of me. I just had to say what I was really feeling. "If all that you said is true, then where was God when I was raped?" I blurted.

The table suddenly fell silent. I threw my sandwich in the garbage and ran from the room.

I knew the Johnsons were stunned. This was the first time I had told my secret to people other than my parents, but the Johnsons were good friends, and I knew I could trust them with anything.

No one called for me to come back outside. Everyone just left me alone. Although I felt some relief after blowing off steam and letting go of some of the resentment, I stayed in my room to avoid discussing the topic further.

I heard the pastor and his wife say goodbye and leave. I was watching TV when I heard my dad mention to my mother that he was going to check on me. I pretended to be asleep, so he closed the door and left me alone.

I knew that I would have to face another day come morning, but until then, I was going to concentrate on my future and the future of my baby. I fell asleep and was grateful for the few hours I was granted to rest my afflicted mind.

Early in the morning, I was awakened by the little blue bird that frequented my window sill. I had learned to love that tiny creature, and I was thankful for its presence. It seemed to know just the right time to sing to me and dance. I got out of bed, took a hot bath, and went downstairs to begin yet another chapter of my troubled life.

Chapter Nine

Time has a way of creeping up on us without notice. Here it was already—fall of the year and time for school to start. I should have been preparing to enter college, but here I was gazing at myself in the mirror. My body was changing. I could no longer fit into my jeans. My belly was starting to protrude, and I had to resort to wearing very long shirts to hide my pregnant stomach. I knew I couldn't hide this much longer.

Our church always had an annual Labor Day picnic. I never missed going to it, but this year was different. I was tempted to stay home, but I didn't want to disappoint my family. I knew I had to get my mind used to the fact that people were soon going to find out my secret.

This particular church picnic was always the biggest one. I guess it was because it was the last one for the year, so everyone made plans to attend. I was hoping Mom would feel okay enough to go. She was trying to be strong and upbeat for her family. She continued to do housework and insisted she was fine and not in any pain. Our church had been very good about praying for Mom and encouraging my father.

The picnic was a huge success. Everyone had a great time, and of course we enjoyed all of the good food the ladies had prepared. The kids had a fantastic time. I watched them play and wondered if my baby would someday be playing and enjoying life to its fullest. My thoughts were put on hold when Jacob approached where I was sitting.

"Boy, I know you must be excited for college to start. When will you be leaving, Beth?" he said.

I had to think of an answer real fast. "I'll be taking some time off from college to stay with my mom," I said.

Jacob said he understood my situation, that he would do the exact same thing. What did he mean? What situation was he talking about? I wondered if Pastor Johnson had let it slip to Jacob that I had been raped. I immediately felt bad for thinking this, since I knew my pastor would never betray my secret like that. I quickly, silently asked God to forgive me for thinking such a thing of my pastor.

Jacob changed the subject about me leaving for school with a proposition for me. He said he noticed I was very good with the young children at our church. Jacob wanted me to be his Sunday School assistant on Sunday mornings. I thanked him for his offer, but explained to Jacob that I was busy helping my mother out and taking care of Jonathen.

"I understand," Jacob said, but he asked me to pray and ask God for his direction about it.

I told him I would pray and give him my answer next Sunday. With that said and done, I said goodbye and walked away.

Mrs. Johnson had seen us talking. "Did Jacob ask you to help in the nursery?"

I was flabbergasted. "How did you know?"

"Well, we need some extra help, and Jacob has been watching you interact with the children. My husband had told Jacob to pray about who would be a good fit to join our children's ministry. I guess Jacob felt like you were the one for the job." Mrs. Johnson smiled. "I'm sure you will know what to do, Beth."

Before I could saunter away, Mrs. Johnson rushed on. "Beth, while you're here, I want to ask you something."

My heart sank. What was she going to ask me?

Mrs. Jonson insisted we go to the church office to talk. I complied, but only because I had a lot of respect for her. We sat down in the office, and I knew exactly where this conversation was going.

"Beth, I have known you all of your life," Mrs. Johnson began. "I have changed your diapers. You have spit up all over my church clothes." She laughed and continued on. "I love you just like my own daughter. You don't have anything to be ashamed of. So, I'm going to ask you: are you pregnant?"

I hung my head and told her it was true.

Mrs. Johnson lifted my chin and told me I had nothing to be ashamed of. "You did nothing wrong, Beth," she said softly, referring to my secret I'd divulged to her and Pastor the other night. "God is going to give you a beautiful baby. This is going to be a happy time for you, despite the circumstances. There is no reason to hide your baby."

Mrs. Johnson reached over to hug me. I felt safe, though I was scared.

"What about the other people in the church?" I said. "What are they going to think?"

"It's going to be okay," she told me. "Some folks won't understand, but most of them know and love you, and they will be there for you. When the time comes to tell them, the Lord will help you and give you the right words to say."

I needed to talk to my parents and see what they had to say about how I would be received in the church if I took the job as an assistant Sunday school teacher.

I told my folks at home about what happened at the picnic. Both of my parents said that whatever decision I made, they would be supportive. I was so thankful that I had such understanding and loving parents. I knew I could trust them with my life.

The following week was a hectic one for me. I had so much on my mind. Sunday morning would soon be here, and I had to be prepared with an answer for Jacob. I wanted to be sure I was doing what I needed to do.

Sunday morning rolled around. The sun was shining brightly through my bedroom window, and it felt so good. I made myself get out of bed and start getting ready for church. I hopped into the shower and was enjoying the warm water trickling onto my face and belly. At that instant, I felt as though something was crawling on my stomach. I wrapped a towel around me and called for my mom. She hurriedly came over, and I tried to tell her what I had felt.

Mom started laughing. I couldn't believe she was making fun of me.

"Beth, honey, that is your baby moving inside of you. I remember the first time I felt you move, honey. It was a time of great joy," she grinned.

I was so embarrassed to have thought something was wrong with me. I should have known what the feeling was, but I guess I was just too scared and dumb. My mother and I both started laughing. After the moment passed, I dressed and joined my family downstairs for breakfast.

It was a beautiful Sunday morning. The bright blue sky was absolutely gorgeous. My heart was bursting with joy. The experience of feeling my baby's movement inside me had made my world just a little bit brighter.

Upon arriving at church, I was so happy that I had noticed Jacob standing on the front steps of the church. I was in my own little world.

I was pulled back down to reality when I heard, "Hey, Beth, are you with us?"

It was Jacob. He was snapping his fingers in front of my eyes. I realized he wanted to know if I had made my decision about working with the children. I apologized for not hearing him.

"Beth, are you going to take that position I offered you? Please tell me your answer is yes," Jacob was saying.

I flashed a smile. "Yes. Yes, I will help you out."

Jacob was ecstatic. "This is great, Beth! I'll help you. Today will be your first day on the job, and we will need to get things ready for them before they come into class. Sis. Miller has said she would help you with all that you need." Jacob walked away with a hearty "good luck" and a huge grin stretched across his face.

The class wasn't a very big one. I knew I would have a lot of fun with the kids. Jonathen was also in my class, so I was used to playing with children his age. Sister Miller stayed with me, since it was my first day "on the job", as Jacob had said earlier. She complimented me on how well she thought I was doing with the class.

Our pastor's wife came into the class after Sis. Miller had left the room. She wanted to know how the class was, and I confessed to Mrs. Johnson that I was actually quite tired. I didn't realize little kids could keep you "on your toes", as the saying goes.

"Speaking of children," Mrs. Johnson said with a small smile. "Beth, I would like to throw you a baby shower."

"Oh, no, I couldn't have you do that," I said with too much haste, and Mrs. Johnson noticed.

I tried to settle down as my pastor's wife was attempting to convince me it would be a good idea. Someone suddenly knocked on the nursery window. I thought we were all alone.

I pulled the curtain back from the window. It was Jacob. He had his nose pressed up against the glass, holding a small stuffed animal and pretending to make it talk.

"Let me in! Please let me in," the toy was supposedly saying to us.

Mrs. Johnson and I burst into laughter. Jacob looked so funny. He came into the room sporting a huge grin and handed me the toy.

"How long have you been there, Jacob?" I tried to ask nonchalantly, but I was secretly alarmed.

"Not very long, why?" he said.

"No reason," I said quickly. I was praying he hadn't heard us talking about my baby shower. He never mentioned anything, so I felt a little better and hoped Jacob truly hadn't heard our conversation.

I thanked Mrs. Johnson for helping me clean the class. She was coming to see Mom during the week, and we discreetly made plans to discuss the baby shower when she came over.

My parents were waiting for me outside the church. I ran to catch up with them so we could head home.

I recognized a blue minivan parked in our driveway. My aunt Sammy was here. Mom sprung out of the car and hastened to hug her sister. Both my mother and aunt were clinging to each other and crying tears of joy. I had not seen my aunt Sammy in a long time, since she had moved to Iowa. I hugged my aunt and told her I would retrieve her bags. Mom was anxious to go inside and visit with Aunt Sammy, so Dad just said I could get my aunt's luggage later.

My father got Jonathen settled in his room with his toys before joining us in the living room.

"How are you doing?" my father asked Aunt Sammy.

Aunt Sammy's husband had passed away right before I had left for college. My mother was also eager to know how her sister was doing. Mom was worried about her because Aunt Sammy was living alone since Uncle Henry passed away.

"I'm just fine," Aunt Sammy reassured my parents.

Mom wanted to know if she was still working, and Aunt Sammy said she had taken a leave of absence from work.

"I want to visit with you for a while and help you if you need me to, Sis," Aunt Sammy said.

I saw relief wash over my mom's face. She had not said anything to Dad and me, but I knew Mom was worried about who would help us out.

"You're welcome to stay as long as you want to," my father warmly said to his sister-in-law, then went to retrieve Aunt Sammy's bags from her car.

Little Jonathen had fallen asleep. I gently picked him up and tucked him into bed. I lay beside him for just a few minutes before I got sleepy as well. During my nap, I had a horrible dream. I dreamt of Brian, and why I even had him on my mind was a mystery to me. I did not want to even hear his name spoken in my presence.

I dreamt that I was back in Brian's car, and he was pinning me down, telling me that I belonged to him. In the dream, I felt like the rape was occurring all over again. I was screaming and crying for Brian to let me go. Suddenly, I was awakened by Jonathen crying and my family trying to get me to calm down and snap out of my nightmare.

My dad soothed Jonathen's crying while Mom walked over to me and looked me square in the eye.

"Now, Beth, I know you are afraid, but Jesus will help you. I promise he will never leave you. He will be there for you any time you need him," Mom said soothingly.

Those few simple words from my mother, along with her gentle stroke on my head, seemed to make everything okay. I hugged Mom and assured her I would be fine.

My aunt Sammy had left the room after she knew that I had calmed down. She did not believe in God quite as much as my family did. Aunt Sammy was still grieving over the loss of her husband, and she was still a little angry and bitter about God taking Uncle Henry away from her. Mom would often try to talk to her about it, but it fell on deaf ears. Even though Aunt Sammy did not want to hear about God and salvation, my mother continued to talk about God and how much she loved him.

My aunt stuck her head into Jonathen's room, announcing to us that she would be cooking dinner. We knew her favorite thing to make was spaghetti and meatballs. Jonathen loved that idea. I had taught my little brother a while back how to make slurping sounds with the noodles. Mom had yelled at me for teaching him that, but we all had a good laugh when we saw how Jonathen had gotten the sauce all over his chubby little face.

Chapter Ten

The evening sun had begun to dip its face below the horizon. All of us settled down in the living room after dinner to reminisce with my aunt.

The doorbell rang, and my father went to see who it was. I was curious to know who could be here without prior notice. Dad notified me that Jacob was here and wanted to talk to me.

"Is that your new beau, Beth?" Aunt Sammy teased.

"No, it isn't," I said sharply, "and please don't say that in front of him."

Pastor Jacob wanted to pray with Mom concerning her health issues. I waited until he was finished to ask Jacob what he wanted to talk to me about. Mom and Aunt Sammy stood up to leave the room, but not before my mother made sure to offer Jacob dinner. She told him we had just finished and would be glad to fix him a plate of my aunt Sammy's spaghetti.

I rolled my eyes at my mother.

"Don't you think that is a good idea, Beth?" my mom said.

To be polite, I said, "It sure is."

I got Jacob his food. After he prayed and ate dinner, he volunteered to help do the dishes.

Boy, where did he come from? He even knows how to do the dishes.

He seemed to read my thoughts because he proceeded to tell me how he could also do laundry.

"I had to do things early, and my mother was a good teacher," Jacob explained.

I wondered why he never mentioned his father. I didn't want to pry, so I just didn't ask about his dad.

Jacob finished helping us and then asked me if I would go out on the porch with him. At first, I almost hesitated to go out on the porch with Jacob. It was dark, and it seemed that darkness brought back a lot of bad memories for me. My parents were here, though, so I decided it would be okay.

Jacob sat down on the porch swing, but I stood up in front of him.

"Are you going to sit down, Beth?" he asked.

I assured him I was okay standing. It sounded foolish, but it was the only excuse I could come up with. Jacob had no clue that he was the first boy I had been alone with since my terrible ordeal with Brian.

Jacob chattered on about how much he enjoyed dinner. He expressed that my family was wonderful and very friendly.

"You don't talk much, do you, Beth?" he finally said.

I plastered a fake grin on my face. "Sure I do. What did you want to talk about?"

"The church has allotted some money for the young people, and I think we should take them to the aquarium before it gets cold. What do you think?" Jacob said.

Before I could answer, Jacob added, "We won't take the little ones. Would you be able to help me out? I'm not familiar with the city, so I'll need you to show me around. I'm not good with directions."

I agreed to help him if my mom thought it was okay and if I was free of any prior commitments. Jacob told me the date we would be going on would be two weeks from now. After he called it a date, I quickly corrected him and explained that I don't date.

Jacob smiled. "I meant a date with the church."

My face turned bright red and burned with embarrassment. I said goodbye to Jacob and slipped back into the house, only to find my parents pretending to straighten the curtains.

I sorta laughed to myself. *Parents actually can get caught spying on their kids!* I thought.

Tuesday morning rolled around. Mom and I were just getting the day started when the phone rang. It was our pastor's wife, who said she was coming over to talk to Mom. I had completely forgotten to tell my mother about Mrs. Johnson and I having a conversation at church. I told Mom just then that the pastor's wife wanted to throw me a baby shower. Mom thought it was a great idea, so I told Mrs. Johnson to come over whenever she could. She told me she would come over at 11:00 a.m. I was relieved that Aunt Sammy had decided to do some early shopping so we wouldn't have to discuss this in front of her. Aunt Sammy was the kind of person that would ask a million questions about any simple thing, and that's exactly what she would do if she found out I was pregnant. Thankfully, she hadn't found out that little detail.

Mrs. Johnson arrived at precisely eleven. Mom greeted her at the door with a hug. Jonathen ran to the door to get his hug from the pastor's wife, too. She gave Jonathen a big hug and kiss. My little brother just loved Mrs. Johnson.

We all retreated to the family room. It was much bigger than our living room, and it had a big screen television for Jonathen to watch. This morning, he insisted on watching *Noah and the Ark*. It was his favorite movie. He adored the animals and tried to imitate the sounds they'd make, and Jonathen's attempts to do so were often hilarious. His favorite part of the movie was the rainbow at the end. I think it was because the bright colors fascinated him. Mom popped the movie in, and Jonathen instantly got excited. My little buddy got his favorite pillow and lay down in front of the television, now calm and engrossed in his movie. I knew this would be the perfect opportunity for us ladies to talk.

I had made my mind up that I was going to refuse for anyone to give me a baby shower. Before I could say anything, Mrs. Johnson told me she had a word from the Lord for me.

For me? What could it be? I thought.

I was very aware that the pastor's wife talked to God a lot. If she had something to tell me from him, I would listen and know it was true.

"First thing: I want us to join hands and pray," Mrs. Johnson declared.

The three of us joined hands. I could feel the hair on the back of my neck stand up as she started her prayer.

"Dear Lord, I know you have made this day, and I know you have sent me to this home for this family. Please help me to have courage and boldness to speak the things that you want me to say. I want to do your blessed will. Thank you, Lord. Amen."

Mrs. Johnson glanced up at me. "Beth, the Lord woke me up last night and told me to pray for you and your family. He told me to give you this Scripture to read. I want you to listen to what the Word of the Lord is saying. The Scripture is found in Jeremiah, the twenty-ninth chapter and the eleventh verse. It reads like this: "*'For I know the thoughts I think toward you,'* saith the Lord, *'thoughts of peace, and not of evil, to give you an expected end.'*"

I was amazed at those words. I was also comforted with each thing she told me. I could tell Mom was too—she had been on her knees praying and praising God the entire time. I just had to hug Mrs. Johnson and my mother. We were crying while Jonathen was still watching his movie, and our little "prayer meeting" had not disturbed him.

My aunt arrived home and came into the room where we were sitting. She said hello to Mrs. Johnson and asked how her family was. Aunt Sammy knew the Johnsons pretty well also. The pastor's wife had sung at Uncle Henry's funeral.

Mom asked her sister to sit down with us, saying the Lord had just given me a message from the Bible.

Aunt Sammy started to walk away. "You guys just do your thing. I'll go into the other room."

I don't know why I asked my aunt to stay with us, but I wanted to tell her about the baby and the shower for some reason. When Aunt Sammy sat down and asked why I looked so serious, I knew it was time to let the cat out of the bag.

"Aunt Sammy, I am going to have a baby," I heard myself say.

My aunt, as expected, rapidly fired questions and comments. "A baby? What do you mean a baby? I didn't even know you had a boyfriend! Are you kidding me?"

"I don't have a boyfriend, Aunt Sammy," I answered her. "I'm not kidding you, either."

She was a little calmer than my parents had been. My aunt had worked at the police station as a 9-1-1 operator and had dealt with a lot of drama.

"I was raped, Aunt Sammy," I blurted.

My aunt was incredulous. "Raped? Did you just say raped?" She glanced at my mother to gauge Mom's reaction. My mother affirmed it was true.

My very calm aunt soon lost her cool and demanded to know who did this to me. She would see that this man was caught and punished. Most of Aunt Sammy's friends worked at the police station, and they would help catch him.

Aunt Sammy wrapped her arms around me and assured me that she would take care of me and my baby. She wanted full details about how this had happened to her little "Be-Be", a nickname my aunt gave me when I was born. No one else called me by that name.

I sat down by my aunt and started to relay to her just some of the details of the rape. I tried to convince my aunt that the father of my baby had left town, and no one had heard from him. She insisted on his name, but I refused to tell her. I did not want Brian close to me or my baby. I shuddered at the thought of someday possibly seeing him again. Aunt Sammy could tell that I was on the verge of tears, so she tried to change the subject.

Mrs. Johnson asked me if I had given any thought about the baby shower. This question really got my aunt started again.

"Have you all lost your mind?" she cried. "Beth has been raped, my sister is sick, and you want to have a baby shower? I can't believe what I'm hearing, especially coming from a pastor's wife!" With that angry remark, Aunt Sammy stormed out of the room.

Mom tried to apologize for my aunt's behavior, but Mrs. Johnson told her she understood and to just forget Aunt Sammy's outburst of emotions.

I walked Mrs. Johnson to the front door and told her we would talk about the shower as soon as possible. I knew she was caught off guard by my aunt, but Mrs. Johnson was used to people and their sudden changes. She had dealt with a lot of hurting folks in our church. We hugged each other goodbye, and after she left, I joined my aunt outside. I hoped I could reason with her emotions. Aunt Sammy had been through a lot of hardships and was just not thinking clearly at this particular time.

I found my aunt sitting under the same dogwood tree that I loved to sit under. She was sobbing, and I begged her not to cry anymore. For some reason, she was blubbering how she was sorry she couldn't be there for me when I was raped.

"It wasn't your fault," I said softly. "I'm grateful you're here with me now."

Aunt Sammy was shaking, and that's when I realized I was trembling too. It wasn't from our ordeal. The wind had started blowing, and it had a chill to it. I got up to go into the house for a sweater, but Mom had met me at the door, holding an old high school jacket of mine. I accepted the jacket and turned to go back to my aunt. I looked where she was sitting, but Aunt Sammy was gone.

I called out to Mom to ask her if she'd seen my aunt. My mother hadn't seen her lately, so she stepped outside to help me look around. Aunt Sammy was nowhere in sight.

"Elizabeth, grab your little brother and come with me," my mother said.

"Where are we going?" I asked.

"We're going for a ride. I think I know where we will find my sister."

And with that, the three of us piled into the car. I strapped Jonathen into his car seat, and then we were off to search for my aunt.

Chapter Eleven

I could tell that my mother was on a mission: to find her best friend and sister.

We drove past the post office and down several back streets. I wondered where we were going. The familiar places I knew brought back many old memories from my childhood.

We were approaching the cemetery. I remember going there with some of my friends a few years back. I never told Mom that we used to go there to play hide-and-seek. My mother would have gotten upset if she knew. Our little group of friends would go there just before dusk. We would hide behind the huge monuments, jumping out and scaring each other. We would each read the markings on the old tombstones, and then we would make up a story about the person we had chosen. Some of our little stories were funny, but some of us could concoct some pretty wild and scary tales. Our favorite tombstones were the ones where you could hardly read the inscriptions because the weather had changed their appearance. We could really tell some weird stories about those folks. My mind was full of memories from that cemetery, but I really needed to slow my thoughts down and help Mom look for my aunt Sammy.

We were driving past the chapel, and that's when I got a glimpse of my aunt. She was kneeling down in front of a somewhat new monument. Mom parked the car and asked me to stay in the car with Jonathen. I watched as my mother got out and wrapped her arms around her sister, kneeling down beside her. I could see that my mom was rocking Aunt Sammy back and forth like a child. I guess at that moment, my mom felt like her sister was a little child. I saw Mom talking to her. After a few minutes, they both got up and came to the car. I asked Aunt Sammy if she was okay, and she told me that she just needed to be alone.

"I'm fine, Beth," my aunt insisted. "But how about we go get some ice cream?"

Jonathen heard that remark, and of course he wanted to go. I told them I was hungry. Before I could say anything else, Mom verbalized the rest of my thoughts.

"Of course you can have your French fries and mustard," my mother laughed.

She knew that I had been trying to stay away from the junk food. She also knew I was craving just one more order of fries and mustard.

We arrived at the ice cream stand. Each of us placed our order and got a seat at the picnic table. It was a good day for eating outside. We were enjoying our food when my aunt noticed someone was looking in our direction. I didn't see who she was referring to, so she pointed in the direction of the couple seated just a few feet away. I saw that it was Jacob and his mother. Jacob quickly turned his head. I guess he didn't want me to know he had been staring at me.

Mom got up and went over to their table. They exchanged a few words.

"Oh, no…they're coming over here…now what?" I said.

"Beth, what is wrong with you? Why don't you want them to come over here?" Aunt Sammy said.

Before I could answer her, Jacob and his mother had made their way to our table. I had to scoot over for Jacob to sit down.

"Who's your friend, Beth?" Aunt Sammy asked with a lopsided smile.

I introduced the Turners to my aunt. I just wondered what Aunt Sammy was thinking. She liked to know details, and I didn't have any details to tell her yet.

I had heard that Mrs. Turner was going to speak at the next ladies' meeting, so I commented about it to her. Before she could answer me, Mom interrupted to hand me a napkin. She tried to point out that I had mustard on the corner of my mouth. My mother discreetly made a wiping gesture, so as to not embarrass me. It was too late—Jacob's mother had already noticed.

Mrs. Turner smiled and told me she also used to eat fries and mustard. "That was a long time ago, Beth. You are the first person I have ever seen do that. I feel better just knowing that I'm not the only strange eater around here."

I smiled and urged her to continue telling us about her upcoming speaking engagement.

Mrs. Turner admitted she was nervous, but that she was also looking forward to doing it.

"The prayer meeting is going to be at your house, I believe. Is that right?" Mrs. Turner asked my mother.

My mom verified that it would indeed be taking place at our home, and that all the ladies were anxious to hear Mrs. Turner speak.

Aunt Sammy had been closely following our conversation. "How long have you been in the community?" she inquired to Mrs. Turner.

"It's a very long story," Jacob's mother informed my aunt. "If you come to the prayer meeting, I'll tell you all about that."

Before my aunt could respond, Jonathen started to get restless and cry. We wished the Turners a good evening and headed for the car. I braced myself for the teasing that was bound to come from my aunt as soon as we got to the car. She did start teasing me, but I played along with her. She was obviously feeling much better, and I didn't want to change her good mood. Jonathen had fallen asleep by the time we arrived home. I picked him up and carried him into the bedroom for Mom. All of us were tired. I, for one, was glad that nighttime had finally settled in.

I said goodnight to Mom, Dad and Aunt Sammy and went upstairs to my room. I relaxed on my bed and tried to go to sleep.

That's when I heard a strange rapping noise on my window. It was a scary sound. I saw weird shadows on my ceiling. I peeped out through the curtains and could see it was just a branch of a tree hitting my window. I was grateful that was all it was, but now I was wide awake and couldn't sleep.

I got out of bed and got my old journal. I hadn't read all of it since I had found it. It seemed as though I did have a lot of good days before college. I had made a note about how excited I was getting ready for school. I was working real hard to get good grades. One of my entries was about how happy I was when Mom told me that I was going to have a little brother. I was thrilled at the news, but at the same time, I was trying to figure out how I would tell my friends. I knew that I would be teased. I was happy for my parents but didn't know how I would react if my friends teased me too much. My reading was interrupted with a knock on my bedroom door.

I yelled, "Come on in!"

It was my aunt Sammy.

"Hey sweetie," she said as she came into the room. "I saw your light on, and I wanted to check and see how you were doing."

I told her that I was fine but couldn't fall asleep. She replied that she was having trouble falling asleep also.

"What are you reading?" she said.

I showed Aunt Sammy the journal, and she told me that she use to keep a diary, too.

"It helped me to get my feelings out," she told me.

I wanted to hear her stories. She closed my bedroom door and started to tell me a few things about our family that I had never heard.

Aunt Sammy remarked that she had to be different from the rest of her siblings. She said it was just her nature to be the "black sheep" of the family.

"I really gave my parents a hard time when I was a teenager. I finally had to change my friends, and that made things somewhat better. My relationship with your grandmother had suffered because of my stubbornness. Your grandmother and I had just begun to mend our problems when she died," Aunt Sammy confessed.

I wanted her to tell me more about how my MawMaw had died. Aunt Sammy informed me that my grandparents had been shopping and were on their way home when a man fell asleep at the wheel, killing both of my grandparents. My aunt told me how angry she was with God for taking her parents from her.

"I was such a mess that I moved away from our hometown," she said sadly. "I still could not recover from losing them. I just quit talking to God. I could not forgive the man who had hit them, the man who caused both of them to be taken from our family. I wish you could have met them, Beth. They were loving parents, and they sure would have loved you. In fact, you have a lot of Mom's traits."

I just had to interrupt my aunt by asking her a very direct question. "Was that whose stone you were kneeling down at today in the cemetery?"

She replied that it was. "I know they aren't there, Beth, but I feel close to them when I go to their graves."

I knew that we both were beginning to get real sleepy.

Aunt Sammy said, "Let's go to bed now, and we'll talk again." She said goodnight and left my room.

I snuggled down under the covers. Auntie had tucked me in before she left. I liked it when she said, "Goodnight, Be-Be." I felt secure in knowing that I had a mom and aunt who loved me and were trying to help me through this chapter of my life.

After a restful night's sleep, I was awakened by the sound of Mom and Aunt Sammy in the kitchen. They were laughing, and I could tell they were happy. It was Friday morning, and this was the day that Mrs. Turner would be speaking at the ladies' prayer service. I hurried downstairs to join in the conversation.

My two favorite women were busy making finger sandwiches for the ladies meeting. I overheard Mom ask her sister if she was going to stay for the service.

Aunt Sammy said, "No, I'll stay upstairs and take care of Jonathen."

Mom told her that she wanted her to stay.

My aunt said, "No, that isn't for me."

"If you change your mind," Mom replied, "please come down and join us."

"I will help you in other ways," my aunt said. "I'm not ready to be a part of prayer meetings."

The doorbell rang, and we knew that the women had started arriving. With a troubled look on her face, my aunt went upstairs to watch after my little brother.

One by one, the ladies started coming in. I was the only one of my age there. I told Mom that I was going to go for a walk.

Mrs. Johnson overheard and asked me to stay. "I have something I want you to hear, Beth. Please join us.

I agreed to stay, at least for a few moments. I hoped I could leave the room before too long.

The women all gathered in the living room. I watched them as they talked and greeted each other.

I could see a lot of love on all of their faces. Mom welcomed everyone and announced it was time to start the service. I sat back and took notice of what they were doing. The ladies all joined hands and began praying. They were praising God for all his goodness to each of them. I could just tell that God was listening to them. The atmosphere in the room had changed. I felt good.

Mrs. Turner got to her feet and commented about how she had been invited to be the guest speaker for that day. "I want to tell all of you how it is that I am here with this church and the community. First of all, though, I must thank my Lord Jesus Christ for his love and mercy, and for bringing me here." No one had noticed that Aunt Sammy had come downstairs. She didn't come close, but she could hear what was being said.

"I know all of you have questions about Jacob's father. I heard that some of you thought that Jacob's father would be the youth pastor. His father and I are not together, and no, we are not divorced." Mrs. Turner paused.

Then where is he? I was saying in my mind.

Mrs. Turner started telling us the story of her life.

"About twenty-two years ago, I lived in the remote mountains of Orado. Our town was small and much like this small city. We only had a few small grocery stores. If you didn't have a car, you had to walk everywhere. I ran most of the errands for my parents. This one particular day, I had been shopping and was on my way home. I only had a few small bags of groceries. I was almost home when a carload of young men went whizzing by me. They drove a short distance up the road, and then they turned and came back to where I was. They stopped the car, and one of the boys asked me my name. I told him my name and he commented that I sure was a pretty girl. He wanted me to get in the car. I politely told him, 'No, thank you, I will walk.' The boys kept driving along beside me, begging me to get in the car. I just kept walking, but suddenly one of the boys jumped out of the car and began walking in front of me. He just kept asking me to go with them for a little ride. He was real close to me, and I couldn't get away. I was terrified. I shouted for him to leave me alone. He grabbed my grocery bags and threw them to the ground. The boy got real angry and demanded that I go with them. I tried to run, but he caught up with me and forced me to get into his car. I had no idea where he was taking me. I just kept screaming and begging them to let me out of the car. The boys were all laughing at me and poking fun because I was scared. The car came to a quick stop. I tried to see where we were. I could see an old abandoned barn in the distance. One of the boys grabbed me by the arm and forced me to get out of the car. For an instant, I thought they were going to let me go home. I soon realized this was not their intention.

"The boys were dragging me in the direction of the barn. Once we were inside, all of them started beating me. I was so terrified that I passed out. When I finally came back out of the fainting spell, the boys were taking turns raping me. I was hurting so much from all of the beatings and rape that I passed out again. The boys were gone when I became conscious again. My clothes were torn, and I was bleeding badly. I had to get home, but how could I? I got to my feet and tried to start walking towards my home. I wasn't sure if I could make it. My mind was so confused that, for a moment, I wasn't sure in what direction my home was. I know it had to be God who helped me find my way home. I finally saw my home and tried to run, but I was so ravished that I could barely walk. I got to my home. As soon as I entered the door, I collapsed on the floor. My parents were so devastated, but they put me to bed immediately. I believe I must have slept for two days."

Mrs. Turner continued to tell us her story, and I glanced around the room. Most of the women were crying. As for me, I was wondering if my pastor's wife had told her of my situation. In my heart, I knew that Mrs. Johnson had not shared my story with Mrs. Turner. My pastor's wife was a very good woman, and she would never tell anyone about my secret, unless I gave her permission to do so.

"You know, ladies, in those days, families didn't talk about such things as rape. Pregnancy was not discussed—ever." Mrs. Turner could see the ladies were taken aback about her last comment. "Yes, ladies, I was pregnant. I had no idea who the father was. All of the boys had raped me, so I had no way of knowing who the father was. My parents were so upset and confused. They had to make plans about what to do with me and my baby. After much thought and prayer, my parents sent me out of state to a home for unwed mothers. I did not want to go, but I had to do as my parents said.

"The months preceding Jacob's birth were a very trying time for me. The administrators of the home I was staying in wanted me to give my child up for adoption. I refused to even think of such a thing. I was a mother now, and I would protect and take care of my child. I could never abandon my baby. After Jacob was born, I had to decide what I was going to do and where I would be living. I couldn't stay at the home much longer. A widowed woman was visiting someone at the home, and I got into a conversation with her. She told me that she needed someone to stay with her. She was beginning to have health problems and needed help with her home. I had already explained to her that I couldn't go home—not yet, anyway. I agreed to stay with this woman, that I would do whatever she needed me to do. This precious lady became like a mother to me. I know now that God placed her in my life. She taught me so much about Jesus Christ. She was a real grandmother to my son, Jacob. I never married. I dedicated my life to God. I wanted Jacob to be raised in the church. My son was my number one priority in my life. Jacob and I have been through a lot of difficult times. The Lord has been so good to us. He has always provided for us."

"Now ladies," she continued to say, "I don't know why we are here in this community. I just know that God has a plan for Jacob and me."

Mrs. Turner finished her story and asked my mom or the pastor's wife to continue with the service. Mrs. Johnson stood to her feet and asked if anyone had any questions or comments for Mrs. Turner. All of us were sobbing, and no one said anything for a few seconds. One of the women, through her tears, stood up and made this profound statement. "I thought I was the only one this had happened to." This seemed to help the other ladies to tell some tragedies they'd experienced in their life. One by one, they told of some sad experiences. I was so shocked to hear all of this. I was crying now. I noticed that my aunt had come into the room. She was crying, too.

I knew it was time to tell my story. With legs trembling and voice quivering, I blurted out, "I was raped a few months ago. I am pregnant." I dropped to my knees with those words.

The women gathered around me and started praying. Some of them were speaking in another language. Others were crying out to God. I don't know how long this went on. I could hear someone saying, "I'm sorry, please forgive me." I turned to see who it was. I couldn't believe my eyes. It was Aunt Sammy. She had come into the room and was now on her knees, praying. I went over and knelt down beside her. There was so much love, joy, and healing in the room. I looked at my mother, and I could see that even she looked different. All of us were overjoyed. We continued talking for a few minutes and, after we calmed down, went to the kitchen to enjoy some of the food that my mom and aunt had prepared for us. Several of the women told me that if I needed anything, to please let them know. I assured them that I would. I felt as though a heavy weight had been lifted from my chest and off my shoulders.

Mrs. Turner had heard someone mention the baby shower.

"I love baby showers, Beth," she gushed. "Please consider having it."

I was so overjoyed that I agreed to let the women have a shower for my baby. I know now that the Lord had worked it out so I could hear Mrs. Turner's story. It helped me to let other people be a part of my life. I knew I would need some of them in the very near future.

Chapter Twelve

Fall was just around the corner. I needed some warmer clothes.

Mom, Aunt Sammy, and I made plans to go shopping. We didn't have a large mall close to our home. There was a new mall across town, near the Turners' home, that had just been completed. Mrs. Turner had told us about this mall, so we decided to pay it a visit. I knew we could find what we were looking for there. I wanted to buy some special clothes.

My dad had wanted to stay home and work on his workshop. He told Mom to leave Jonathen with him. Dad could keep my little brother busy, and my father wanted his wife to get out and enjoy the day.

We ladies stopped at the local diner and consumed a light breakfast before heading out to shop. The new mall was huge, and none of us knew where we wanted to go first. We agreed to meet in the middle of the mall around noon. I went in one direction; Mom and Auntie went the opposite way.

After about an hour, I was getting tired and thirsty. I found my way to the food court, where I got myself something to drink and found a table to sit and rest at. I saw several people from our church. We said our hellos and exchanged a few words. It was mostly just small talk. They all left, but I glanced back at them as they were walking away. Two of the girls I knew were looking back at me and whispering. One of the girls made a gesture with her hands around her stomach, and both of them erupted into laughter.

Oh my gosh, I thought. *Someone has told them about me.*

I could feel embarrassment bubbling up inside me. How could they do this to me? Who told them my secret? I suddenly felt like everyone in the mall was staring at me.

I pitched my drink in the garbage and fluttered from store to store, looking for mom and Aunt Sammy. I found them in the check-out line at the baby store. I just stood there and waited for them.

I tried not to speak, but the words tumbled out. "Mom, they know, they know!" I cried.

The cashier made a weird face at me. Aunt Sammy came out of the store and guided me to a bench in front of the store. My mother finally checked out and came over to where we were sitting.

"What's wrong with you, Elizabeth? Why are you so upset?" my mother demanded.

I replied to my mom that I just didn't want to talk about it. "I just want to go home. Please, Mom, just take me home."

We left the mall and went to our car. My aunt and mom got into the front seat. I just sort of slid down into the backseat. I guess I thought I could hide.

"Elizabeth, I am not leaving this parking lot until you tell me what's wrong with you," my mother said. Mom usually didn't raise her voice, but this time, she was persistent on finding out what the problem was. I relayed to my mother how the two girls from our church had laughed at me and held their stomachs, mocking me.

"They know my secret. What am I going to do?" I wailed.

Aunt Sammy spoke up. "Tell me who they are, and I will take care of this one."

I couldn't tell her. She was too hot-tempered. Mom was the calm one who took control of situations. I sat up in my seat and asked my mother to please turn the radio on. Music would surely help us feel calmer and more clear-headed.

Mom leaned over to turn the radio on but gasped. "Boy, that hurts!"

Could reaching hurt that much? I thought.

I asked her what was wrong, but she just shrugged and said it was just normal aches and pains. My mother dismissed it as old age, but I sure didn't. As soon as we got home, I found my dad in his workshop and explained to him about what had happened with Mom, since I knew my mother wouldn't bring it up to him. My father commented about how he had noticed Mom's appetite wasn't very good. He told me to let him know in the future if something didn't seem quite right with Mom again, but that I shouldn't be concerned this time around. I assured my father I would keep a close eye on Mom. I hugged him, and Dad told me to check on Jonathen.

I went upstairs to see what my little brother was up to. There was silence in his room. I thought this was strange, because Jonathen always made noise in his room. I slowly opened his door. There he was, sound asleep. Dad had left my little brother's favorite CD playing for him. The song "Jesus Loves Me" was softly playing over and over. I lay down on the bed beside Jonathen.

"Little brother, you are the best thing that has happened in my life, and I promise I will always be here for you. I pray to God that he will help me protect you," I whispered, kissing Jonathen's forehead and telling him how much I loved him. I stroked his blonde curls and held my baby brother close. Then I fell asleep, exhausted from the events of our day.

I was awakened about two hours later with Jonathen making a funny slobbering noise on my arm. I used to do that on his little fat belly when he was younger. I started laughing with him. I flipped Jonathen over onto his back and started making the funny sounds on his belly. He loved it.

Our time of fun was interrupted when Dad yelled to me that I had a phone call. It was Jacob. Jonathen followed behind me to the phone.

"Hi, Elizabeth, how are you?" Jacob asked.

"I am fine. How are you?"

Before Jacob could answer me, I had to ask him if he would talk to my little brother. Jonathen was yanking on my skirt and wanted to talk on the phone. I handed Jonathen the phone. He just kept saying, "Hello? Hello?" I had to laugh when I saw that my baby brother had the phone upside-down. Jacob said a few little words to Jonathen. Then I called for Dad to come and get my brother so that I could finish talking. Dad came for Jonathen, and I got back on the phone with Jacob.

Jacob wanted to know if I was going to help him take the kids from church to the aquarium. I told him I would go and help out. We were only taking the junior and senior high kids. Jacob and I both thought that we could handle them. Of course, we had a good laugh because neither of us had ever been in charge of so many young people, but we ready for the adventure. We said our goodbyes, and I went into the kitchen to check on Mom.

Mom reminded me that we both had doctor appointments on the same day. We had purposely scheduled them at the same time so that we could go together. I especially wanted to go with Mom to hear what the doctor would say. My mother had this way of not telling us what the doctor said unless we pressured her into telling us.

The day for our doctor's visit came too soon. It was now Monday morning and time to go. Mom's appointment was first thing this morning. My appointment wasn't until after lunch. My aunt Sammy was going to take care of Jonathen for us. She would take him to the play room at the mall. Mom and I had our appointments in the same building. All of our day was planned out, and we headed for our doctor's visit.

I waited in the waiting area for my Mom to see her doctor. She wasn't in the office very long. She came to get me. The doctor explained to us that he wanted Mom to take a few shots for her blood, since my mother's blood was a little on the low side. Mom reluctantly agreed to take the shots. One of my mother's weaknesses was the thought of getting a shot. The nurse gave Mom her shots and we left the office, since it wasn't yet time for my appointment. We decided to have some lunch while we were waiting for my appointment. We both loved Mexican food—Mom especially liked their fried ice cream. Consequently, we ended up going to our favorite Mexican restaurant. The waitress seated us, and we placed our order. I could hardly understand what she was saying. Her English was sort of broken. I was flabbergasted when the girl made a comment about me being a "little mama."

"How did she know that?" I asked Mom.

I hadn't gained very much weight, so I wondered how she knew. Mom replied that it was the glow on my face that had made the waitress aware of me being pregnant.

"Glow, what glow? I don't have a glow."

If I had a glow, I was sure I would be the first to notice. Mom just smiled at me and explained that when a woman is pregnant, she has a different glow on her face, and that I would be seeing a lot of different changes in my body.

I felt apprehensive and in awe at the same time. This was all new to me. I was glad I had my mother to help me through this time in my life.

We finished lunch, left the waitress a tip, and left the restaurant. As my mother and I were leaving, the girl that had served us said to me, "Congratulations, little mama!" I thanked her on my way out the door.

We arrived at my doctor's office. I had to wait for the doctor to come in, and the nurse informed us that the doctor would be just a few minutes late. The doctor had to rush to the hospital and deliver a premature baby.

The nurse took me back to the room, where she would be checking my blood pressure and weight. I told the nurse that I had been feeling well most of the time, but that I had started having some severe headaches. She wrote this on my chart, excused herself, and said the doctor would be in shortly. A few minutes later, I could hear someone outside my door, flipping through some papers.

Knock, knock, knock.

The door opened, and the doctor came in. He asked me how I was doing.

"Miss Reed," he said, "your weight is beginning to change, and your blood pressure is higher than it should be."

He explained that he wanted to monitor my BP. "Sometimes when you are pregnant, high blood pressure can develop. Now, don't get alarmed," he said. "We will take care of you."

"Will it hurt the baby?" I cried.

"It can cause a problem," the doctor admitted, "but don't worry; I will take care of you and the baby.

My doctor listened to the baby's heartbeat. It sounded really good. He instructed me not to eat a lot of junk food. He gave me a brochure about healthy eating. Needless to say, it did have French fries and mustard on the list of foods I should avoid. I made an appointment for the following month and joined my mother in the waiting room. I told Mom what the doctor had told me to do and gave her the food list to look at.

Mom said to me, "Beth, I will make you a deal. If you will help me to endure taking my shots, I will help you with your cravings."

We had a good laugh at her remark. We both knew were going to have a hard time keeping our promise to each other. Mom was getting tired, so we headed for our car to go home.

At home, when I went into the TV room, I could see Aunt Sammy and Jonathen watching cartoons. She loved them almost as much as my little brother did, especially the older ones. I watched television with them for a little while. I was real tired and sleepy afterwards, so I told everyone goodnight and went to my room.

It was early, but nightfall seemed to come quickly. I soon fell asleep.

Sometime in the middle of the night, I awoke with a very dry mouth. I made my way down the hallway, past my parents' room. I tried to be very quiet, so as not to awaken my mom and dad. To my surprise, the light in their room was shining under their door. I heard my mother's voice, talking to my father. I couldn't hear what she was saying, but I could hear my father.

"Hannah, I love you," he was saying. "Sweetheart, don't be afraid. I'll take care of you. You are not going anywhere, at least not without me. We are in this together, and I don't want you to be scared."

I think I heard my mother say, "Okay, James."

With that, the light went out, and I quietly went to my room. I didn't want them to know I had heard them talking. For some reason, I didn't feel thirsty any more. I crawled into bed and cried myself to sleep because of the conversation I had overheard. I guess the crying had made me very tense, because I woke up with a severe headache. I never mentioned this to my parents. I didn't want them to be concerned about me, so I pretended like everything was fine. They never suspected that anything was wrong with me. I knew I just had to shield Mom from some of my problems. She had enough issues of her own to worry about.

Chapter Thirteen

The entire week had gone by so quickly. Here it was, almost time for our trip to the aquarium. Jacob had called me the night before, and we discussed our plans for the next day.

I found myself feeling pretty good after talking to Jacob.

We made plans to leave early, the next morning. We all met at the church. Jacob's mother was going to be driving the church van. Everyone piled into the van, and away we went for a day at the aquarium. We laughed, talked and sang songs until we arrived at our destination. Of course, some of the teenagers just had to tease me about being an "old person"—though, truth be told, I wasn't much more than three years older than most of them.

Jacob told the kids that he wanted us to meet in front of the ticket booth before we went into the building. We had decided that the high school kids would be okay to go in by themselves. They were instructed to meet us in the lobby at twelve o'clock for lunch. They promised to behave, and that they would meet us at exactly noon.

Jacob, Mrs. Turner, and I would take care of the junior high kids. The aquarium had a guided tour. We thought that would be fun to try—plus, the tour would allow us to interact with some of the animals. We were having a good time until we arrived at the underground tunnel. Our ears started to pop as we went down. Jacob gave me some gum, which seemed to help with the popping.

Our tour guide was talking and explaining to us about all the different mammals. They were beautiful creatures that swam in the tank above our heads. It was so neat to watch them swim around and look down at us. We all had to laugh because we felt like we were the ones on display, instead of the mammals.

While we were sight-seeing and listening to our guide, I noticed that her voice was beginning to sound strange to me. I looked at her, and she had become a blur. I felt my face starting to become flaming hot. I asked Jacob if he was hot.

"No, but are you okay, Beth?" he said.

The next thing I remember was waking up on the concrete floor. Everyone was staring down at me. A man was leaning over me and calling my name. A young man in the crowd said he was a nurse, so Jacob's mom scooted over and let him take a look at me. Mrs. Turner told me she would call my parents and that she would stay with me.

The ambulance arrived. The EMTs started asking me how I felt. I told them I was okay, but that my head was really hurting me. Jacob's mother told me to lie still so they could check me out. I was getting scared.

The other kids had heard about what had happened, and they came to where we were. Jacob assured them I was okay, but he still knelt down beside me to pray. All of our teens joined him in prayer.

The EMTs took my blood pressure. One of them asked how I was feeling. He was close to my head, so I very quietly whispered to him that I was pregnant. I didn't want anyone to hear what I was saying. The kids did not hear anything, and neither did Jacob.

The young EMT left my side for but a moment, returning with an IV.

He explained that I would feel just a small needle in my arm. He was preparing me to go to the hospital. Before I could actually realize what was going on, I was in the ambulance and headed for the nearest hospital.

When we arrived at the hospital, I felt like everyone was firing questions at me and poking me with more needles. The ER doctor entered the room and introduced himself. He reassured me that he thought I would be alright, but that they needed to do more tests to make sure. He asked me how many months I was pregnant. I notified him that I was about three months along. He listened to my heartbeat, and then to my baby's. He told me that I probably passed out because of my blood pressure. He would know more when the blood work came back from the lab, he informed me. As we were talking,

Jacob and his mom came into the room. Before I could introduce them, the doctor went over to Jacob to shake his hand.

"I guess this is the father," the doctor said to Jacob. "Congratulations, young man. I think everything will be fine."

I peeked at Jacob. His eyes were as big as saucers. He looked at me without saying a word, but I knew he was wondering what was going on.

I was absolutely mortified. I covered my head with the bed sheets.

"Did I say something wrong, Miss Reed?" the doctor asked.

I very timidly replied, "He is not the father."

The doctor apologized for his assumption. I explained to him that Jacob was our youth pastor at church, and that the woman with him was his mother.

"We were at the aquarium together," I said lamely.

No one said anything else.

The nurse came into my room and told us that my parents were here. Jacob said he would go get my mom and dad. When he left the room, Mrs. Turner came over to my bed, took me by the hand, and told me that she would explain everything to Jacob.

"You are going to be alright, Beth. Jacob will keep your secret as long as you want him to."

I just had to believe her. I wasn't ready to tell anyone that I had been raped and was now pregnant.

My parents and Aunt Sammy came into the room. Mrs. Turner left so we could be alone.

My mother came to my bedside and kissed my forehead.

I started crying. "Mom, everything is going wrong. I'm sick, and now Jacob knows my secret." I was beginning to get hysterical.

Mom took my trembling hand and told me to calm down. She knew it would cause my blood pressure to spike.

"Come on, baby girl, we are all here," my father said. "You're going to be okay. Let's just take one day at a time. Everything will take care of itself. We'll talk about it later. Okay, honey?"

I said okay just as the doctor came back into my room. He instructed me to make an appointment to see my OB-GYN as soon as I could. I told him I would do that, and I was released from the hospital. I met Jacob and his mother in the waiting room and mentioned what the doctor had said. Everyone made me promise that I would do a follow-up with my doctor.

Jacob looked concerned, but he assured me that things would be alright. His mom would help take the youth group home. I had forgotten that all of our young people had come to the hospital with me. I just hoped that none of them had heard anything the doctors had said. I left the hospital. Jacob loaded all the kids up and headed for home.

I called my doctor first thing Monday morning. I explained to his receptionist what had happened to me over the weekend. She told me that my doctor was booked up for the next two weeks. I asked to speak to the doctor, and he came to the phone. I notified him about my incident and how the ER doctor wanted me to see my OB-GYN immediately. The doctor told his nurse to get me into the office as soon as possible. She said she would call if there was a cancellation any time before my visit.

We scheduled my appointment in ten days, with the exception of there being an early opening. I hung the phone up and went to join my parents in the kitchen.

I told Mom that we needed to try and schedule our doctor's visits on the same day, if we could. She agreed with me. Mom needed someone with her, and I sure wanted her to be with me.

My mom had been doing fair. She was having some problems with being very fatigued sometimes. I tried to help with the chores and Jonathen. Mom would try to do everything by herself.

She was so strong and determined. I once asked her where she got all of her strength from.

She just smiled and said, "The Lord Jesus is my strength. He is the One that keeps me going, no matter what happens in my life."

Mom had faced many challenges in her young life. Her parents were killed in that awful accident. Aunt Sammy and Mom were moved to another state so that they would have a place to call home. Relatives took care of them, but they had to grow up quickly. It was not an easy life.

Mom said she had always believed that God would take care of her, no matter what she had to face. She had cried many tears, but she was the "glue" that helped keep our family going. She always seemed to know what to say or do. If she didn't have an answer, you could hear her praying and asking God for his guidance. Her faith was unshakeable.

Mom left the kitchen, while Dad headed for his favorite spot: his work shop. I did the dishes and a load of laundry. I had not heard Mom and I was concerned, so I went to find her. I found her in her favorite spot: the large garden tub. When she was tired from caring for Jonathen and doing other chores, she would sneak off and head for the tub. My little brother had fallen asleep.

I tried to be really quiet when I knocked on the door, where Mom was enjoying her time alone. Mom didn't answer me. I started to get scared until Mom apologized for not answering me. She been running her bath water and hadn't heard me knock. She said she would be out in a little while, and then she would talk to me.

"Okay," I answered, before making my way outside to find my father.

Dad was supposed to work today, but he told Mom he had some things to do, so he was taking the day off. I really think he didn't go to work because of the things that had happened at the aquarium.

The door to his workshop was ajar. I could hear my dad's favorite music blaring on the radio. He loved bluegrass tunes, saying it reminded him of his hometown in the hills of Kentucky. That's where my parents met. After they married, my parents moved to Georgia. Dad had been promised a job there. He was going to go to Georgia just as soon as he and mom were married. They moved there immediately after they said "I do."

I didn't see Dad, so I just followed the music. I came around the corner of the shop.

There was my father, kneeling by the work bench, praying. I didn't want him to see or hear me, so I hid behind one of the large tables, out of his sight. I definitely did not want to disturb him. I just wanted to hear what he was saying.

I could tell my father was crying. He kept wiping his face, and it wasn't hot in the shop. I decided to go to the house because I didn't want him to know that I had been there. I walked into the house just as the phone was ringing. Mom yelled for me to answer it; Jonathen had woken up and needed her.

I picked the phone up. It was the pastor's wife. She wanted to know how I was feeling, and she asked about Mom. Mom was expecting a visit from her that day, but Mrs. Johnson asked me to inform my mother she was going to be a little late. Something had detained her at the church. I assured Mrs. Johnson that I would give my mother her message. I said goodbye and hung up.

Dad came into the house, just as I hung the phone up.

"Who was on the phone?" he asked.

"The pastor's wife," I replied.

"Oh, yes, that's right," Dad said. "She's supposed to be here to visit with your mom. Is everything okay?"

I told him Mrs. Johnson was going to be late and how she would be here later on. Dad was going to take Jonathen out for a drive, and possibly go get some ice cream. I wanted to go with him, but he wanted me to stay home with Mom. He also thought that I needed to rest; I agreed. I hugged my dad and Jonathen as they left for their little ice cream excursion. Then, I went to tell mom that I was going to take a nap: if she needed me for anything, she was to yell for me. She promised me she would.

I don't know how long I have been asleep, but I was awakened by the doorbell. I heard Mom talking to someone: Mrs. Johnson. Mom called for me to come down and join them. Why would she want me to join them? I grabbed a small blanket and threw it across my shoulders. It had been a lazy day, and I was still in my pajamas. I walked into the family room where Mom and her best friend were talking. Mrs. Johnson commented that I looked a little tired.

I said I was a bit sleepy, but I would be okay.

I sat down on the couch by my mom. The pastor's wife handed me a bright yellow bag.

What is this? It isn't my birthday, I thought.

"It isn't a special holiday. What is this?" I asked Mrs. Johnson with curiosity.

"I think you'll understand when you open it," Mrs. Johnson replied.

I quickly took the vibrant tissue paper out of the bag. I put my hand inside the bag, trying to figure out what it was. I felt something soft and fuzzy. I took the gift from the bag. It was a beautiful stuffed lamb. I was excited just looking at it. Pastor's sweet wife told me to turn it over.

There was a key on the back side of the lamb. I turned the key. My favorite children's song, "Jesus Loves Me", started to play. It was so pretty and soft to the touch.

"I hope your baby will like it," Mrs. Johnson said eagerly.

"My baby? I thought it was for me." At the look on Mrs. Johnson's face, I laughed and tried to make my comment sound like a joke—but I really did think it was for me. I had always loved stuffed animals, especially lambs. Mom must have told her.

I thanked her and gave her a big hug. I smiled and promised Mrs. Johnson that I would be sure to give it to my baby.

I was not taken by surprise by Mrs. Johnson's next statement. "Beth, have you thought any more about letting me have you a baby shower?"

I paused for a second and glanced at my mother to see what she was doing.

"Beth, honey, let us do this for you," Mom pleaded. "It will be a lot of fun. I know you're concerned about what other people will say, but please don't let anyone take your joy from you."

I didn't understand what my mother meant, but sometime later, I came to realize what she was talking about. I agreed to have the baby shower—mostly for my mother's sake, because she was so thrilled with the idea. I would do anything to make her happy.

"Just leave it to us, Beth! We will take care of everything," they said gleefully.

Mrs. Johnson and my mother were so busy talking that I don't believe they even took notice when I left the room. I took my little lamb and went to my room. I just kept playing it over and over. The music was so sweet and soothing.

It wasn't very long before I heard my father and little brother come in the house.

"Come down here, Sissy! We have pizza," Jonathen said happily. He couldn't pronounce pizza very well, but he sure knew how to eat it and get it all over himself. He loved pizza and I did, too. I came down from my room and joined the family.

After we ate, Dad wanted to watch a movie. Jonathen was still wound up and making noise. I hurried to my bedroom to retrieve my little lamb.

Maybe this will keep Jonathen occupied while we watch the movie, I decided.

Jonathen spotted what I had in my hands. He grabbed for it immediately. "Mine! Mine, Sissy! This is mine!" he said.

I almost told him it wasn't his, but I knew he wouldn't understand. I let him play with it until he fell asleep.

My aunt Sammy had been gone for most of the day. She went to visit some of her old friends. Before the movie was over, my aunt finally came home. She watched the end of the movie with us.

Dad asked her how her day went.

"You know, James, it went great!" Aunt Sammy gushed. "I had a really good time, and I got to see a lot of my old classmates. One thing I did come to realize, though, I am not as young as I used to be." She made a face. "I am exhausted. I'm ready for a good night's sleep."

We all laughed at her. The movie soon ended. We all said our goodnights and went to bed.

I had not been sleeping very well, so Mom let me sleep in that morning. It was late when I came downstairs. Mom had fixed me some breakfast. She kept it on the stove to stay warm until I felt like eating. I splashed my face with some cold water to wake up. That felt a lot better. I ate my breakfast and went outside to sit on the front porch.

I was enjoying the warm sun as cars went by. Some would drive past our house and wave to me. I would return the hello and wave back. It was customary here in Georgia to do that. Our little community was very friendly, and most everyone knew who their neighbors were.

I had only been sitting there for a short time when a car I didn't recognize pulled into our driveway. At first, I didn't see who it was. The gentleman stepped out of the car. To my surprise, it was Jacob.

He smiled at me and came onto the porch.

I said hi and asked if he wanted to see my parents.

"No, Beth, I came to see you," Jacob said.

My heart started hammering inside my chest, and I could feel myself blushing. Why would he want to see me? Jacob could tell I was getting nervous. He told me to relax, that he just wanted to talk. He asked if he could sit next to me. I said yes and scooted over.

Jacob wanted to tell me he was sorry for leaving the hospital without saying goodbye. I reassured him it was okay. I knew that he was embarrassed when the doctor thought that Jacob was the father, so I told him I was the one who should be sorry.

"No, Beth, I wasn't embarrassed," he said, after catching my implication. "I just didn't know you were going to have a baby. I didn't even know that you were seeing anyone."

"I'm not seeing anyone," I insisted. "The father of my baby doesn't even know that he's having a child."

Jacob looked at me with concern. I could tell by the look on his face that he didn't understand. He told me that when he heard it from the doctor, he was shocked.

"It did shake me up a lot, Beth," he admitted. "I just had to leave and be alone so I could talk to the Lord."

I sort of felt sorry for him. He had a package in his hand. He handed it to me.

"This isn't much, Elizabeth, but I felt I should give it to you."

I opened the package, and I could not believe what I was seeing. It was a brand new journal. I knew I had not told Jacob about how I had kept a journal when I was much younger. Jacob explained to me that he had something he wanted to tell me.

"Beth, when I was born, my mother kept a journal, and she still does. When I got older, my mom would let me read some of the pages. She would write how she was feeling. It helped her get through a lot of rough times. I know this isn't an easy time for you, but I just want to help, if you will allow me to."

This is too much of a coincidence. Or is it? I thought while he was talking.

I almost told Jacob my story, but I just couldn't—not yet, anyway. Jacob finished explaining about his mother's journal before excusing himself, saying he had to go somewhere with our pastor.

"Thank you for the journal, Jacob," I said.

"You're quite welcome," he said with a smile. "Bye, Beth."

I watched him as he drove down the street. I heard a noise behind me and turned to see my mother at the screen door. She was just standing there, looking out at the street.

"Mom, did you hear us talking?" I asked her.

"I did overhear you talking, Beth. I'm sorry; I thought you were out here by yourself. When I came to the door, I heard Pastor Jacob speaking to you. I didn't mean to intrude on your conversation, honey. I just didn't know you had company."

I handed the journal to Mom and asked her what she thought about Jacob giving it to me.

She said it was very nice and considerate of him to get the journal for me.

"Mom, I just could not tell him about the rape. I don't know how to tell him," I moaned.

"Child, you don't owe anyone an explanation," my mother said firmly. "The Lord knows all about this, and he will help you. I am so proud of you, Beth. You have a lot of courage."

With those words, we hugged one other and went back into the house. We both needed to get to bed early. Our doctor's appointments were in the morning, and it was bound to be a long day tomorrow. Everyone settled in for the night.

What will tomorrow bring for our family? I mused to myself.

I crawled into bed and soon fell asleep.

Chapter Fourteen

Today was the morning of our appointments. My aunt was going to take care of Jonathen while Mom and I were gone. We arrived at the office, signed in, and waited for the nurse to call us.

Both of our appointments were at the same time. My doctor was across the hall from Mom's.

I went over to the waiting room close to my doctor's room. I was so glad that both of us had doctors that were located in the same medical complex. It made things so much easier for me.

My doctor was somewhat pleased with my health, except my blood pressure was much too high. He cautioned me to limit my salt intake and try to relax during my visit. I guess he could tell I was a little apprehensive. I told him I would really try to do what he asked.

Mom was finished with her exam before I was. She was waiting for me in the hallway when I came out of the office. I told her what the doctor had ordered me to do, and she encouraged me to follow his instructions. I wanted Mom to tell me how her appointment went. She said she was doing fine, but that she would be glad when her series of shots was finished.

We stopped by the grocery store before we went home. Little brother was out of his favorite cereal, and Mom had told him that she would bring it home after she was finished with the doctor. Jonathen met us at the door when we got home, excited to see what mom had got for him. Of course, Mom had gotten Jonathen exactly what she had promised him. I recalled back to when I was a child, and even then, Mom always tried to keep her promises.

My mom and I were both exhausted from our doctor's visits and going to the grocery store. We chatted a few minutes with Jonathen and my aunt Sammy. Then Mom and I decided to go to our rooms and relax before Dad got home from work. I was still wondering what this week had in store for all of us. I was going to try and take it just one day at a time. Mom had always tried to stress that point to me. She would often quote Matthew 6:34 from the Bible to me:

"Don't worry about tomorrow. Tomorrow will worry about itself. Each day has enough trouble of its own."

"Take one day at a time," my mother would say to me. "We have no promise that tomorrow will ever come."

I had not always listened to her, but I have realized that it is a true saying to live by.

Sunday morning soon rolled around before I even gave it much thought. I had tried to stay busy and keep my mind occupied with good thoughts. I had learned to love being with my little Sunday school class. I was learning a lot about children, and how they behaved and communicated with each other. I enjoyed just watching them. As I observed them, I couldn't help but let my thoughts wonder and wish that the adults of this world would become more like my little class. Children are so innocent and trusting.

The morning service soon ended. Everyone was shaking hands and greeting each other. Most of the women would ask both me and my mother how we were feeling. The ladies each wanted to know if there was anything they could do to help our family. Mom politely said no and thanked all of them for asking.

I could hardly believe that Thanksgiving would be here in two weeks. Where had the summer gone? My parents had always loved the holidays. It was a special time for them. Mom always had the tradition of inviting someone new to the community, or sometimes a homeless family, to dinner. This year, my mother apparently decided our guests would be Jacob and his mother. I was initially a little upset when mom told me this. I really liked Mrs. Turner and Jacob—truly, I did—but I was still very uneasy around Jacob. I just felt like Jacob could read my mind, and I didn't like that. I knew that he was aware of my secret now, but it was still very hard for me to see him.

Thanksgiving was finally here. I was concerned that no one would be able to make it to dinner, considering the weather was beginning to look pretty bleak. The weather channel was calling for our first snow of the season—a light snow, anyway—but then again, the weatherman isn't always accurate.

Mom and I had been up really late last night. Mom always fixed a few items the night before. Last night, we both had made a batch of pumpkin cookies and cornbread for our stuffing. The house smelled so good. I could hardly wait to eat. Mom and I were tired from all of the dicing, slicing, and chopping, but at least we had prepared some of the food last night.

We were supposed to eat around four, and the Turners arrived right on time. Mrs. Turner had made some fried apple pies. Jacob's mom knew that I loved peanut butter fudge and, even though I wasn't supposed to eat it, she had made me a big container of it. I couldn't wait to dig into it.

Mrs. Turner smiled at me. "Now, the fudge is for everyone," she told me. "I don't want to be the one to blame for you not following your diet."

I just laughed. "I won't eat it all. I'll try to share the fudge with everyone."

Mom had to snicker when she heard me say that. She knew how I was when it came to sweets.

My mother called all of us into the kitchen. Dinner was ready. She asked Jacob to pray over the food and thank God for another day of life. Jacob prayed and we all sat down to a wonderful meal. Dad tried to carve the turkey and, like every year, made a mess. He wanted to carve big, juicy pieces of the turkey, but it just never seemed to turn out that way. Dad could carve out wooden items, but he sure couldn't carve a turkey. It was the yearly joke in our family about Dad and the turkey. We all loved to tease him. He didn't mind. Dad thought it was funny, too, but that didn't keep him from trying to carve it.

Everyone had finished dinner. We went into the living room to relax and talk. Our conversation was interrupted with Jonathen calling for his daddy to come there. Dad went to see what he was so excited about, and I followed him. It was snowing. Little brother was so happy—he had never seen snow. Dad tried to explain it to him. I told Dad I would get my coat and hat on and take Jonathen outside. My father bundled my little brother up in warm clothes; then, little brother and I ran outside in the beautiful snowflakes.

I let Jonathen play for a few minutes before Dad wanted me to bring him back inside. Jonathen had never played in the snow, and my dad didn't want him to get too cold. I took him inside and went back out to the front porch by myself to enjoy our first snowfall. I hadn't noticed, but Jacob had followed me. I noticed something move out in the yard. It was a mama deer and her baby. I stood really still and watched them. I didn't want to scare them away. I thought Jacob had seen the deer, too, but he said he was looking in the other direction.

"I guess you are the lucky one today, Beth," he joked.

I just smiled and started for the front door. I was getting pretty cold myself. Before I could go inside, Jacob urged me to stay so he could ask me something. I was used to him asking me things about church, but this question I definitely wasn't ready for.

"Elizabeth," he said, "I would like to get to know you a little better. Will you go out to dinner and a movie with me?"

I was caught completely off guard. I could not believe what my ears were hearing, what Jacob was saying. I even asked him to repeat himself

"Why, Beth, did I offend you? If I did, I didn't mean to," Jacob replied.

"No, I'm not offended," I said quickly. "I'm just curious to know why you want to go out with *me*."

Before I could say anything else, Jacob smiled. "I don't care that you're pregnant. I think you are a beautiful girl. I would like the chance to get to know you better. I hope we can become good friends. I hope you will allow that to happen. You don't have to answer me now. I'll talk to you about it later. Just think about it."

I agreed to think about it, and we both went back into the house.

Everyone in the house had retired into the family room. Jacob and I joined them. Aunt Sammy and Jonathen were snuggled up together on the oversized chair by the fireplace. I could see they were getting sleepy—both of them were beginning to doze off. My mother had retrieved some of our old photo albums out of the attic. She was showing them to Jacob's mom and telling her a story about every single one of them.

"I want to see them," Jacob said, pulling up a chair and looking at old pictures of me. I was so embarrassed. He just had to see all of the crazy hair styles I had when I was a teenager. He didn't tease me, but occasionally I would see a silly smile flash across his cute face.

It was beginning to get very late, and Jacob's mom said she had to work the next day. She thanked my mom for having them for dinner and told her how wonderful it was, and how much she had enjoyed it. We all said goodnight. As my family walked to the door to see the Turners off, Jacob flashed me a smile.

"I hope I will be seeing you soon, Elizabeth," he said. I could feel myself blushing profusely. I wondered if anyone else noticed. All I could think to say to him was, "See ya later."

When they were gone, my father said to me, "What was that all about?" He said it as only a father can. I really didn't want to tell my parents that Jacob had asked me out.

"Oh, it's nothing," I said in the most nonchalant manner I could muster.

All of us were jaded from the day's events. I immediately told Mom I was going to take a hot shower and go to bed. I kissed my parents, told them how much I loved them, and headed for my room and the shower. I hurried to get upstairs, because I knew if I stayed any longer, my dad would surely interrogate me about Jacob. He had a way of getting things out of me.

It seemed as though the days were flying by. I was starting to gain a lot of weight. My belly was getting bigger and bigger. There was no way I could hide my pregnancy any longer. I still had not told Mrs. Johnson that she could throw a baby shower for me. Mom reminded me that I should talk to her the following Sunday.

"What's the rush?" I asked my mother. I still had four months to go before the baby was due.

"I want to have the shower before Christmas, which is right around the corner," she insisted.

Christmas was always a busy time at our house, so I promised mom that I would talk to the pastor's wife on Sunday morning.

After the service Sunday morning, I informed Mrs. Johnson that I needed to talk to her about the shower. Mrs. Johnson could not contain her excitement. I think she was more excited than I was.

"Now, Elizabeth, I want to take care of all the plans. It will be my gift to you. Please say you will," Mrs. Johnson chattered.

I agreed to let her take care of everything. Then, I thanked Mrs. Johnson for her kindness and joined my parents out in the car.

The shower was scheduled for the second week in December. Mom was getting excited as the days until my baby shower drew a lot closer. I was apprehensive, but I was also looking forward to it. I did worry about who would attend and what they might ask me. I also was concerned that Mom might not feel like doing this. I always did have a way of letting my mind take over all of my thoughts and imagination. I told myself that I just had to settle down and keep myself busy. If I was busy, I didn't have time to try and solve everything for myself or my family.

The day of my shower had finally arrived. I had slept a little later than usual. It was a girl's day today; Dad had taken Jonathen to see Santa Claus at the mall. I remembered when he used to take me—such fond memories.

Mom and I had been up real late the night before. Aunt Sam had gone shopping and got a lot of decorations and prizes. All three of us had worked late, trying to get the room decorated. It was so cute, what with all of the little baby things hanging from the ceiling. The party was set for 2:00 p.m. and it was already 1:30 p.m. We made sure everything was in order and went to the kitchen for coffee before our guests arrived.

The back doorbell rang. It was Mrs. Johnson. She needed help getting the cake out of her car. I grabbed my coat and told her I would be right there to help her. The cake was in several boxes. I couldn't wait to see what it looked like. We went into the family room, where Mom had prepared a table to sit it on. Mom and Aunt Sammy were waiting for us.

We all were anxious to see what the cake looked like. I couldn't believe that the women made me turn my back until they unpacked the cake and got it all set up. This just didn't seem fair. After all, it was my baby shower. However, I did as I was told. Mom put her warm hands over my eyes. Mrs. Johnson took me by my hand and led me to the table.

"Now you can open your eyes, Beth," Mrs. Johnson said.

The room seemed so quiet, as I opened my eyes to the most beautiful and colorful work of art.

The cake was a barnyard scene with all sorts of baby farm animals. All of them were in their special places, and there was a brilliant rainbow suspended over the barn. I was so happy that I started to cry. I looked at mom, Aunt Sam and Mrs. Johnson. They were crying, too.

Mrs. Johnson explained that she had chosen the farm animals because she knew that I was an animal lover. She also said that the rainbow represented hope for a brighter tomorrow. I thanked her for being so kind and thoughtful.

"How did you keep this a secret from me, Mom?" I wanted to know.

She just shrugged her tiny shoulders and smiled at me.

The guests soon began to stream through the door. They all carried colorful bags and packages. Some of them even had boxes and baskets. I had never seen so many gifts. The house was full of women. Mrs. Johnson appointed Aunt Sam to be in charge of the games.

Games? I thought.

I didn't know we were going to be playing games, but it was hysterical to see a bunch of older women acting like children. It was a lot of fun. I didn't know that the church ladies could be so much fun. After the shower, I could see these church ladies in an entirely different light.

I opened all of my gifts. I was overwhelmed at the things these women had given my baby. One by one, we admired the presents. Each was more beautiful than the previous one I had opened.

I was being asked a lot of questions about my baby, but the main question was what I had chosen for my baby's name. I had not decided what her name would be. The ladies laughed and told me I'd better hurry and pick a name before the baby arrived. Only one of the women asked me about the father. I simply told her that the father was not involved in my life any longer. I know the other women were curious, too, but no one else said anything about the father. It wasn't until late in the evening that we got around to eating our cake and ice cream.

The ladies were all giving me advice about how to raise children. Some of them wanted to tell me all about childbirth. Needless to say, I had a lot of questions for my mother just as soon as the last guest left our driveway. Mom assured me I would be fine. I wanted to believe her, but these ladies sure had made me a little scared about the birthing process.

I went into the kitchen to help mom finish cleaning up. As I entered the kitchen, I saw my mother slumped over the kitchen sink. She was holding onto the faucet and splashing cool water on her face.

"Mom, are you okay?"

She didn't answer me. I asked her again if she was alright. She raised her head and looked at me.

I immediately knew something was not right. Her face had drained itself of all color, and she had a strange look in her eyes. I started screaming for Aunt Sam, who had gone to empty the trash. When my aunt heard me yelling, she ran back into the kitchen. She saw that I was clutching Mom and trying to get her to sit down.

Aunt Sammy was frantic. She screamed at me to call my father, so I went to call Dad.

I could hear my aunt saying, "Oh, gosh, Hannah, what's wrong?"

I watched as Aunt Sam took a cold wash cloth and began stroking my mom's face.

Dad came to the phone. I told him what was going on, and made sure to let him know that he needed to come home immediately. My father said he would be home just as fast as he could.

I hung the phone up and rushed to my mother's side. I knelt down beside her chair and again asked her if she was okay.

Mom just said that she had gotten a little dizzy and felt sick to her stomach. She wanted us to think it was just too much partying. That was my mom's way of pretending she was alright. I knew something was seriously wrong, but I didn't push the issue. I knew when Dad got home, he would handle things. He had a way of doing that.

It wasn't long before my dad got home. He wanted his wife to go to the hospital, but she refused. "I'll be okay after I go to bed and rest," Mom protested.

When my mother made up her mind about anything, you could not change her mind. We all just listened to her and tried to honor her wishes.

Aunt Sam and I finished cleaning the kitchen. I promised Mom I would take care of Jonathen and see that he got to bed at his normal time. I told Auntie that after I got Jonathen to sleep, I would come back downstairs and spend some time with her.

Jonathen was worn out from his day at the mall. He usually went to sleep quickly, so long as I pretended I was asleep.

That night, little brother caught me with my eyes open several times. This made him not want to go to sleep.

Jonathen tried to close my eyes with his little hand. "Go to sleep, Sissy!" he admonished.

It was hard for me to keep a straight face and not laugh at him. If I laughed, he would not go to sleep for a long time. He wanted to play "sleepy time" with his sissy. After about forty-five minutes of pretending, Jonathen finally fell asleep. I quietly slipped out of his bed and went to join Aunt Sammy in the family room.

My aunt had started a fire in the big, open fireplace. We both loved to sit and talk by the fireside. She had made some hot chocolate and motioned for me to sit next to her. I couldn't keep from crying as she handed me my cup of the hot chocolate.

"Come here, Be-Be," Aunt Sammy cooed, as I started to cry even more than I had wanted to.

I finally calmed down, and we both snuggled up under the big blanket that Mom kept near the fireplace. We talked about the days ahead, and how excited my parents were about the baby. We discussed a name for the baby, but Aunt Sam insisted Mom help name her. Every time Mom's name was mentioned, I had the urge to go check on her. However, I didn't want to disturb my mother, so I tried to brush the urge away. I knew I could pray for her. It seemed I was doing a lot of that now.

The fire started to dwindle down. I told my aunt that I was tired and ready for bed. We said goodnight and went to our own rooms.

The night was long, and I could not get comfortable. I tossed and turned frequently. I even got up a few times and kept pacing the floor. I had a feeling that something bad was going to happen. I couldn't understand what I was feeling. The house was so quiet. My mind was racing. All I could think about was Mom and how she had looked after the party. I knew she was not telling us exactly how she felt. I finally fell asleep after a very long time.

I was awakened by Aunt Sam. She was hovering over me.

"Elizabeth, wake up. You're dreaming," she was saying to me.

"Dreaming?" I muttered. "What is going on, Aunt Sam? What's happening to me?"

My aunt tried to explain that she had heard me screaming for someone but couldn't understand exactly what I was saying. I couldn't remember what I had been dreaming. All I knew was I was exhausted and felt like I had been running a country mile. I asked her what time it was. She told me it was noon.

"Twelve o'clock?" I shouted at her. "What about Mom? How could I have slept that long without checking on my mother?"

I nearly scrambled out of bed to check on her, but Mom had heard me call out her name and was at the door to check on me. She wanted to know where I was going in such a big rush. I made an excuse because I didn't want my mother to worry about me. I had to admit, she did look a lot better today. Mom said she was fine and proceeded to tell me that I needed to calm down or she would be taking me to the hospital, instead of her.

I did calm down when Mom reminded me about my blood pressure. The doctor had warned me about getting overly excited.

"After all, Beth, you are going to have a baby. You need to be thinking about these things," Mom reminded me.

I apologized for getting overly excited and said I would try to do better. I asked Mom how she was doing.

"I'm fine, Beth. Your father prayed for me last night, and the Lord has touched me. This is another new day, so let's enjoy it."

I looked at my aunt Sam. She was smiling, and so was I.

Mom had lunch ready. She wanted me to come downstairs and eat with her. I told her I would just as soon as I took a good hot shower. I grabbed a couple of oversized towels from the linen closet and headed for the bathroom. I decided to use my parents' bathroom. Their shower was bigger than mine, and it had a great showerhead. The water pressure was so much better, and I liked the way the showerhead had several settings on it. I could set the pressure to suit me, and that made me feel so warm and relaxed. I was just beginning to enjoy my shower when I heard my mother at the door.

"Beth, can you come here?" she said in a low voice.

"Why are you talking so quietly?" I said.

I peeked at her from behind the door. Mom's face had a strange look on it. With her finger to her lips, she motioned for me to be quiet. She whispered for me to grab my robe and come to the phone. I asked who it was, but she didn't answer me. I sat down on her bed, and Mom sat down beside me.

"Hello?" I spoke into the phone, to whoever was on the other line.

I heard a familiar voice say, "Hello, Beth."

My heart plummeted. Brian.

I felt the rage boiling up inside my chest. I hung the phone up without hesitation.

I looked at my mother now. "Oh, no, Mom, it's Brian," I kept saying. "It's Brian! Do you understand what I am telling you? It's Brian, Mom! It's Brian."

I started pacing the floor. Hot, angry tears sprang from my eyes. I didn't want to ever talk to him again. How could he be so cruel and call me after what he had done?

The phone rang again, and I knew it was Brian calling back. I was still fuming. Mom knew how upset I was, so she answered the phone and started talking to him. How could she be so calm?

She knew he had raped me. Mom told him to hang on for just a few minutes. She approached me and asked me to talk to him. My mother assured me that I could always hang the phone up if it was too uncomfortable. With great reluctance, I agreed to talk to him.

Chapter Fifteen

I wasn't sure how I was going to talk to Brian after what he had done to me, but I bitterly took the phone from my mother.

I was so scared that I could hardly hold the phone. I was shaking almost uncontrollably. Just the thought of hearing his voice made me sick to my stomach. I put the receiver to my ear.

"Beth, are you there?" Brian said. "Please don't hang up. Please, Beth, I need to talk to you. You don't have to say anything. Just listen to me, okay? Beth, are you there?"

I could barely get out a very low grunt, but it was enough to let Brian know that I was on the other line.

Brian started talking to me. He told me that he had been incarcerated in Florida for several months, after having been arrested for drunk driving. He wanted me to know that he was coming back to our hometown.

"You can't come back here!" I snapped. "You can't do that to me."

"Beth," he went on, "you don't understand. I have to come back."

"What do you mean, you have to come back?" I screamed at him.

I felt Mom rubbing my back, trying to keep me calm.

"Brian, you have exactly five minutes to explain yourself, and then I never want to hear from you again," I said.

Before he started talking, I motioned for Mom to get the other phone and listen in on our conversation. I wanted her to hear what he would say to me. At first, Mom shook her head. I just kept shaking my head yes, so she quietly picked up the other phone.

Brian began by telling me how sorry he was that he had hurt me. "I know what I did was wrong. In the beginning, after I left town, I didn't think much about what I had done to you. When I had to go to jail, I met an older gentleman, who was the chaplain there. We became friends, and the chaplain, for some reason, confided in me. He told me the story of his daughter, who had been raped and killed by her boyfriend on her sixteenth birthday. I couldn't believe he was telling me about his child, but it made me realize what I had done to you. I felt so bad that I just opened up to the chaplain and told him about how I had hurt you. We talked for a long time before the chaplain talked to me about Jesus Christ. I listened to him, and he led me to know the Lord as my own personal Savior."

I could not believe what I was hearing Brian say to me. I started to interrupt him when I heard him say, "Beth, I am coming home to turn myself in. What I did to you was wrong, and no girl should be treated, the way I treated you. I know your mom is listening, and I want to tell her also how sorry I am for what I did."

Before I could answer him, I heard the phone click. Brian had hung up.

I hung the phone up and looked at Mom. We just stared at each other. I walked back into the bathroom to put my clothes on, but I collapsed on the floor. I was beside the bathtub on my knees, asking God what was happening. Mom had followed me. She helped me to my feet.

"Now, Beth, we are going to take one thing at a time. Get dressed and we'll talk," Mom said.

I got dressed and joined my mother in the kitchen.

"Mom," I said, "what about Brian and my baby? I don't want him to know I'm pregnant. He will know, Mom. Anyone can look at me and tell that I am going to have a baby."

My mother took her hands and gently turned my face toward her. "Beth, the Lord knew that this day was coming, and he will help us get through it, one day at a time."

That was my mother's favorite quote. She explained that it would take Brian a few days to arrive back in town, so that would give us time to pray and ask God for his direction.

Aunt Sammy, Dad, and my little brother were in the family room. I tried to act as though everything was just fine as I entered the room.

I put on a fake smile and said, "So what are we doing today?"

Jonathen blurted out, "Kissmus tree, Sissy, kissmus tree!"

I had to laugh at his little crooked smile and the way he pronounced Christmas. I loved Christmas trees as much as he did.

Jonathen was jumping up and down and going around in circles. "Kissmus tree! I get a kissmus tree!" he yelled, clapping his hands with glee.

All of us joined in on his little game and started clapping our hands, too. It was so funny, but it made everyone feel better.

Mom finally got Jonathen's coat and gloves on him. Dad said he would go start the truck. The truck was old, and it would take a few minutes for it to warm up. We had to take Dad's work truck so we could put the Christmas tree on it.

The weather channel had predicted this was going to be a brutal winter. As we piled into the truck, we all knew that the weather was really getting bad. Georgia didn't have a lot of bad winters. This one looked like it was a first for our state.

We arrived at the local farm, where the trees were sold. My family climbed out of the truck and gazed at all of the big, beautiful trees. We found one that Jonathen liked that would also fit into the family room. The attendants at the farm helped my dad put the tree on his truck.

We all were having so much fun. Despite all the excitement of looking for a tree, drinking hot chocolate, and listening to the local churches sing Christmas carols, I still could not get my mind off the phone call I had received from Brian. I dreaded him coming home and wondered how long it would take him to arrive back here in town. I was getting really tired and was anxious to get home, since I knew that my little brother would want me to help put the tree up.

At home, Mom and Dad had already brought in the decorations to hang on the tree. I was so glad they had done that part already. All of us helped Jonathen hang the ornaments and lights on the tree. It was really pretty, and Jonathen loved it. This was the first tree that he had ever helped decorate.

When the last ornament was hung, I said goodnight to my family and went to my room. I needed the rest and was still worried about Brian. I fell asleep quickly. Thank God for that.

I had a very restful night. My alarm woke me up very early. I hit the snooze button and considered lying there for a few more minutes longer, but I got out of bed and made my way downstairs to join my family.

It was time for usual Sunday morning routine. We always attended church on the Sabbath.

I wanted to go, but I was feeling a little sick to my stomach. I didn't tell any of my family members this, but I did silently wonder if something was wrong with my baby. I dismissed it from my mind and finished getting ready to leave for church.

When I walked into the sanctuary, I looked around for Jacob. I needed to talk to him. I didn't see him and assumed that he was just running late. Pastor Johnson asked us all to be seated. He had something to say to us before we went to our classes. He opened the service with a peculiar prayer:

"Our Heavenly Father, we know and accept your divine promises to us. You told us in your Word that you would never leave us or forsake us. You promised us that you would see us through all things. We believe your Word, and we thank you for all your many blessings. Help us to always be mindful of your plans for our lives. We pray in the name of your Son, Jesus. And the whole church says amen."

Pastor Johnson continued to speak to us. He told us that Jacob was at the hospital and would not be able to attend services today. The hospital needed Jacob to be there. A multi-car accident had occurred on the interstate. Pastor told us that a family from our church needed a lot of prayer. One of the victims in the accident was the family's son. I could not believe what I was hearing when he said the young man's name is Brian Saylor. I felt a huge lump rise in my throat. I could hear a lot of commotion from everyone in the church. We were asked to calm down and please pray for this boy.

Mom grabbed my hand. "Are you okay, Beth?" she whispered.

I told my mom that I was so sick to my stomach. I got up and headed for the back of the church. I had to get some air. My mother followed me. She wanted to take me home. I was crying and could not tell her that I wanted to leave. I knew people were staring at me, but this time, I didn't care what people thought about me. Mom asked the assistant teacher to take care of my class. Mom said she would tell my father that she was taking me home, and she would return later to pick up our family from church. We left the sanctuary. Before we could get to our car, I glanced behind me. My father, little brother, and aunt were hot on our heels.

The phone was ringing as we opened the front door. My dad answered it. I heard him say, "I don't know if she can talk." It was Jacob, and he wanted to talk to me. I just stood there for a few seconds. I didn't know if I would be able to speak, but something inside me compelled me to accept the phone from my father to talk with Jacob.

"Jacob, Jacob," I blubbered, crying into the receiver.

Through my sobbing, I heard him repeating the words, "Beth, I'm here."

I asked Jacob if he had seen Brian. Jacob told me he had.

"How is he doing?" I inquired.

"He's not doing very well," Jacob confessed. "That's actually the reason I called. He is in serious condition at the moment. It will be a miracle if he lives. Brian's parents are here with him now. Brian has been asking for you. We need to know if you can come to the hospital to see him."

I couldn't think rationally. "What does he want? Why does he want me to be there?"

"Please, Beth, try to come," he begged. "Brian wants to tell you something. I'll be here, don't be afraid. They're calling for me. Beth, please come quickly, if you can find it in your heart to do this for Brian." Then Jacob hung up.

I turned around to see that my parents were donning their coats. They were handing my coat to me. How could they have known that I would even go to see Brian? I slipped into my coat, and we headed for the emergency room.

On my way to the hospital, I was extremely nauseous. I had to keep a plastic bag with me.

I was overwhelmed with everything that was happening. With so many constant changes, I knew that it would be a miracle from God if my baby survived.

We arrived at the hospital. Dad asked the lady at the front desk what room Brian was in. She directed us to where Brian was.

I heard someone calling my name—it was Jacob. He hurried to where I was. For the first time, Jacob wrapped his arms around me and held me tightly, stroking my hair and murmuring how glad he was that I had come.

Jacob cupped my face in his hands. "I know you're scared, but God is here with us, and he is with Brian, too. Are you ready to see Brian?" he said.

I told Jacob I was afraid, but that I was able to see Brian if Jacob promised to stay with me.

Jacob promised he would not leave my side. "His parents are with him, Beth. He told them what he did to you. He also told me, too, so please just let him talk."

Brian was in ICU, so I knew that he had to be in critical condition. I agreed to Jacob's request.

My parents and I followed Jacob. A lot of people were standing outside Brian's room. Some of them were relatives, but most were friends from school. I tried to smile when I passed by everyone.

I walked into the room and thought Brian was sleeping. I gasped and tried to quickly turn my head—Brian looked so different with all the wires and needles protruding out of him.

Brian's mom came over to me and wrapped her arms around me. "Beth, we know what happened. Brian told me. I am so sorry." She was weeping as she continued to hold me and rub my back.

Mom came over to console both of us and pointed to a small couch over by the window. My mother wanted me to sit down and talk with Brian's mother. I was reluctant, but my legs were really weak. The baby was moving more than usual.

When I walked past Brian's bed, he seemed to stare at me more than usual. For a moment, I thought he had seen me. He never said a word. Brian shut his eyes again and fell asleep.

I sat down beside Brian's mother. Jacob and my parents pulled up chairs and sat down with us. Brian's father had left the room to go get a cup of coffee.

Brian's mom talked to my parents about her son's condition and prognosis. It was in the Lord's hands if Brian survived. I watched to see if Brian was sleeping or about to wake up. The nurses were constantly coming in and out of the room to check on his vital signs. All they ever said was, "No change."

My legs were beginning to go numb from sitting for such a long time. I asked Jacob to show me where the cafeteria was so I could stretch my legs and purchase a drink. Before we could leave the room, Brian opened his eyes, which were now round as saucers.

"Beth, are you there? Beth, are you here?" Brian stammered.

His mother and Jacob walked over to Brian's bed. Mrs. Saylor told him to calm down, and that I was here.

Jacob got real close to Brian. I heard him say, 'Brian, calm down for me, and I will let you see her."

I couldn't believe what Jacob was saying. He would let me see Brian? What if I didn't want to see Brian at all? And why was Jacob making decisions for me?

Jacob took me by the hand and led me to Brian's bed. "It's going to be okay," Jacob swore to me. "I'm here with you, Beth. I will never leave your side or let go of your hand, I promise. Did you hear me, Beth? I promise you that I will always be here."

Jacob and I, my parents, Brian's parents, and two nurses were now standing in Brian's room, which was almost occupied to the fullest. I gazed down at Brian.

Brian stared at me with those swollen, bruised eyes. "Beth, I am so sorry that I hurt you," he said softly. "Please forgive me for raping you. Please forgive me, Beth."

My heart was heavy in my chest as his words soaked in. That's when I saw the tears dripping down his mangled face. I don't know how my hand was holding to Brian's. I don't remember taking his hand, but the hot tears from his swollen eyes were hitting my hand.

"It is okay, Brian. It's okay. I forgive you," were the only words that I could say.

Brian turned to face Jacob now. "It is okay now, Preacher, except for one thing."

Jacob asked him what the one thing was.

Brian said, "I need for you to take care of Beth and my baby."

Before Jacob could answer, Brian closed his eyes.

I panicked. "Is he okay?" I yelled to the nurse.

The nurse checked his vitals and told us he was alright for the moment, but that it was looking grave. The nurse requested us to leave the room so they could work with him. Several doctors were parading in and out of his room. Things were not going well.

I wanted to go to the chapel. I asked Mom if she knew where it was, and she told me how to find it. I think she wanted to go with me, but I asked her to stay there and be with Brian's parents. I started to go to the elevator when I heard Jacob call for me. He caught up with me and said that my mother had notified him of where I was going.

"Do you need some company, Beth?"

I said yes and asked him why he continued to stay in Brian's room, even after the nurse said that we should leave.

"I just wanted to make sure Brian was okay," Jacob said. "And remember, Beth, I do work here."

He smiled at me, and I found myself reciprocating. It felt good to smile for a change.

Chapter Sixteen

Jacob and I slipped into the chapel. It was beautiful.

In front of the room, there was a built-in waterfall. The lapping sound of the water was so soothing. Jacob and I were the only people in the chapel.

"What's going to happen?" I asked Jacob softly.

"I don't know. Everything is in God's hands now," he said to me.

I made a strange remark to Jacob. I told him that I didn't want Brian to die.

"Jacob, at one time, I wouldn't have cared if Brian died," I admitted. "When he raped me, Jacob, I hated him."

"I know, Beth. I understand what you're saying," Jacob said kindly.

We both knew that God's forgiveness was the reason my feelings had changed towards Brian.

I knelt down at the altar and started asking God for healing upon Brian. I also asked God to please help me know what his will for my life was.

Jacob was kneeling beside me. He knitted his hands in mine, and we continued to pray for Brian. Before we even realized it, we had been in the chapel for more than an hour. We needed to get back to the room, so we quickly got a drink of water and made our way back to Brian's room.

On the elevator, Jacob's pager beeped. He had told the nurse to page him if there was any change with Brian. I was terrified. A huge lump formed in my throat.

I did not see anyone in the hallway on Brian's floor, and I soon figured out why. As we entered Brian's room, I saw that everyone was there with him.

Brian's mother was leaning over him, stroking his hair and swollen face. "I will see you again, my baby boy. You know you have always been my little boy. Jesus is here, and he will take care of you. You won't ever have to hurt again."

Brian's father was clutching the bed and trying to comfort his wife at the same time. Tears streamed down both of their faces. I knew that Brian was gone.

I scanned the room for my parents or a familiar face. I didn't see anyone I knew. Everything was blurry, and I suddenly felt very strange. That was the last thing that I remembered until I woke up to my mother's voice. She told me that I was in the emergency room. I had fainted, so they put me in the emergency room and hooked me up to an IV. I was even wearing a hospital gown.

"Do you remember what happened?" My mom peered at me with curiosity.

Tears stung my eyes. "I don't remember. Brian is gone, isn't he, Mom?"

My mother said yes, Brian was gone. She pleaded with me to lie back and relax.

"Brian is with the Lord now. God will help us get through this ordeal," my mother said gently.

Mom always had a way of comforting me. She had a very soothing voice. I had not always listened to her when I was a child, but now that I was an adult, I tried to honor her wishes.

I was exhausted. The doctor had told Mom that he wanted me to stay at the hospital overnight. He wanted to keep an eye on me and my baby. I agreed to stay. I didn't want any harm to come to my child.

The staff barged in my room early the next morning and released me to go home. I asked my mom where Jacob was. I hadn't seen him since Brian's passing. Mom said that Jacob had stayed right by my side after I passed out. He only left long enough to check on Brian's parents. When Jacob knew that I was going to be alright, my mom said she told him to go home and get some rest. He had suffered sleep deprivation for many hours and needed to go home.

"I told him that I would stay with you. I said if I needed him, that I would call him, and he could come back, to the hospital," Mom explained.

I finished dressing. I was more than happy to get rid of the most beautiful "gown" I had ever worn. I giggled to myself at my lovely hospital attire. As my mother and I strolled down the hallway, I saw none other than Jacob. He was sprawled out on a couch in the family waiting room. Mom just had to laugh. He was hanging halfway off the sofa.

He's so adorable, I thought. Wait, was I actually thinking that?

Mom interrupted my thoughts. "Elizabeth, you have a real friend in Jacob."

I agreed with her.

Jacob heard us and got off the couch. With a boyish grin, he jokingly ran and got a wheelchair for me to ride in.

I shook my head and pointed my finger at him. "I can take care of myself," I laughed. "The doctor only told me to take it easy and rest, not become an invalid."

There was no doubt in my mind that I would become lazy if I allowed everyone to wait on me hand and foot. I didn't want that to happen. I wanted to stay active and keep my weight under control.

The next few days were going to be hectic. Brian's funeral would be soon, and I knew for sure that my mother would be willing to help Brian's mom, if she was able. Mom had not said anything, but I could tell she wasn't feeling well. I had noticed that she had been taking a lot of showers. I interrogated my mother about it, but she insisted that it was just normal hot flashes, that the cool showers helped her to cool off.

I wanted to talk to Dad and Aunt Sammy about Mom. I waited for Mom to take a nap to tell them about my concerns. Both of them decided that something wasn't quite right with my mother, but we all agreed not to say anything to Mom until after Christmas. Christmas was Mom's favorite time of the year. It was just a couple of weeks before the holidays, and I knew that Mom would be preoccupied with cooking, baking, shopping, and decorating the house. I loved the smell of our home during Christmastime. It always smelled of cinnamon and peppermint.

I finished talking to Dad and my aunt. I passed a mirror in the hallway that was hanging on the door. I stopped and took notice of my belly. I could really see that it was getting a lot bigger.

I pulled my shirt up so I could see a little more of my stomach. It was amazing to think that a baby could actually live in there, I mused. I wondered if all women thought about pregnancy the way I did. Mom was a bit on the older side when she had Jonathen, but not once did I hear her complain about her belly or how much weight she'd gained.

I looked one more time in the mirror. *If only I could be like my mother,* I thought.

The day for Brian's funeral had come. I was hesitant about going, but I attended nonetheless. I don't have a lot of things to say about Brian's funeral. Pastor Johnson and Jacob conducted it; Mrs. Turner did the song service. I didn't dare approach Brian's coffin. I was scared that I would get too upset. As soon as the benediction was given, I went to my car. My parents exited the building shortly after. Not a word about the past few days was spoken on the drive home.

The days were getting shorter; the nights, longer. The weather for our area was unusual. We were not used to cold weather, but we residents of Georgia were adapting to the change in climate.

The spirit of Christmas seemed to be everywhere. The youth group at our church was having a Christmas play that Jacob had written. It was about a homeless child who not only found a home, but also found a family that loved him and decided to keep him. The parents won their petitions to the court and adopted the young child. The play was a real tearjerker, and you could feel the spirit of God in the church. I tried to approach Jacob after the play, but he was so busy talking to everyone as they were leaving. Occasionally, I could see Jacob watching me and smiling. Mom and Dad went to the car. I told them I wouldn't be long. I would join them as soon as I got to talk to Jacob.

Jacob finally made his way to me. I stuck out my hand out to congratulate him. "You did amazing," I said.

He grinned and shook my hand. Of course, he just had to say something unexpected.

"Thank you, Beth. By the way, you look beautiful tonight."

I could feel my face getting hot. I knew it had to be at least ten shades of scarlet. I turned my head and giggled to myself, then hoped he hadn't seen. He saw. Jacob and I both started laughing. It felt like we were the only ones in the church, but I soon found out that we were not alone. I heard someone calling my name. It was Jonathen.

"Come on, Sissy, let's go home!" my little brother cried. He ran up the middle isle of the church.

"Okay, okay, Jon!" I laughed. I turned and smiled shyly at Jacob. "Goodnight."

He gave me a smile that made my heart do somersaults. "Goodnight, Elizabeth. I'll be calling you."

I secretly did want Jacob to call me, but I didn't want him to know that.

It was pretty late when we got home. We were all tired, so we said our goodnights and headed for bed. I got into my PJs, climbed into my warm bed, and snuggled up in a soft fleece blanket. It was difficult to fall asleep. I could no longer sleep on my stomach like I normally did. I tried to get into a comfortable position, not just for me, but for my little baby girl. I moved from side to side and would try to sleep, but the baby would start kicking inside me and move around. It was a weird feeling, but it was a nice one, too.

I finally fell asleep. Sometime in the night, I was awakened by a tapping on my window, which startled me. I got up to peer out the window. It was just a tree branch. I should have known that, since it had scared me a few times in the past. I switched my light off and shuffled back to bed.

My insomnia got the best of me, so I decided I would go downstairs and help myself to some of my mother's homemade peanut butter fudge. I thought someone had left the hall light on, so I went to turn it off. I tiptoed past my parents' room. I tried to quickly sneak past Jonathen's room. I sure didn't want to wake him at this hour.

I made my way downstairs. I glanced in the direction of the glowing fireplace in the family room. I saw someone curled up on the couch, sitting in the dark—Mom. I crept close to the couch but didn't say anything. The fire was just bright enough that I could see she had something lying in her lap. It was her Bible. I watched her for just a few minutes. I made a slight noise in my throat, so I would not scare her. Mom turned to see me standing there.

"I couldn't sleep," Mom whispered. "What are you doing up?"

"I couldn't sleep, either."

Mom motioned for me to come and sit beside her, so I did. Mom took her blanket and spread it over both our laps. She curled her arm around me, and I felt just like I was "mommy's little girl" again.

"Why are you sitting here all alone?" I said.

She smiled at me and replied that she was just praying and talking to the Lord.

"Elizabeth, the Lord has been showing me a lot of things," my mother declared.

This caught my attention. I wanted to hear what Mom had to say. I knew that she had a close relationship with God. If she had something to tell me, it was for good reason.

My mom took my hand in hers. She told me about a dream she had a couple of weeks ago, and that the Lord had talked to her about my baby. I got so excited. I wanted to hear what my mom had to say.

"Beth, the Lord didn't say anything to me, it is what I heard and saw."

"Tell me what you saw," I urged her.

My mom said that in her dream, she had seen herself holding a newborn baby. It had coal black hair. She couldn't see its little face, but she knew she was handing the baby to me. In the background, Mom said she could hear church bells ringing. My mother listened for a while, and then the dream ended.

"That was a quick dream," I said. "What do you think it meant?"

Mom rubbed my hand. "I'm not sure, but there is one thing that I do know. Beth, I am not going to be here much longer. I want you to know that I will always be with you."

I couldn't believe what I was hearing. How could my mother say this to me?

I couldn't choke back my sobs. "How do you know that, Mom? Maybe you are wrong. I need you here with me. Please ask God to let you stay with us. He'll listen to you, Mom. Maybe he will change his mind. Please, Mom, you just have to ask him. Promise me you will."

My blubbering had reached a crescendo—so much so, in fact, that I woke my dad and aunt up. They groggily stumbled into the family room.

"Dad, please have Mom tell you what she has just told me," I sobbed to my father.

Dad asked me to calm down. "Baby, we have known this for some time, but I just didn't know how to tell you," my father said tenderly.

I hadn't told him the dream that Mom had just told me, but I knew from what Dad was saying that he already knew all about it. My aunt started to cry. She sat down by my mother. Mom said that it was so hard to try and cope with all that was happening. I knelt down in front of my mom and promised her that I would never leave her side.

My dad finally coaxed all of us to settle down and go back to bed. We didn't want to, but for Mom's sake, we obeyed. Needless to say, I could not go to sleep. The tears would not cease. I was so scared for my family.

When daylight came, I was awakened by Jonathen. He knocked on my door. He announced that Mom had breakfast ready. Everyone wanted me to come and join the family. For a moment, I thought to myself that maybe, just maybe, I had imagined the dream Mom had told me. I soon realized it wasn't my imagination when I walked into the kitchen and saw my mother. I felt weak in my knees. When Mom looked at me, I could tell she was thinking about our conversation last night. I didn't want to show any negative emotions, so I said good morning and smiled at my family. Dad told me to sit down, and he would pour me a glass of orange juice. Aunt Sammy was helping Mom get Jonathen's food. My dad said the blessing, and we ate in silence. I was sure that all of us were thinking about last night.

Finally, my mother broke the silence. She asked my dad if he would watch Jonathen for a couple of hours. She needed to finish wrapping some gifts, and she also wanted to go to the post office to mail some Christmas cards. Dad volunteered to go to the post office. My aunt was busy doing the dishes. The three of them were holding a conversation as if nothing had happened last night. How could they be so calm after Mom had told us that she was going to be leaving us soon? How could they even think about Christmas? Was I the only one who was concerned? I just could not understand why they seemed to be so calm. Was I the only one who could see what was happening?

My concentration was broken when Dad asked me why I didn't finish my meal. I didn't want to be disrespectful and say something wrong to my father, so I excused myself. I told my dad that I was tired and was going to go back upstairs to my room. I was confused over a lot of things and didn't want to upset my mother. I could feel the tears welling up. I knew that if I stayed downstairs any longer, Mom would be asking me questions about how I was feeling. I knew I wouldn't be able to answer her without letting my emotions get out of control. I had to be strong for my mother. She had a lot to deal with already.

I went upstairs and closed my bedroom door. I just wanted to be left alone. I played some of my favorite music. I turned it up really loud so no one would hear me cry. I just wanted to scream, but if I did, they would all come running to my rescue. I didn't want that. I sat down on the side of my bed, and before I realized what I was saying, I was asking God why he was doing this to me. I was so angry with God that sometimes I had even thought about giving my baby up for adoption. How could I take care of a baby by myself now that I knew that God was going to take my mother from me?

Was God being cruel to me and punishing me for being pregnant? Maybe God wanted me to give my baby away.

Every time I would start thinking these bad thoughts, my baby would start kicking and moving around in my belly. Could it be possible for her to know what I was thinking? I lingered in my bedroom for about an hour, going over all this in my mind. I knew I should get up, wash my face, and go downstairs to join Mom. I knew she had started baking—I could smell her famous sugar cookies in the oven. I washed my eyes; I definitely did not want my mom to know I had been crying.

Chapter Seventeen

I had just stepped into the kitchen when the phone rang.

Mom had cookie dough on her hands. She asked me to answer the phone. To my surprise, it was Jacob. I was so happy to hear his voice. I thought he was out of town visiting relatives for the Christmas holidays.

"Jacob, is that you? Where are you calling from?" I said.

"Well, Beth, I believe it's called a telephone," he laughed.

"Ha-ha, very funny. You know what I mean, Jacob. You were supposed to be out of town."

"I am out of town," he said. "I'm at a truck stop. I just wanted to hear your voice."

It seemed that Jacob's timing was always perfect. He knew just the right words to say. I needed to hear a lot of positive words right about now. I was so glad that he had called me, but I didn't want him to know how delighted I truly was.

Mom came over and tapped me on the shoulder. She wanted to know who was on the phone.

I asked Jacob to hold on for just a minute.

I covered the mouthpiece and whispered to Mom, "It's Jacob. He's calling from a truck stop in another state."

My mother smiled brightly and went back to her baking. Apparently, I wasn't the only one who was happy Jacob had called me.

I went into the family room, away from Mom. I wanted to tell Jacob about Mom's dream and about the conversation our family had last night. We talked for a long time, and he tried his best to comfort me.

"I can't wait to see you, Jacob. Please hurry home as soon as you can," I suddenly heard myself saying. Was I actually saying that to Jacob? The words had spilled out of my mouth before I even thought twice about what I was saying. I told Jacob that I needed to go back to the kitchen and help Mom. We said goodbye, and I went back to the kitchen to help my mother finish making the sugar cookies.

We finished the baking, and I told Mom I would clean up the mess we made. As a rule, Mom would never leave the kitchen without cleaning it herself. This time, she agreed to let me handle it. She grabbed a couple of warm cookies and a glass of cold milk before shuffling into the family room. I almost forgot that Mom was sick when I saw her get her little snack. Mom wasn't one to eat a lot of sweet snacks, so I was hoping this was a sign that she was feeling better. Before she left the kitchen, she had wiped flour off of my nose, just like she did when I was her "little girl." Mom had laid her apron on one of the chairs. I picked it up and held it close to my heart. Mom just can't leave this family, I kept saying to myself.

I heard the television and a very pretty Christmas carol. I hurried to finish cleaning so I could join Mom. I grabbed a small bowl of cookies and took them with me. I thought maybe Mom would be feeling better, and she could help me eat them all. When I got into the room, there she was, sound asleep. She looked so peaceful. I didn't have the heart to disturb her, so I peeled her quilt from the back of the couch and gently covered her. I pulled the rocking chair up next to the sofa, just so I could sit and watch her sleep. She did need all the rest she could get, I decided. I watched several little Christmas programs before I got sleepy and decided to go bed.

Oh, yeah—I ate all of the cookies. After all, I was eating for two people now.

It wasn't time for bed. It wasn't even dinnertime. I was just tired and wanted to take a brief nap before dinner. My dad and aunt had been gone for a while. They were taking my little brother to see a live manger scene on the courthouse square. Jonathen loved the animals. I knew he would be so happy when he did come home.

I heard someone knocking on the front door. I squinted through the peephole but couldn't see anyone.

"Pizza delivery," a voice said.

"You must have the wrong house," I told the guy. "We didn't order pizza."

I started to open the door. Before I could open it, I heard some giggling.

It was just Dad, Jonathen, and Aunt Sammy fooling with my mind. I decided to play along with their little game.

"No one ordered a pizza. Go away," I argued, stifling my giggles.

"Come on, Beth, open the door! It's freezing cold out here!" my father yelped.

I burst into laughter. Jonathen ran past me, calling for Mom. I tried to grab him, but it was too late. He had already shaken Mom and woke her up. She said the shaking didn't wake her; it was my yelling at Jonathen that had aroused her from sleep. I think that was first time I had actually scolded my little brother. I realized what I had done and apologized to both Mom and Jonathen.

I scooped Jonathen up in my arms. "I'm sorry, Jon. Your sissy does love you, you know."

Jonathen planted a big, wet kiss on my cheek. "It is okay, Sissy. It is awwight."

He was such a joy to our home, even if he did still have problems saying his words correctly. Even we had trouble sometimes trying to figure out what he was saying, but it was okay; we all had a ball doing it, especially Mom.

Dad had brought the pizza into the family room. We finished the night talking and eating pizza. We had a lot of things to talk about. So much had happened to us in the last few weeks. The main question was: "What are you going to name the baby?"

In my heart, I knew my baby was going to be a girl, but I had not been told that by the doctor. My father just had to give me a list of boy names, even though he said there was no way I could be sure it was a girl. I guess he wanted another boy to keep Jonathen busy.

Mom and Aunt Sam had a lot of names picked out. Most of their names were for girls, obviously. I had always heard that most women want their first baby to be a girl. I didn't know if that was true, but I kind of thought it was.

Little brother wanted to help with the names. He had picked out a list of cartoon characters for me to name my baby after. It was hysterical. After we all finished our game of names, I reminded everyone that I wouldn't know what the gender was until I went for a sonogram.

Mom quickly spoke up. "Now, Beth, it is your decision if you want to know what the gender is, but I can tell you that there isn't anything like the feeling of being surprised when you find out after the baby is born."

I told Mom I wanted her to go with me for my next appointment, if she felt like it. She promised me she would go. I gave my mother a great big hug.

She patted my belly and said, "We will love the baby no matter what it is, boy or girl—or maybe one of each," she added with a cute smile. I loved when my mother smiled.

My family had been gabbing for a long time. It was already ten, and I was ready for bed. We watched the weather report before going to sleep, since my dad had heard that a huge winter storm was heading our way. That worried me, because I knew that Jacob and his mom were somewhere traveling. I hoped that they were on their way home.

The weather finally came on. The reporter announced that a big storm was almost upon us. It would consist of strong winds and a drastically dropping temperature. I asked Mom if she would pray for the Turners. I wanted them to be safe, wherever they were.

"Of course, Elizabeth. Your dad and I will pray for them before we go to bed."

"I love you, Mom," I said, before saying the same thing to my father. "I thank God for you and Dad."

I hugged my parents and said goodnight.

Sometime during the night, I woke up to the wind rattling against my bedroom window. I was also freezing, which was strange considering I had two quilts on my bed. I snatched up yet another blanket and crawled back into bed. It didn't take me very long until I fell asleep.

I don't know how long I was asleep before I heard Jonathen crying for his mommy. I heard my parents talking to him. A few minutes later, his crying died down, but I was now wide awake. I was also cold again. What was going on? I made my way to the bathroom. It was so cold that I could almost see my breath. The overhead lights began to flicker. I grabbed my housecoat and warm booties. I went to my parents' room to ask them about it.

To my surprise, my parents were not in their room. I then went to my aunt Sam's room. She was gone, too.

I heard a sound coming from the family room. I hurriedly made my way there. My dad was standing in front of the fireplace. He was putting several logs onto the fire. I found Mom, Jonathen, and my aunt huddled together on the couch.

"Why are you all up so early? And why is it so cold?"

They just had to laugh at me. "Beth, we are up for the same reason you are. We're cold. Grab another blanket and join us in our homemade tent."

By this time, the lights were beginning to flicker a lot. Dad turned the TV on, hoping we could hear the news. The weather channel was giving out warnings about a huge winter storm that was headed for our vicinity. They were predicting snow, and possibly an ice storm. I just couldn't fathom such severe weather.

They must have it wrong, I thought. We're in Georgia. We don't have bad weather.

I was on the verge of panicking. I had a doctor's appointment, and Jacob was somewhere traveling. I prayed he wasn't out in all of this mess. What if Mom got sick? What would we do?

My father could see that I was freaking out. He wrapped his arms around me. "You don't want to make our grandbaby early," he said. "Relax. Things will work out for us, Elizabeth."

I snuggled close to my father. He always knew the right things to say.

Dad went to go prep some hot chocolate. While he was in the kitchen, I got under the "tent" with Mom and Aunt Sammy. Jonathen had gotten too warm, and he had fallen back to sleep. I guess the hot chocolate made me doze off also.

When I woke up, no one was in the room except Jonathen, who was still sleeping soundly. I went into the kitchen; Mom and Dad were talking and staring out the window.

"Come and look, Beth. It's beautiful," my mother said.

I went to the window. It was a beautiful sight indeed.

The ground was completely covered with snow; I was in awe. We'd never gotten this much snow in Georgia. The trees were decorated in time for Christmas. Icicles were strung on the tree limbs; sparse leaves were dusted with snow. My mom and I lingered at the window for a little while, just amazed at what we were seeing.

"It is so beautiful, Beth, but I hope the electricity stays on," Mom said.

She barely spoke those words, when the lights started to flicker on and off again.

"If anyone needs to shower, you'd better do it now," my dad warned us. "The lights could stay off for a very long time."

That was my cue. I hurried to the bedroom and got a change of clean clothes. Just as I finished showering and dressing, the power went out. I was just about to dry my hair. Dad said the lights would be back on in a few minutes. The power didn't come back on for a while. My hair was still wet, and that made me even colder. I wrapped my hair in a big towel. I was walking to my room when I saw Mom coming down the hallway, looking for me. She wanted to make sure that I was bundled up, and she inquired if I still had my battery-operated radio. I hadn't seen or used the radio for a very long time, but I told her I was sure we could find it.

I got to my room just as Aunt Sam was coming down the hall carrying Jonathen. He was upset by all the commotion and too young to understand what was happening.

I reached for my brother. "Hey, Jonathen, do you want to see the snow?"

His little eyes lit up, and that got him really excited. I knew I needed to find the radio, but at this moment, I wanted Jonathen to see what was outside. I carried him to my bedroom window. Even though he was so young, I could tell from the glow on his face that he thought it was beautiful also.

Jonathen had his eyes fixed on the snow. For a second, he didn't say a word. A smile spread across his little dimpled face. He pressed his nose against the cold glass and only had two words to say: *Christmas snow!* Jonathen was the only one who remembered that Christmas was almost here.

Mom excitedly came into the bedroom. "I found it, Beth! I found the radio! Let's see if it still works."

Aunt Sammy just had to make a cute remark about finding the radio in my messy closet. Some of my things had been packed up for a very long time. Jonathen got down from the window and started playing with some of my old stuffed animals. While Mom looked for some batteries, I started looking through some of my old pictures that I had stored away, back before I left for college. It was hard to believe that so many changes had taken place since my old high school days.

I continued rummaging through my stuff. I found an old picture album. A handwritten letter from Brian, still in the original envelope, was tucked in the front. The words "Brian loves Beth" were scribbled on the front of the envelope. My heart started to race, and my hands trembled. I still thought about Brian and his death. This was bringing back a lot of really bad memories. I guess I was crying, because Mom and Aunt Sam gathered around me. Mom tried to take the album from me, but I couldn't let go. Jonathen was confused by all of us, and he started crying.

Aunt Sam picked him up and assured him that his "sissy" was going to be okay. Aunt Sammy took him downstairs to find my father, and then sent Dad upstairs to where Mom and I were.

Chapter Eighteen

Dad came to my room, where Mom and I were still talking. He sat me down on the bed and told me to calm down. We just sat there for a few minutes. Dad got up, kissed me on top of my head, and asked me to please stay calm. He had to go take care of a few things, just in case the lights were to stay off for an extended period of time.

My mom said that I needed to stay calm for the baby. I had noticed that every time I got excited, the baby seemed to move around a lot more. I tried to take my mother's advice. She had been through two pregnancies; I was sure she knew what she was talking about.

We were still sitting on the bed when my father returned. He wanted us to come to the kitchen. He was listening to the news and wanted us to hear what they were saying.

Mom and I followed him into the kitchen. My aunt had breakfast ready for us. She had made instant oatmeal and orange juice. Dad had heated her some water in the fireplace. My father laughed and said we were going to be roughing it for a while, if the weather didn't get better.

A shrill noise interrupted the news. We knew that this could only mean one thing—a special newscast was coming on. It was a storm warning. The weatherman said that the heavy snow and ice had hit several of our surrounding counties. The electricity was off all around town and wasn't expected to come back on for several hours, maybe even days. The newscaster asked everyone to stay indoors. The temperature was so low that it would not melt the ice. We were advised to stay tuned for further updates. The only ones who were to be on the roads were the emergency workers or the police. This storm was really beginning to get frightening. No one was prepared for all of this.

I remembered I had a doctor's appointment. I knew that there was no way I could go. I tried to call the office, but their phone service was out. I would have to call back after the weather advisory ended. I almost automatically started to worry again. How would we manage without electricity? What would we do about cooking? What would we do if one of us had an emergency and had to go to the hospital? In the midst of all these thoughts, I suddenly heard my mother's voice telling me to calm down, remember the baby. I took a deep breath and tried to relax.

I hadn't heard Jonathen or Dad for a little while. I asked where they were. My aunt told me to look out the window. There they were. Dad was outside with Jonathen. He had bundled my little brother up from head to toe. My father was showing my little brother how to make snowballs, but poor Jonathen was bundled up so much that he could hardly move. It was funny to watch. His little nose was so red that I told Mom he looked like Rudolph the red-nosed reindeer. Jonathen was so happy. I could recall when I was his age, Dad and I would go play, but I had never gotten to play in the snow. My brother was lucky that he had got to see so much snow.

I went to the kitchen, where my mother and aunt were getting some vegetables prepared for a big kettle of vegetable soup. We made enough to last a couple of days. It would be so much fun if we could cook it over the fireplace, since we would have to cook on an open fire. I was anxious to try it.

Dad and Jonathen came back into the house. It was a sight to watch everyone trying to get Jonathen out of his wet clothes. Jonathen didn't like all the attention. Mom got him into his footed PJs. Then my little brother lay down on a small mat in front of the fire. It wasn't fifteen minutes before he had fallen asleep. Mom had so many covers on him, he could hardly breathe. She knew he was chilled, and she didn't want him to catch a cold.

I sat down to watch the fire. It was so relaxing. I was enthralled watching the flames when there was a knock at the door. It was Jacob.

I was so shocked to see him that I just stared at him without saying anything.

Mom finally came to the door and said, "Elizabeth, let them in. It is freezing cold."

I hadn't realized that I was just standing there looking at Jacob and his mother.

"Please, come in," I said quickly.

"We will if you let us," Jacob teased.

I was embarrassed, but I moved away from the door so they could come inside. Mom led the Turners over to the fireplace and went to get them some coffee or hot chocolate. I still had not said anything to Jacob, but he was smiling at me. I started to leave the room, but Jacob asked me to stay with them for a few minutes before they had to leave. I went back over by the fireplace, where the Turners were attempting to warm themselves.

"Are you surprised to see me?" Jacob questioned.

I told him I sure was, because he wasn't supposed to be home until after Christmas.

Jacob chuckled and gave me a little wink. He had beautiful blue eyes. "I wanted to be home for Christmas. I left my relatives' place early so I could get ahead of the storm," he explained.

I apologized for being in sweatpants. My hair was still a mess, and my face was red from standing too close to the fire.

"Don't worry about how you look, Beth. You always look beautiful," Jacob told me.

I liked his compliment, but I was nevertheless ashamed of my appearance. Mom knew I was dumbfounded, so she quickly changed the subject. Of course, our topic was the weather. Mrs. Turner said that the roads were very hazardous and that traffic was almost at a standstill. They had passed several accidents. It was only the hand of God that helped them to get home safe and sound. Mrs. Turner said Jacob wanted to get home so he could check on our family. He thought my dad might need some help, what with the power going out. Mom assured Jacob we were okay and asked him if they wanted to spend the night. Jacob said he needed to get home and check out things there. He left to go start the car, which would take a few minutes to get warm enough for the Turners to leave. He wasn't outside very long until he came back inside looking for dad. Jacob's car wouldn't start, and he needed help getting it running. I told him that dad was out back, getting some wood for the fire. I took Jacob to the window and pointed in the direction of my father. Jacob was gone for a few minutes, but I hadn't heard his car start.

I heard a knock on the door, so I opened it. There was my father, leaning on Jacob for support. Jacob had his arms around him, and Dad was limping. I could tell my father was in pain. We helped get Dad inside. Jacob had gone to where Dad was gathering wood. My father had fallen down and couldn't get up by himself. His foot looked as though it might be broken: it was starting to swell. I called for Jacob's mom. She was a nurse, so maybe she could tell if his foot or ankle was broken.

My mom had heard us talking, and she came to see what all the commotion was about. When she saw her husband and realized he was hurt, she got upset. My father assured her he was alright. Jacob's mom told my dad to sit down so she could see if his injury was bad. Mom tried to roll my dad's pant leg up. She couldn't get the fabric to roll, so she grabbed her scissors and cut his pant leg all the way to his knee. It was great to see everyone was working together as a team.

"I don't think it's broken," Mrs. Turner finally said, "but he does need to keep it elevated to keep the swelling down.

The Turners helped get Daddy to a nearby chair. I wanted my father to tell me he was okay. Dad told me to quit worrying; he was going to be alright. I just didn't want to see my father in a lot of pain. He told us that he wasn't in a lot of pain, but I could see by his expression that he was very uncomfortable.

"I think the Lord sent you our way, Jacob," my mom said to him. Mom knew that if we had been alone, neither she nor I would be able to do very much lifting.

While Mrs. Turner and Mom were attending to my father, Jacob had gone outside to fetch more firewood. I helped Aunt Sammy put the big iron kettle on the fire. We needed to cook our vegetable soup.

My father was now propped up in his recliner and seemed to be doing okay. The house was getting colder and colder. It would take a long time for our soup to cook, and I think everyone needed something warm in their bellies right about then.

Everyone sat around talking until dinner was ready. Aunt Sam and I made sure that Mom and Mrs. Turner ate first. We had been taught that our elders always were the first ones to be served. Of course, that also included my father.

I dished out a bowl of soup for my little brother, who was greatly amused at the moment. He thought we were having a big Christmas party.

My father had asked Jacob if he would go down into the basement and get the air mattresses. Jacob obeyed and brought the mattresses into the family room. At first, Jacob and his mom said they would try to make it back to their home, but my parents insisted they spend the night with us. They agreed to stay. Everyone helped get more blankets and pillows for the mattresses. Dusk had begun to creep up on us, and we needed to get prepared for the long, cold night ahead. We lit a couple of oil lamps. The fire would give us some light, but we still had our flashlights handy.

Jonathen snuggled up to Mom; and Dad, who had taken a couple of pain pills for his ankle, was dozed off on the recliner. The rest of us just sat around talking. Mom and Aunt Sammy wanted to reminisce about their childhood; Jacob and I listened intently. He and I would just glance at one another and smile. We stood by the fire to warm our hands. It was just awkward for Jacob to be spending the night with my family. I thought it was fun, too, but I couldn't say that.

After much conversation, we all decided to call it a night and go to bed. We all dreaded trying to hunker down and keep warm. Aunt Sam and Jacob offered to take turns putting wood on the fire. We all knew that it was going to be a long, cold night.

It seemed as though the night lasted forever. I was so restless: I tossed and turned constantly. I had a backache and a lot of pressure, which caused me to keep going to the restroom. I tried to be quiet. I didn't want to wake everyone up. The final time I had to get up, Mom had heard me. She wanted to know if I was alright. Before I could answer Mom, my aunt and Mrs. Turner told my mother that

I had been restless for a long time. They knew I was getting up a lot—they even counted how many times I was up. I just could not relax. Mom wanted to know if the pain was constant, or if it came and went. I told her it sort of did both. The women knew what was happening, but I didn't. I was only seven months along; it was too early for the baby to come, or so I told myself. Mrs. Turner was a nurse, and informed me that I was in the beginning stages of labor. Mom wanted me to tell her when the pains would start and stop, so they could time them.

I tried to dismiss this as just a bad pain, but by now I knew what was happening to me.

I could see the concern etched on the women's faces. Sometimes my mother and aunt would slip into another room, but I could still hear them talking. They knew I was in trouble.

The commotion had awakened Dad and Jacob. The angels must have kept Jonathen asleep; he didn't need to see what was going on with me.

My dad couldn't help much, but he did try to keep me calm. He told me not to be afraid, that sometimes this would happen before it was time for the baby to be born. His words made me feel better. For a moment, it seemed like the pain was easing up. I tried to pretend it was going away, but I just couldn't hide the fact that the pain was getting a lot stronger. I cried and told everyone that I knew something was wrong, and I was scared.

They all wanted to call an ambulance. This time, I agreed with them.

Everyone hastened to get dressed before the paramedics showed. I was sporting my flannel pajamas, and I didn't even try to change into something else. The paramedics took a while to get to the house because of the road conditions. As soon as they arrived, they took my vital signs and asked a series of questions. The paramedics said I needed to go to the hospital, and I didn't argue with them. The Turners drove my parents to the hospital, and Aunt Sam stayed at home with Jonathen.

We all arrived at the hospital after a long time of maneuvering the slick, icy roads. The doctor immediately ordered a heart monitor to check my baby's heart rate. I was hooked up to several IVs, and questions were once again pelted at me.

My hospital room was filled with a whole team of personnel by the time my parents arrived. The pain was beginning to get worse. The doctor explained that he was sure I was having premature labor. He wanted to start me on a medicine that would stop the labor if it was false.

"What's happening to me?" I asked the doctor.

He took me by the hand. "Little lady, you are in God's hands now, and you are in mine also. He will help me know what to do, and I can assure you that I will listen to what he has to say. God knows what you need, and he will help me to help you. Just relax and let the medicine do its work."

I said I would relax.

The doctor patted my hand. "I'll be back in just a few minutes. I'm going to the nurses' desk to order your medicine," he said.

I could feel the hot tears starting to drip from my eyes. I didn't want everyone to see me cry, but I was scared and in pain, and I just couldn't help my emotions.

Jacob stood up from where he was seated and walked over to my bed. He had a Kleenex in his hand, and he wiped the tears from my eyes. "Now smile for me, Beth. Save those tears for another time. You need your strength now," he said softly.

I told him I would try to contain my tears. He smiled and turned to walk out of the room. I believe he was crying, too.

I glanced over at my father, who was sitting in a wheelchair at the moment. I could see that he was still in some pain. Jacob's mother, assuming I wanted to be alone with my parents, started to get up and leave.

"No, please stay here with us," I insisted. "Would you please go find Jacob and tell him that I want him to come back into my room?"

Mrs. Turner went to go find her son. Jacob walked back into the room with his mother and came to my bedside once more.

"Jacob, I want you to stay with me. Please don't leave me," I said.

I knew my parents wouldn't mind Jacob staying with me, but I asked them anyway. Both my parents said that whatever I wanted was fine with them. Mom and I discussed what the doctor had told me about the medicine he was ordering. She was familiar with what he was saying about the premature labor. She had problems like I was having before my little brother was born.

While we were waiting for the doctor to come back in, I asked if anyone had called Pastor Johnson. I was told that he had indeed been called, and that Pastor wanted me to know the entire church was praying for me. I felt better just knowing that.

I turned to Jacob. "Will you pray for me and my baby now?"

"Sure I will, Beth," he said earnestly. "Let's join hands and pray together."

Everyone clustered around my bed and joined hands. I will never forget the prayer that Jacob said for me and my baby. It went a little something like this:

"Dear God, Creator of all things, we humbly call upon your holy name. We thank you, Lord, for all of your many blessings and mighty works. You have made known these works in our lives, and we thank you for that. We thank you for your Son, Jesus Christ, and the precious sacrifices he made for us. I am asking you to protect this innocent child, and to help Beth to teach this child who you are. I also ask that you surround Beth and her family with your love and mercy. Let your angels be with her, and help her to lean on you. I ask these things in the name of your Son, Jesus. I know you always hear us when we pray. We love you, Lord, and we once again thank you for being with us. I know you are in this room because we can feel your presence. Amen."

I opened my eyes and saw that the nurse had slipped into our room. She had been extremely quiet while Jacob was praying.

"That was just beautiful," the nurse said to me. "It gave me goose bumps. I can sure feel that someone is surely watching out for you and your baby."

With that, she asked everyone to step out of the room. She needed to do a couple of things for me. I knew that everyone wouldn't go much further than the hallway. I was so blessed to have them in my life.

Chapter Nineteen

My nurse continued to check my vital signs. She made another comment about Jacob's prayer. She wanted to know who he was and how I knew him. I told her just a little portion of our story. I wasn't very comfortable talking very much about Jacob and me. I didn't want to get embarrassed again if she thought that Jacob was the baby's father. She gave me my medicine and told me that I would start to relax very quickly. I was hoping that I would fall asleep; my body and mind were exhausted. Turns out, I did actually fall asleep. I don't know if it was the medicine, but I would like to believe it was Jacob's prayer.

Everyone entered the room again. I'm not sure how long they watched me sleep. I could only hope I didn't sleep with my mouth wide open. I assumed that I hadn't, since no one said anything.

I asked all of my visitors to go down to the cafeteria for a bite to eat. I just wanted to continue resting. Mom didn't want to leave me by myself. I tried to convince her that I would be fine. Jacob volunteered to stay with me, and I gladly accepted his offer. Dad, Mom, and Mrs. Turner went to the cafeteria. They insisted on bringing Jacob some food, but he said no. He did tell them he would take something cold to drink. I told my mom to take her time, relax, and get something good to eat. Jacob reassured my parents that if I needed anything, he would get it for me. They agreed and left my room.

Jacob turned the lights off and settled in the recliner close to my bed.

"Thank you for staying with me," I said to him.

He just smiled. "Beth, I'm here, and I am not going to leave your side."

That was so good to hear. I got into a relaxing position and fell asleep again.

I don't know how long I had been asleep, but I was awakened by a stabbing pain in my back that radiated to the front of my stomach. The heart monitor alarm was suddenly wailing, and nurses flooded into my room. I had another sharp pain and sat straight up in bed. What was happening to me? Frightened tears raced down my cheeks. I had another sharp pain, and by this time, I was almost hysterical. The nurse tried to calm me down. She told me that I was in labor. \

One of the new nurses said, "Your husband has gone to get your family."

There we go again, I thought. *Everyone just assumes that we're married.*

"It isn't time, it isn't time for my baby," I kept saying.

The nurses tried to explain to me that sometimes things like this happen. When it is time for the baby to come, nothing and no one can stop it, they said. The doctor finally got to my room. He checked me and told me that it was time for the baby to be born. He assured me their hospital was prepared to care for premature babies.

While he was explaining what he would be doing, my parents and Jacob were allowed to come back into my room. They let Jacob in because the doctor thought he was my husband. The doctor said the baby was coming really fast. He said he would probably be doing a Csection.

They were getting me prepared for the delivery room. My labor pains were getting closer, and I guess that was a sign the baby would be here soon. The nurse went out of the room and returned with two men.

"We have to go now, Beth," the nurse urged me.

"Why do we have to go now?" I asked.

"Your monitor has alerted us that your baby is having difficulties. We need to go now."

As I was being wheeled down the hallway, I spotted my parents. Jacob had gone to get them from the cafeteria. Mom and Dad were telling me they loved me and that things were going to be okay. I could feel Jacob touching my hand ever so slightly.

I was rolled into the operating room. I was shaking from what I thought was the cold room, but I learned later that I was in shock of all that was happening to me.

I don't know how long I was in the delivery room, but my parents and Jacob were hovering around my bed the moment I opened my eyes.

The first thing I asked was, "How's my baby?"

I looked at Mom. I could tell she had been crying. "Mom, how is my baby?" I repeated.

"She is fine, Beth, she is just fine," my mother said.

I knew then that God had sent me the little girl that I had believed I would have. I was so happy that I forgot about the pain for a few minutes. The pain had been replaced with the joy that Mom had told me I would feel when my baby was born. She was right.

I had an almost uncontrollable longing to hold my baby. I asked if I could see her, but the nurse told me she would have to call the head nurse in the prenatal unit. She went to call the nurse and then she came back and told me that the head nurse would be in to see me very shortly. The nurse assured me that my baby was fine, that I didn't have to worry. I kept asking Mom a lot of questions.

"What does she look like? How big is she? Is she alright? Does she have hair?"

Mom hadn't seen my baby, so she couldn't answer my questions. I couldn't wait to see for myself. Jacob left the room to go find his mother. She worked at the hospital, so maybe they would let her know the answers to all of my questions.

It seemed like hours had passed before the doctor got back in to see me. He still had on his surgical clothes and explained to me that he had delivered several babies that day. He got me up-to-date about my little girl and told me that I would be staying in the hospital for a few days. He said my baby would have to stay a little longer than me.

I felt my heart sink. "What's wrong with her, and why does she have to stay? Please tell me she is alright," I said to my doctor. I could feel a lump of tears lodged in my throat, and they ran down my cheeks without warning. My doctor took me by the hand and said,

"Beth, God has blessed you with a beautiful baby girl, but she needs you to be strong for her now."

Those were the comforting words from my doctor. My motherly instincts kicked in, so I listened to what he had to say.

Doctor Daniels continued to tell me that my baby was just a little underweight and that her lungs were not completely developed. She would have to be hooked up to a machine to help her breathe better until she was able to breathe on her own.

I was trying my best not to get emotional again. I knew I had to listen to what he was telling me.

"What are you going to name this little princess?" the doctor asked me with a smile.

I looked at mom, she looked at me, and the doctor just stared at us. In all of the things that had been going on, I had not picked out a name for her. The doctor said it wasn't a rush, but to let him know as soon as I decided on a name. I told him I would do that.

I hadn't seen Jacob for a few minutes. The doctor had given me a shot for pain. I knew I would fall asleep, but I wanted to see Jacob first. I tried to stay awake, but I could feel my eyes getting heavier and heavier. I closed my eyes completely but told myself not to go to sleep until I talked to Jacob. Somewhere in the distance, I thought I heard a noise—or was I dreaming?

"Beth, honey, you have a visitor." My mother's voice seemed to be coming from a great chasm.

A visitor? I don't need a visitor.

I slowly tried to open my eyes and focus them, but it was hard to do. The medicine had made me much too groggy. I looked around, and there was a little clear cart by my bedside. In the cart was a tiny baby wrapped in pink. I knew then that I was looking at my beautiful baby girl. My motherly instincts sure did come flooding over me. I desperately wanted to hold my baby. The nurse explained that my baby was hooked up to a machine, and I wouldn't be able to hold her just yet. She rolled the cart closer to my bed, allowing me to tenderly rub my little girl's head and touch her little face. My baby could only stay for a few seconds. The nurse had to get her back to the preemie unit as quickly as she could. My mom followed the nurse out of the room and down the hallway. I desperately wanted to go with them.

Without even thinking, I swung my legs off the bed and placed my bare feet on the cold floor. I was feeling a little dizzy, but I just had to go with my baby. I don't know how I made it to the door, because I was still in a lot of pain. I knew if I could find Mom, she would help me go see my baby. The lights on my monitor started blinking. A warm sensation washed over my body, and that's the last thing I remember.

When I regained consciousness, I felt my mother wiping my face with a cold cloth. She was praying and asking God to help her through this trial, to please help her grandbaby and bring healing to her little body. My mother told him that she knew he had everything under control and would never fail her. I did not say a word while my mother was praying.

Maybe things weren't getting any worse with my mother's health. Maybe the Lord had healed Mom, and she would be here to help me raise my baby.

Mom came closer to me and kissed me on the forehead. She wanted to know how I was feeling. Before I could give her an answer, she looked at me square in the eyes, and demanded to know why I had gotten out of bed. She reminded me that I had just given birth.

"You are lucky that you didn't hit your head and do serious damage. Please promise me that you won't do that again. Elizabeth, you scared me to death." Mom inhaled. "I'm just thankful you're okay."

I tried to explain to my mother that all I could think about was being with my baby. I guess I was crying pretty loudly, because the nurse came to see what the problem was. I was crying uncontrollably now, and my mom was trying to console me. The nurse talked to me and said she would call the doctor. She wanted to ask the doctor if I could have medication that would help me to relax. My mother was doing her best to help me keep my emotions intact. She said that I needed to rest, so I would be able to see my baby when the doctor gave me permission to. I then realized that I had to calm down for my baby's sake.

I had not seen my father or Jacob for quite a long time. I asked my mom if she knew where they were. She said that she thought they were together and would be back shortly.

My mom told me to look out the window on my door that faced the hallway.

I could not believe what I was seeing. A brilliant pink sea of balloons bobbed up and down outside my door. I thought it was the florist delivering them to me, but as the door opened, I could see that it was Dad, Jacob and Mrs. Turner. They were so funny. I just had to laugh at them.

"I was wondering where you all were," my mother said with a smile.

Jacob made a face. "Do you know how long it took me to blow these up? I'm out of breath!"

Everyone erupted into laughter.

Dad and Jacob tied the balloons in every corner of my room. It was beautiful.

"How are you feeling?" Mrs. Turner said, sidling up next to my bed.

"I'm hurting a lot," I confessed. "But the worst pain is not being able to see my little girl."

She said she understood how I felt. I thanked her for helping with the balloons. Jacob's mom told me that if I needed anything, to let her know and she would try to help me.

Jacob wasn't saying much. He sat across from my bed, just listening to us talk. I caught him sneaking a peek at me every now and then, a small smile tugging at his lips. He tried to be discreet about it so that no one saw him, but I saw him out of the corner of my eye, and I liked it.

Wait—did I really just say that?

The nurse came into the room with the medication the doctor had prescribed. She said it was a sedative; it would help me to sleep. Before I took it, I asked her if I could speak with the nurse in the preemie unit. She picked up the phone and dialed the number. The head nurse answered. I told her who I was and that I just wanted to see my baby.

"Miss Beth, I am your baby's nurse," the woman stated. "I promise you that I will be with your child all through the night. She is going to be just fine. You try to relax and get some rest. When you awake in the morning, you will see that everything is alright."

I thanked her for talking with me. She promised me again that she would take care of my little girl. She hung the phone up before I could ask her what her name was. Mom cautioned me once more to let the medicine help me to relax. I could see that mom was getting real tired.

I told Dad to take her home, and if I needed them, I would call them immediately.

My mother initially refused to leave, but my father used his sore leg as an excuse to get her to leave. She finally gave in and agreed to go home. They needed to check on Jonathen, anyway. I guess all of us had been so concerned, we forgot about little brother and Aunt Sammy.

I really wanted someone to stay, but I knew that was selfish of me. My parents kissed and hugged me, and then reassured me they would check on the baby before they left the hospital.

Jacob told them he would stay with me until the nurses kicked him out. I tried not to laugh because the stitches hurt too much. After my parents left, I thanked Jacob for staying with me.

"Beth, I would do anything for you," Jacob said.

The air thickened with nervous silence. This was the first time we had been alone since the baby was born, and I had so much I wanted to say to him. I could feel my heart beginning to pound.

I was trying to muster up enough courage to tell him what I was thinking.

Before I could say anything, the nurse came into the room. She needed to put a vial of medicine in my IV. She instructed Jacob to leave so that I could relax and sleep.

Chapter Twenty

After the nurse disappeared, I asked Jacob if he would stay with me as long as he could. He smiled and winked at me with those twinkling, big blue eyes of his. He leaned back in the chair and folded his hands behind his head.

Jacob yawned. "I am suddenly feeling a little sleepy myself."

I knew that was his way of telling me that he wasn't going anywhere. How long it took for me to fall asleep, I don't know. I do remember getting tired. Jacob was holding my hand and telling me how small they were.

I could hardly see my nurse, but I heard her say, "Just relax and close your eyes."

I thought my nurse had left, but she came to my bed and introduced herself.

"My name is Isabella. I am going to care of your baby," the nurse said. "I promise you that she is going to be fine, and God is going to take care of her."

For some reason, I didn't feel like crying anymore. I felt at peace. I thanked her for talking with me. Isabella smiled and left the room. I thought about how young she was. I had not met this nurse. I guessed she was a new one to the unit.

I looked for Jacob, but I didn't see him. I figured he had gone to get something to drink. My eyes fluttered closed. If I rested well tonight, maybe the doctor would let me see my little princess tomorrow, on Christmas morning.

I guess I had slept all night when I heard a voice saying, "Good morning, Beth! Merry Christmas! Wake up, you old sleepy head."

It was my doctor. I couldn't believe that I had slept all night long without moving. My doctor asked me a few questions. I tried to answer them as best that I could.

I listened to my doctor for a while, and then I asked him if he had seen or talked to the prenatal nurse. He told me he hadn't seen anyone but my regular nurse, who informed my doctor that I had slept the entire night. She also told the doctor that my "husband" had stayed with me all night. My doctor pointed in the direction of Jacob, who was sleeping with his mouth wide open.

I started to laugh, and he woke up. He had not even heard the doctor come in. I continued to tell the doctor that I was feeling a lot better since the prenatal nurse had come to see me and told me my baby was fine.

The doctor appeared puzzled. "I don't know what you're talking about, Beth, but I am glad you are feeling better."

I was still thinking about why he had not known about the prenatal nurse. I guess I just assumed my doctor would be aware of when they were in my room to check on me.

Jacob had dashed out of the room to freshen up a bit. I know he was embarrassed that the doctor and I had witnessed his unfortunate case of bedhead.

He walked back into my room with a cup of coffee for himself in one hand and a breakfast tray for me in the other. I had to admit, he did look better with his hair combed.

Jacob helped me with my food tray. While he sipped his coffee, I questioned him about the nurse who had visited my room last night.

His brow furrowed in confusion. "What nurse?" he said.

"The prenatal nurse who's been taking care of my baby," I clarified.

Jacob gave me a strange look. "Beth, I did not leave your side last night. I didn't go out of this room, not even once."

He went back to drinking his coffee. I was beginning to get aggravated. The doctor didn't know about the prenatal nurse, and now Jacob was telling me he had no idea what I was talking about, that he had never left the room.

"Well, if you didn't leave the room, then you must have been in the bathroom when she came in," I faltered.

I could tell that Jacob didn't want to upset me. Why hadn't he seen the nurse? I even told him what she said her name was. He told me that he would talk to his mom and see if she could get the same nurse to come back and talk to me. He called Mrs. Turner, and she came to see me. She had stayed all night in the waiting room.

I explained to Mrs. Turner about the prenatal nurse, who told me her name was Isabella. Jacob's mother said that she would ask around for this nurse.

After Jacob's mom left my room, Jacob did tell me that he had heard me consistently mumbling something that sounded like the word "bell." He said I have said that for a while, and then I went back to sleep. While we were talking, the prenatal nurse came into the room. She introduced herself as Mrs. Reynolds and told me that she had been taking care of my little girl during the night.

I could not believe what I was hearing. I just stared at the nurse while she told me how my baby was doing. I couldn't stand it any longer; I just had to ask her about Isabella.

"Who?" Mrs. Reynolds said. "I don't think I know her."

I told Mrs. Reynolds about the nurse who had come to my room and told me about my baby.

Mrs. Reynolds gave me an odd look. She told me that sometimes the medication would cause me to imagine things, and that I probably just had my names all mixed up.

I suddenly realized that no one was listening to me. I knew in my heart and mind that the nurse had visited me. Jacob had heard me saying something, so that should be proof enough to everyone that I had talked to a nurse named Isabella. I would get to the bottom of this. I would find out who was taking care of my baby. I needed to know, and I wanted to know right now.

I asked if I could go see my baby. The nurse said I could go after I ate breakfast and got out of bed. I would have to take a shower and stand on my own without help for a moment, so the nurse could see how strong I was. They didn't want me to get up too soon and fall, like I did before. My child was the most important thing to me now, so I did as the nurse requested.

I ate breakfast and got ready to go see my baby. I called my family on the phone first. I knew Mom wanted to know how I was feeling. We talked for a minute, and then Jonathen just had to talk to his "sissy." He got on the phone and was so excited that I could hardly understand what he was saying. I did manage to hear about all of his toys under the tree.

"Sissy, there are pwesents for you," my little brother declared.

I smiled at the way he had pronounced "presents." I told Jonathen I loved him and that I would be home in a few days. He hung up the phone rather quickly. I guessed he was too excited about Christmas to say much more. I was anxious to see him and have the opportunity to introduce him to his new little niece. That sounded too strange to think that my little brother was now a full-fledged uncle. That just didn't seem possible. It was only yesterday that I was becoming his "big sissy." Time sure does have a way of creeping up on all of us.

Jacob had stepped out of the room so the nurse could help me get ready to go see my baby. By the time he returned, I was out of bed and wrapped in a blanket. Jacob had gotten a wheelchair for me. It hurt for me to move, but I managed to get into the chair. Jacob helped the nurse get my IV situated on the wheelchair, and I was anxious to go by then.

"Are you ready, Beth?" Jacob teased.

I laughed. "Of course I am, but do you know where we're going?"

Jacob pretended to glare at me. "Okay, now, don't be funny. I do work here, remember?"

The prenatal unit was on the same floor as my room. I know it didn't take long to get there, but it seemed like it took us forever. We had to go slow because of the IV. If Jacob pushed the wheelchair too quickly, the pain was awful. He tried to wheel me there slowly; he knew how uncomfortable I was.

When we arrived at the unit, I had to call the nurses' station before I could get through the locked doors. I told the nurse who I was, and she immediately buzzed the door open. The nurse brought us to a small room, where we were told to wash our hands and don a sanitary surgical gown. We even had to put gloves and a mask on.

"When you are finished dressing, I will take you to see your baby," she said.

I thanked her, and Jacob helped me put on the gown. We had a good laugh after we got into our garb, and I wished I had a camera.

Jacob and I left the small room and went to the nurses' station. A handful of nurses were sitting at the desk. I studied each one of them and soon realized that none of them looked like the nurse who had been in my room last night. I asked one of the nurses if Isabella was working there today. She sort of looked at me in a curious way and said that she didn't know of a nurse called Isabella. However, she said she would check my baby's chart—it would have the nurse's name on it.

We went down the hallway to a large room. I sure wasn't prepared for what I saw. My precious little baby was dressed in pink from head to toe—pink shirt, pink hat, pink booties. She was even wearing mittens, which looked like socks covering her tiny hands.

My little girl was surrounded by several noisy machines. She had a tube coming from her nose. I knew this was oxygen to help her breathe better. I was so overwhelmed.

The nurse sensed that I was scared and confused. She tried to calm the atmosphere in the room by explaining everything to me. The nurses had been calling my nameless baby Angel, since she was born on Christmas day.

Jacob smiled in a way that made me wonder if he knew about my baby's nickname all along.

The staff told us she was really a good baby, and her vital signs were all very good. I just wanted to hold her. The only thing I was allowed to do was hold my little girl's hand. I rubbed her tiny, frail arms and thanked the nurse for taking care of her. She simply said she was just helping her to get better—it was God who was doing all the work.

I couldn't stop the tears from flowing. I was concerned that maybe my little angel was in pain, and I couldn't help her. Jacob seemed to know what I was feeling. He took my hand and knelt down beside my wheelchair.

His eyes softened with compassion. "Beth, I know that your heart is hurting and you want to help your baby, but the best thing we can do is leave her in God's hands. He will not only help her; he will not leave her side. I promise you."

I'm not sure where the nurse went, but she wasn't in my room anymore. It was strange, but at that moment, it felt like someone had stepped into the room. I didn't see anyone, but the room seemed to be so much brighter. I felt a warm breeze drift past me. I wasn't sure how that was even possible. There were no windows in the room.

I hesitated before asking Jacob if he felt something different in the room. He said he had felt something, too, but he didn't know what it was. We both just sat there, still and silent.

After a few minutes, the nurse came into the room. She said our visiting time was up and that we could come back later that day. I really ached to stay with my baby, but I knew that I had to obey the rules. The quicker I got back to my room and rested, the quicker my time for my next visit would be. Jacob helped me to my feet. I leaned over the crib, kissed my baby's forehead, and told her how much I loved her. I remember looking over my shoulder, stealing one last glance at my little girl before I left.

There was a note on my table in my hospital room. It was from the nurses' station. Mom had called and wanted me to return her call.

Jacob helped me get back into bed. "I'm going to go get a soda," he said.

"Bring me a candy bar. Just don't let the nurses see it," I laughed.

He grinned. "I'll hide it under my coat."

Jacob left the room. I think he wanted me to talk to my mother in private.

As soon as I got comfortable, I dialed my parents' home phone.

Jonathen answered the phone. "Ho, ho, ho! Merry Christmas!" he said happily.

I had to laugh at him. I told him to give the phone to Mom, and he did.

My mother came to the phone. "Honey, how are you doing?"

I told her I was okay. I wanted to know if she was doing alright, and she said she was. I told her that I had gotten her message and hoped everything was okay at home.

"Beth, honey, I'm okay, but I have something I need to tell you. I would have called earlier, but with the excitement with Jonathen and Christmas, I couldn't talk. It was just too hectic." Mom giggled.

"What is it, Mom?" I said.

Mom paused for a second.

Oh, no. What's happened now? I thought.

"I had a visitor last night, Beth," my mother said.

"Who was it?" I supposed it was someone from church or maybe even Brian's parents. I hadn't heard from the Saylors since the funeral. Mom had tried to call them to announce my baby's birth to them, but Mrs. Saylor hadn't been feeling well. Mom found out that they had gone to New York on vacation so Brian's mother could recuperate.

It didn't take me long to understand that Mom's visitor had nothing to do with anyone from church. There was complete silence on the other end. When my mother did speak, her voice had completely changed. It was a sound I will never forget. It sent chills up on my arms when she did finally speak.

"Beth, God sent me an angel last night."

I desperately wanted to say something, but I just couldn't speak. I could feel a warm presence come over my entire body. I almost felt paralyzed for a second. I waited for mom to speak again. She asked me if I heard what she had said. I told her that I did hear her, and she began to tell me about the visitor she had last night. I wasn't prepared for what I was about to hear.

Mom began telling me about the angel. At first, Mom thought she was dreaming and became frightened. It didn't take her long before she realized it wasn't a dream. The angel was in her bedroom.

"Beth, the angel addressed me by name," my mother recalled. "The angel said 'Hannah, I have a message for you from God. Your Heavenly Father has sent me to tell you something very special. I will always be near you and watching over your family. I am a special angel that has been appointed to watch over the baby that your daughter just gave birth to. This child will become stronger and stronger. I will always be present to watch and protect her. God wants you to know that he is pleased with the life you have lived and how you have tried to be close to him and serve him every day. Your Heavenly Father wants you to know that he will always be true to you in all things. He will keep his promises to you."

Mom said that was the message the angel had told her. My mother said the angel turned to the side, as if looking at someone. Mom watched the angel vanish out of sight.

I just had to know more from Mom. I wanted her to describe the angel to me.

Without hesitation, my mother described the very same woman who had visited me last night, right down to the angel's hair color.

"Mom, I just have to know. Did the angel tell you her name?" I asked.

"Oh, yes, Beth, she did tell me her name. I will never forget it. She told me her name was Isabella. Isn't that a beautiful name, Beth? I wish you could have seen her."

I got so overwhelmed that I began yelling. "I did see her! I did, I did!"

Mom kept asking me over and over what I did. I could not answer her for a few seconds.

I tried to tell her about the nurse who had come into my room. "The nurse told me that she would be taking care of my baby. She even told me that her name was Isabella," I said excitedly.

"Beth, are you telling me that a nurse came to you last night, and her name was Isabella?"

I said, "Yes, Mom, that is what I am telling you."

We were both crying. It was so unbelievable that each of us had been visited by the same angel. We were so blessed that God would send a special angel to bring us a message from him. I just could not wait to tell everyone that an angel had visited both me and my mother on the same night.

We didn't want to hang up, but Mom wanted me to get in bed and rest. I knew Mom was weary from all the excitement, especially with Jonathen and his new toys. I told Mom I would be home in a few days. I told her how much I loved and appreciated her. I promised her that I would call her if I had any news about our little princess. My mother said okay. She told me that she loved me and was anxious for me to come home. We said goodnight and hung the phone up. I thought it was strange that no one had come into my room while we were talking on the phone.

Jacob had not even come back from the snack shop. This had to be God's way of making sure my mom and I had time alone to talk about him and the angel he had sent to visit us. I turned the TV on, listening to Christmas carols and watching the evening sun as it slowly melted the snow off of the hospital roof. I thought how beautiful it was to have a white Christmas, but I also knew that it would bring havoc to our little town. We had never seen so much snow and ice. I was thankful that I was safe and wouldn't have to go outside for a few days. Maybe it would all melt before the doctor released me to go home.

Chapter Twenty-One

Listening to the soothing music from the Christmas carols had relaxed me. I didn't want to go to sleep yet. It wasn't bedtime, and I wanted to wait until Jacob got back from the snack shop. I was ready to go see my little girl again, before it got too late in the evening.

Suddenly, I was awakened by someone calling my name and saying, "Wake up, sleepyhead. You have visitors."

I brushed the hair from my eyes and tried to see who my visitors were. My father and little brother were standing at the foot of my bed.

"How long have I been asleep, and Daddy, how did you get in here with him?" I asked, motioning to Jonathen.

My dad chuckled. "I have connections. We can't stay very long, Beth. We just came to have breakfast with you."

"Breakfast?" I repeated. "But I just had breakfast this morning! What day is it?"

"December 26," my father replied.

"What are you talking about? I just fell asleep a little while ago! It's still Christmas day. I know I haven't been asleep that long!" I said.

Jacob spoke up. "Beth, you've been asleep for a long time. I wanted to wake you, but the nurse told me to let you rest. I left for a little while, and when I came in this morning, you were still sleeping. I don't know who you were talking to, though. You just kept calling for Bella. Who is Bella, Beth?"

I tried to ignore what Jacob was saying because I was so mad at myself for sleeping and not checking on my baby. What kind of a mother was I? I was so disappointed at myself.

My father had let Jonathen move closer to my bed. He wanted to get up on the bed with his Sissy. Every time he would move, I could feel sharp pains racing through my sore body. He had started to get whiny right then, so Dad said they would go home. My father promised to come back later on without my little brother. I kissed both of them goodbye and gave Jon one of my balloons. He left a happy little camper. Jacob told Dad that he would stay with me, a little longer.

"Don't worry, she will be fine," Jacob smiled to my dad as they walked out of the room.

The door had barely closed when Jacob said he wanted to talk about what I was saying in my sleep. I ate my breakfast, and tried to tell him who I was talking to in my sleep. First, I had to go back to the beginning to tell of the angel, who had visited Mom and me.

I explained to Jacob that I was talking to my own child. I told him about the angel and what she had said to me and Mom. I told Jacob that the angel had visited my mother also, and that the angel had even told us what her name was.

"Jacob, I know what I am going to call my baby," I said to him.

"What are you naming her?" he asked.

"The nurses have been calling her Angel, and I want to keep that name. She is my angel from God," I said.

Jacob nodded his head in agreement that she was a little angel. "Why are you calling her Bella, though?" was his next question.

I relayed to Jacob how the angel who came to my room told me that her name was Isabella. I thought that Isabella Angel would be a very good name for her.

I saw Jacob's eyes widen. He looked very happy with the name I had chosen. That's when he leaned over my bed, kissed me on the forehead, and told me that he knew I was going to be a great mom.

I thanked him and said, "Jacob, we know that she is an angel, and my visiting angel's name was Isabella, so my baby has the right name."

Jacob smiled in agreement.

While he was still leaning over my bed, I felt compelled to throw my arms around his neck and hug him. I lost my nerve, though. It's a good thing I chickened out. There was a knock on the door, and in walked our pastor and several kids from the youth group. I heard some of the girls giggle.

My pastor said, "Hey, kids, maybe we came at a bad time. They seem to be in deep thought."

I could feel my face growing warm. If I had a mirror, I wouldn't have been surprised if my face was fire engine red.

I was speechless, but as usual, Jacob came to my rescue. "How are you doing, Pastor?"

"I'm doing alright, but how is our patient?" my pastor said.

"I'm just fine. Have you seen my baby?" I asked him.

Pastor Johnson said, "I haven't seen her today, but I saw her the day she was born."

"You did?" I exclaimed. "I didn't see you."

"I know you don't remember seeing me, Beth. A lot was going on that day. I want you to know that a lot of people have been praying for you and your baby. God has been with you, dear."

A lump of tears gathered in my throat. I felt so hopeless and grateful at the same time, just knowing that I had many people concerned about me and my baby girl. Mom's words which were, "I promise you, Beth, God is going to help you. I promise" kept ringing in my mind.

The conversation topic changed when the kids told me they had something for me. I hadn't noticed each of them had their hands behind their backs. In unison, they started piling baby items all over my bed. My bed was now covered with gifts.

I was astounded. "How in the world did you guys get all of this together in such a hurry?"

Jacob told me that the group had planned to have a surprise baby shower for me, but I surprised them and had the baby too early. Everyone laughed.

"I guess I should say that little Bella surprised all of us," I admitted.

"Yeah, she sure did!" one of the girls said.

Pastor Johnson said, "Is that what you are going to name her, Elizabeth?"

"Yes, it is," I answered.

The girls in the group loved her name, especially when I told them her full name would be Isabella Angel.

"That is a beautiful name," Pastor Johnson said.

If he only knew the complete story, I thought. I'm sure someday I will tell him.

The young girls were getting excited. They were waiting to go see Bella. I asked Jacob to go with the pastor and the girls while I got a shower and put a clean gown on. Jacob wanted to know if I would be okay. I assured him that I would be fine.

"Just go check on the little princess for me," I said.

It was almost time for my doctor to come in, and I wanted to be up before he got here. I tried to dress and got ready by myself, but I was still in a lot of pain. I didn't dare let anyone know how weak I was. I was afraid they would make me stay in bed, and I wouldn't get to see my baby. I brushed my teeth and attempted to fix my hair. The hair was a lost cause, so I just got back in my bed.

Just as I crawled into bed, my doctor came in the room. Doctor Daniels asked me how I was feeling and if I needed anything. I told him I was doing well. I sure wasn't about to volunteer any extra information about my sore belly.

"Beth, your baby is coming along very well. I just saw her and read the reports. I also read your progress reports. You seem to be doing well, too. I am going to release you to go home in the morning. Your baby will have to stay just a little longer, though."

I couldn't believe what Dr. Daniels was saying to me. I guess I got rather upset when he said Bella couldn't come home with me.

"I can't leave my baby here without me," I protested. "I just can't go home and not take her with me. I just can't, Dr. Daniels. Please tell me you are wrong."

"Beth, I am not wrong. Your baby has a few problems, and she need to stay just a little longer than you do. I know you're scared, but it is what I have to do," he said.

"But I am her mother, and I have to be with her. A good mom wouldn't leave her little girl in the hospital by herself," I said. I was hysterical right about then.

Doctor Daniels said, "Now, you have to calm down. I haven't made the orders yet. Are your parents here with you?"

I told him no, and he wanted to know if anyone was with me. I told him Jacob was, but that he had gone to the nursery to check on my baby.

"Okay," my doctor said. "I will wait until tomorrow to talk about it. Right now, I want you to get plenty of rest. Your little girl is going to need you."

I watched my doctor leave the room. I still wasn't satisfied with his decision to send me home without my baby. I was so confused. How could I leave her in such a huge, strange place?

The aide brought my lunch in. I told her I wasn't hungry. I was hungry, but thought that if I went on a hunger strike, maybe the doctor would change his mind. I was so mad it was getting me upset with Jacob. Where was he, and why had he been gone so long? How could he leave me, and didn't he know that I needed him right now? I even tried to call home, and no answered the phone. Now all I could do was just sit there and wait for somebody to help me.

When Jacob returned from the nursery, I didn't give him a chance to say anything before grilling him. I do believe it shocked him to see me throw a fit. He had never seen me act so foolish. I just kept rattling off about the doctor and what he had said to me. No one in the room knew what I was talking about. Jacob asked me to calm down and asked me to tell him what I was so upset about. I told him the doctor was going to send me home without my child, and I refused to leave her.

"I will just sleep on the floor of the hospital if I have to! I am not leaving without my Bella!" I cried.

Jacob tried to comfort me. I just could not get past the fact that I wasn't going home with my baby, so he just quit talking and let me settle down. I had to calm down, it was almost time to see my child, and if the doctor heard me fussing and crying, he would not let me go see Bella.

My heart started to sink when I recalled older moms in the past telling me that a baby knew when his or her mother was scared. I didn't want to scare or upset my angel. I tried to pretend like I was okay, for her sake.

I tried to eat my lunch but I couldn't peel my eyes away from the clock. I still had a while to go before I could see her. Jacob and I were just sitting there, looking at each other. Neither of us spoke. Pastor Johnson and the kids had gone home, and we were there alone. I guess we both were a little confused. After all, neither Jacob nor I had ever been a parent. The phone rang, and it broke the silence. It was the assistant RN in the prenatal unit calling. She asked how I was and told me that she was the nurse that helped with Bella's care. She told me I could come down and see Bella if I wanted. Elated, I thanked her and told her I would be there in a few minutes. I was so happy I could shout for joy, but I wasn't able to. I was just too tired and sore.

Jacob grabbed a small blanket and covered my legs. I had already gotten in the wheelchair before the nurse called; I was ready to go immediately. Jacob wheeled me to the elevator. I asked him why we were getting in the elevator, when the preemie unit was on my floor.

He just smiled. "I am going to take a detour, but don't worry; we will still end up in the prenatal unit."

I said, "Jacob, tell me where are we going."

"It's a surprise," he said. "You'll see—just be patient."

We went from the third floor down to the first floor. We took several turns down the hallway. Jacob rolled me into the lobby of the hospital and parked me directly in front of the most beautiful Christmas tree that I had ever seen. It was decorated with crystal stars, and they glowed so brightly that I could feel the warmth radiating from them.

Jacob came around to face me. "I have another surprise for you."

"What are you talking about?" I said.

He reached into his pocket and handed me a small, black velvet box. "Merry Christmas, Beth. I hope you like it. I've been holding on to it for a while now, just waiting for the right time to give it to you. I just can't wait any longer."

My heart started to beat really fast. I don't know if anyone else was in the lobby, but at that moment, I just didn't care. I felt like something very special was about to happen.

My hands were trembling; I could hardly open the box. I looked into the box finally, and there was the most beautiful diamond heart necklace I'd ever laid eyes on.

Jacob took my hand and turned my face to look at him. He was kneeling by my wheelchair.

I wanted to say something, but I was frozen in time.

His blue eyes searched mine. "Beth, I know you have had a lot on your mind, and a lot of things have been happening, but I just had to get you alone. I can't wait any longer to tell you how I feel about you." He took a deep breath and continued. "Beth, do you remember the first time we met? It was the day that your dad brought your mom to the hospital. I was the attendant that directed your family where to go with your mother. I knew right then that I just had to find out who you were. I prayed that very night and asked God to let me meet you. I just knew he would answer my prayer. I could feel it in my very soul. It wasn't but a very short time before I became the youth pastor at your church. I knew then that it was meant for me to meet you. Beth, I can't help it. I can't get you off my mind."

I don't know what happened to me, but I suddenly lost all of my inhibitions. Jacob reached for me. He drew me close to him. Before I could say anything, he kissed me.

It was just a second before I pulled away from him. It was like lightning had gone across my body. The memories of what Brian had done to me came flooding back, and I started to choke up.

"Please get me out of here," I begged him. "I can't do this now, or ever. Just take me to see my baby. We have been here too long already."

Jacob looked scared. "What is it, Beth? Did I do something wrong?"

He stood to his feet and paced the floor for a few seconds. Then he knelt down in front of me and repeated his previous question. He tried to get me to look at him, but I just couldn't. I turned my face away and asked him to please take me to see Isabella.

"I would never hurt you," Jacob swore to me, "and I make you this promise: I will always be here for you."

He took the small blanket and put it back on my lap. I did ask him if he would hold onto the necklace for me until we got back to the room. He slid it back in his pocket, and he wheeled me to the elevator to see my little Bella. Jacob and I never spoke as we were going to the nursery. I wanted to tell him that Brian was still in my head, but I just couldn't say it. I didn't want to hurt him again. I had been hurt and abused so terribly by Brian, that I was afraid to let another man hurt me. I didn't think Jacob would ever do that, but I was still scared to let my emotions show.

The unit nurse met us at the nurses' station. She smiled at me and commented that my baby must have sensed that I was coming to visit her. I asked her why, and she told me that they were having trouble getting my baby to take a nap.

"Maybe she wants her mommy to get her to sleep," the nurse suggested.

I liked that comment. I asked her if Bella was sick, and she said, "Oh, no. I think she just wants her mommy and daddy." I still had not told anyone that Jacob was not my baby's father.

I walked over to her little bed. I could only rub her tiny hands and arms, or her beautiful little face. The more that I tried to console her, the louder she cried.

"What am I doing wrong Jacob? What should I do?"

Jacob looked as puzzled as I did. With a slight grin, he replied, "You could sing to her."

"Oh, no," I said. "I can't do that, where everyone would hear me. There has to be another solution."

Bella began to cry even louder. It seemed as though she knew what we were saying. Maybe she did. I considered singing to her like Jacob had suggested, but I was almost too afraid to do so. I hummed a little tune to her, but it did not help. I had to try something else. I got close to her little face and I sang a very soft rendition of "Jesus Loves Me." She didn't stop crying, so I sang a little louder. I guess she was satisfied with me being loud, because she soon fell asleep.

Bella's nurse came into the room when her crying had just stopped.

The nurse smiled at me. "You have a beautiful voice."

I knew my face was getting red. I told her that I didn't know anyone could hear me. I didn't realize I was singing that loudly.

"Don't be embarrassed, honey. Your song was beautiful, and it was just what your baby needed to hear," the nurse affirmed.

She checked all of the machines and Bella's vital signs. All was well, so she suggested that Jacob and I go back to my room and rest while she was asleep. She assured us that if she needed anything, she would call us.

"You do know that someone is watching over her besides me, don't you, Beth?" the nurse said.

I nodded. I took my two fingers, kissed them, and placed them on top of my little girl's head. I told her that I loved her more than life itself, and that I would be back very soon to see her.

Jacob also told her that he would be back to check on her. He helped me get into the wheelchair again, and we started back to my room. I was exhausted and getting hungry. It was almost time for dinner. The excitement from earlier in the day had taken my appetite away. I knew Jacob had to be hungry, too.

We got back to the room, and for some reason, it had been rearranged. Someone had brought a small table in, draped a white tablecloth overtop it, and placed the table in the middle of the room. There were two small candles and a vase of pink carnations on the table. I didn't know what to say, because I didn't know what was happening. Jacob wheeled me over closer to the table.

There was a typed note. "Congratulations on the birth of your baby girl, little Isabella Angel" the note read. "The hospital staff would like for you and your husband to enjoy a private dinner on us tonight. Again, we offer our congratulations, and please enjoy your dinner. Dinner will be served at 5:30 p.m. Thank you." It was signed by the hospital staff. I picked the card up and handed it to Jacob. We exchanged confused looks. Neither of us knew what to say or do. I guess Jacob could tell that I was uneasy, because he said he would call the nurse and have her take the table away if I wanted him to. I told him no, that it would only cause the staff to ask a lot of questions. Besides, we were both hungry, so why should we let the meal go to waste?

I wanted Jacob to stay and eat. I needed to explain to him about my behavior from earlier that day. He agreed to stay.

It wasn't very long before our dinner arrived. Our dinner consisted of rib-eye steak and all of the trimmings. Jacob held my chair out for me. He lit the candles and pretended we were in a luxury restaurant. He pretended to be a server and asked if he could cut my steak for me. He was such a goofball. He knew exactly how to get me to smile and forget about my worries, at least for a little while. I guess that's what attracted me to him. We had so much fun that Jacob didn't even talk about how he had kissed me back in the lobby.

We were greatly enjoying our dinner, when the nurse came in and told us that Jacob needed to leave so I could get some rest. She told him he should go home, or at least go to the lobby and rest like he had been doing. I was shocked to hear that he had not been going home to sleep. The nurse said she thought that I knew he had been staying at the patient's lobby ever since I had come to the hospital. I felt so ashamed that I had yelled at him earlier, but now he had some serious explaining to do.

Chapter Twenty-Two

I could feel the tension in the room. I asked Jacob if it was true that he had not been going home to rest. He tried to dodge my questions and get me to rest in bed.

"Jacob, where have you been sleeping?" I demanded, trying to get him to look at me. "Have you not gone home at all? Please tell me. I need to know why you haven't told me that you were staying here all this time."

He slowly turned his head, ran his fingers through his hair, and sheepishly met my expectant gaze. "I could not leave you, Beth." His voice began to crack. "I was afraid you might need me when I was at home. I couldn't leave you."

He walked over to me now and looked me straight in the eyes. I started to talk, but Jacob put his pointer finger over my mouth and insisted he had something that he needed to say. He asked if he could sit on the bed beside me. I told him yes. I scooted over to make room for him to sit.

"Beth, I want you to listen to me. Please don't say anything. Just listen, while I have the courage and we're alone. I can't stand it any longer. I have to tell you something. I can't keep it inside anymore. I think you are the most beautiful girl that I have ever known, and I would do anything for you. My feelings for you have gotten stronger and stronger these last few months. I know we've become good friends but I just have to tell you that I love you, Elizabeth. I've been falling in love with you for a long time now. There is nothing you can do to stop it or to change it. I love you, and I also love that little baby angel of yours." Jacob finally went quiet. He stared at me, gauging my reaction.

My heart was pounding. I could hear the words I wanted to tell him in my head. *I love you. I love you, too. I hope you kiss me again.*

I couldn't say it out loud. Our eyes met at the same time. I wanted to respond, but before I could say anything, he put his arms around me. Our lips brushed again. I had never felt this feeling in all of my life. It was as if we were the only two people on earth.

I slowly removed myself from his warm embrace and shyly spoke the words that I had been hiding in my heart. "I love you too, Jacob."

He gently threaded a hand through my hair, kissing me tenderly and murmuring how much he loved me. We were two people who didn't know what to do right at that moment.

Jacob broke the silence. He said that he wanted to stay with me, but it was getting late and he wanted me to rest. He said he would go check on Isabella one more time before he left. I was so glad to hear him say that. He said he would call me from the prenatal unit and let me know how she was. He started out the door when the nurse walked in. I could tell by the expression on her face that something wasn't right. The nurse told me that my baby was in trouble, and I needed to come to her room just as soon as I could. I started to tremble, and I kept asking her what was wrong with my baby. All that the nurse would tell me was, "You need to come now."

I felt as if my life was drained from me. What was wrong with my child? I was terrified. The nurse said that Bella was having trouble breathing, and her oxygen level was too low.

"The doctors are with her, but you need to go now," the nurse cautioned.

Jacob had already gotten the wheelchair ready for me. When we arrived at the unit, the nurse asked us to stay outside the door until she checked on Bella. While we were anxiously waiting on the nurse, I asked Jacob if he would call my parents. He could hardly see his phone; the room we were in was dimly lit. Jacob did call my family, and I heard him talking to my father. He tried to tell him as much as we knew about her condition.

Jacob assured my dad that we would see him soon.

I wanted to go to Bella's room, but I still wasn't allowed, and it seemed as if I was frozen to the wheelchair. Jacob hung the phone up and rushed to my side. He rubbed my hand and assured me that things were going to be alright. He said my dad was calling everyone at church, and they would be praying, too. My mom was coming but she would be a little late in getting here. I guessed she had gone to take care of some errands with Aunt Sammy and Jonathen.

No one was coming to talk to me about my baby, and I was starting to get upset. Jacob and I tried to be strong and trust that the Lord was with us, and that things would be alright. It was so hard not to be able to be with my little girl. The nurse did finally come out and tell us that the doctor was coming out to talk to us just as soon as he could. I don't know if I felt better or more worried after she talked to us. I just remember that I was terrified.

The doctor finally did come to where we were. He still had his mask on so I couldn't tell anything about his expressions. I was surprised when he did remove the mask and a small smile crossed his face. He introduced himself and pulled up a chair beside me.

"Your baby is doing much better, but she is having a problem with one of her lungs," the doctor said. "She is a real little fighter, but she needs a different kind of medicine. We have a new medicine that has just been released for us to use, but we have to get your permission, to try it."

I gave him permission to do whatever he felt was necessary to help my baby. The doctor thanked me and said he was sure Bella was going to be okay—she just needed a little extra help with her underdeveloped lungs. He told me I could go in for a few minutes to see her. The nurse came to get Jacob and me as soon as they were through working with Bella.

Jacob had been unusually quiet while the doctor was in the room. I could see that he had tears in his eyes, too. He came over and knelt down beside me.

"Beth," he said, "God is going to see us through this. He has never failed us, and he never will." He then laid his head on my lap, and I stroked his beautiful hair. I cried and told him that I, too, felt as though things were going to be alright, but that we would have to be strong for our baby. I didn't realize I said "our" baby until I had already spoken it. I wondered what Jacob thought. The nurse came to get us, so he didn't have time to respond to my statement.

It was just a short distance to the unit, but the closer we got to it, the faster my heart was racing. When we came to the door, I knew something was different. There were several nurses outside the door, and all of them were jotting down notes. There were a lot of new machines sitting outside of Bella's room, and the atmosphere was unusually quiet. The machines and the nurses coming in and out of Bella's room were the only sounds I could hear. I could only peep into the room. I could see there were more needles in her tiny arms. My baby didn't seem to be in distress, but I felt so helpless. I guess the nurse could almost tell what I thinking. She came over to me and asked me if I wanted her to tell my little princess that I was here.

I tried to keep my voice calm. "Please do, and make sure that she knows I'm still here."

I could see the nurse lean over and whisper in my baby's ear. I don't know what she said to her, but I could see Bella's little tummy rise up and down more frequently. I counted every breath my baby took. The nurse did let me go over to her bed, but she guided my hand to the only spot that I was allowed to touch. I softly touched my little baby's warm skin.

The tears started to flow. Jacob and the nurse tried to console me. I just wanted to be the only one taking care of her. It was my place to care for her: I was her mommy. I asked God to please help and keep my little girl alive.

I don't know how long I stayed by Bella's side, but a familiar voice caught my attention.

It was my dad. I wanted to go to him, but I knew that I couldn't stay much longer with Bella. I needed to stay with her as long as I could. I kept my eyes focused on her beautiful little face. I didn't want to take my eyes from her.

I felt a warm hand on my shoulder. It was my father. He whispered in my ear, "Don't worry now, Elizabeth. Everything is going to be alright."

That was all it took for me before I turned and fell into my dad's arms. He picked me up and put me back into my wheelchair. I was still weak from the surgery.

The head nurse entered. She commented on what a good family I had. She didn't want to ask us to take turns coming to see the baby, but we needed to let Bella rest all that she could. The nurse knew that all of us wanted to stay close by my little girl's side, but we knew we couldn't do that. The nurse suggested we go to the family waiting area. If she needed us, they would come and get us. I didn't want to leave, but the nurse told me that one person at a time could come back occasionally to check on her.

All of us touched Bella's little hand and told her how much we loved her. With much reluctance, we headed for the family room.

Jacob stopped at the snack room to get each of us something cold to drink. When we got seated and settled down a bit, I asked my father how Mom was doing. He told me that she was coming to the hospital with the Johnsons, but she first had to take care of Jonathen. Aunt Sammy had gone to the grocery store, so Mom had to wait for my aunt to return before leaving my little brother.

I asked my father once again how my mom was feeling.

"She seems to be doing okay, but you know your mom," he said. "She never complains, and that makes it difficult to know exactly how she is feeling."

I tried to relax and not show how concerned I really was, but I just kept watching the clock and listening to my father and Jacob talking. I could not tell you one thing they were saying. My mind was on Bella and how long would it be before I could go see her. I got a magazine and tried to slow my mind down by reading, but nothing worked.

My back had begun to hurt terribly. I didn't want them to know, so I pretended to be doing fine. I guess I wasn't good at pretending, because my father wanted to know if I was okay. He had noticed I was in pain by the expression in my eyes. He suggested that I go to my room and lie down for a while. I thought if I left the area close to Bella, I would be a bad mother. I had to stay close by her. Dad and Jacob finally persuaded me to go to my room. As we were walking out of the waiting room, the phone started ringing. At first, no one moved to answer it. My dad walked over to the phone and said hello, introduced himself, and started talking to someone.

All that I could hear him say was "yes" and "okay." When he hung the receiver up, I just knew he was going to tell us that something had happened with Bella. I was wrong. He told me that I was going to have some visitors. They were in the lobby downstairs and trying to locate my room. Dad had told them where to come and that we would be waiting for them in front of the elevator.

We strolled down to where the elevator was. I was pushed in my wheelchair. We waited a few seconds before the elevator door opened. There stood my mother and several other people. I started to say something to Mom, when out from behind her stepped two familiar faces: Brian's mom and dad. It was sad seeing them; both of them had aged and didn't look as if they were in good health. I had not seen them since Brian's death. Mr. Saylor reached out to shake my father's hand.

Brian's mom came to where I was and leaned down close to me, tears streaming down her face. With a gentle smile and tender voice, she told me she was sorry that she had not been with me when the baby was born, but that she was here now and would help me and my baby get through this crisis.

I embraced her and thanked her for coming. I turned to look at my mother. My mom could tell that I needed her. Her beautiful eyes were watching every move I made. When Brian's mom moved over just a little bit, Mom sidled up next to me. My mother took my hand and, as usual, assured me it was going to be alright. She asked my father to take everyone back to the waiting area so we could visit and be more comfortable. Mom knew how to take charge.

I didn't remember seeing Pastor Johnson and his wife, but Mom told me they were there. They came down to the waiting room to wait for us. I felt so bad that I had not spoken to them, but things were happening so fast that I almost felt like I was losing my mind.

Jacob tried to make everyone comfortable. He led all of us to a group of chairs when we arrived in the room. He was so thoughtful and polite. Mom started asking how Bella was and what the latest doctor's report was. I told her that we hadn't talked to the doctor in about an hour, but that as far as we knew, Bella was holding her own. Everything seemed to be going well. Dad said he would walk down the hall and ask the nurses if there were any changes in our angel.

I observed that Brian's parents were very quiet and didn't join in on the conversation. His mom looked so tired. I wondered if her health was bothering her.

Jacob and my father came back into the room. Jacob had walked to the prenatal unit with my dad. They were not alone: Bella's doctor had tagged along. I was about to say something. Before I could, the doctor introduced himself to everyone.

The doctor turned to where I was sitting and came over to my wheelchair. He knelt down beside. "Beth, your little girl gave us a real scare, but she is holding her own now. The new medicine has just arrived, and we are going to start her on it immediately. Most of my experience has been that it works well on preemie babies."

The doctor wanted me to try and be strong for Bella. She would have a lot of days that she would have to try and breathe on her own. He asked me if I had any questions for him.

The first thing I wanted to know was when I could see Bella again. I wasn't prepared for any other questions, I was too upset. I began to cry almost uncontrollably. I was so scared. Just the mere thought of losing my child was more than I could bear. My mom and others tried to console me. I just wanted to protect my baby, and right now I couldn't help her.

Pastor Johnson asked everyone to gather around me and pray. He said a beautiful, touching prayer. It touched my heart and made me a little more at ease. Pastor Johnson said, "Precious Lord and Savior, we are asking you to help Elizabeth to lean on you. We need you to help heal her, so that she can be strong enough to take care of this precious baby you have given to her. We ask you to visit little Isabella's room and heal her little body. Help her to be able to breathe on her own. Please help the doctor's to know exactly how to help her. We thank you in advance for all of the many blessings we believe you are going to bring to this family. I know that this is all in your hands, and miracles are not too hard for you to perform. We praise Yyou and bless your holy name. We ask all of this in the name of your Son, Jesus." And everyone said, amen."

After Pastor Johnson finished praying, I had started to feel a lot calmer. I was no longer crying. When I raised my head and looked around, I wasn't the only emotional one. Everyone in the room was wiping tears from their eyes. The Lord Jesus had surely been in this waiting area. I decided right then and there that I was going to try my best to keep all of Pastor Johnson's prayer in my heart and mind. I knew that the Bible told us that God would never leave us or forsake us. I knew that God had already seen that my child was in desperate need of him. His Word promises that if we trust and believe him, He would hear our earnest prayers. Little Bella was having a lot of prayers being said for her now.

Before everyone had sat back down, the nurse came into the room and told me that I could go see my baby. Only two of us at a time could be in her room. I immediately looked at my parents. It seemed like everyone wanted Mom to go with me. I turned to Brian's parents. They nodded in agreement that my mother should go in first. I thanked them and told them I would hurry back so they could go see their grandbaby.

Brian's mom smiled at me. "Elizabeth, go to your baby. We will be here when you get back."

Jacob wheeled me down the hall with my mother by my side.

Chapter Twenty-Three

As we were nearing Bella's room, I noticed that my mother was having some difficulty breathing. She sat down in the first chair she came to. I started to say something to her. She put her index finger to her lips, as if to tell me to be quiet, and then pointed to Bella's bed. She mouthed the words "I'm fine" and gave me a quick smile.

I was now at my baby's bedside. Mom came over as soon as she got control of her breathing. My mother was looking at Bella intently, and I was looking at my mom. I could sense that Mom knew I was watching her, but she didn't say a word. Mom whispered to my little princess that she was beautiful and a gift from God to our family.

"The good Lord is helping you, Bella," my mother said softly. "Your mommy is standing here by your bedside waiting to hold you as soon as you get a whole lot better. Your Maw-Maw loves you—I always will." My mother gently touched Bella's little arm, telling my baby how blessed we were to have her in our family. I was so proud to hear those words.

We just stood there for a while and watched Bella sleep. Jacob walked into the room and told us that our visiting time was up. I reluctantly left, but I leaned down and promised my baby that I would see her again real soon.

"I promise you, Isabella Angel. I promise you."

As my mother and I walked down the hallway, I asked Mom how she was feeling. She took me by the hand and told me to quit worrying about her, that she would be alright. I let my fears subside because I believed what my mother had said to me.

When we got back to the family room, Mom sat down and dad got her something cold to drink.

Brian's mom wanted to know how her granddaughter was doing. I told them she was resting peacefully. They were so happy. I heard Jacob tell them that he would take them to the prenatal unit. They left the area, and I could see concern on their faces as they started down the hallway. Dad was pleased that the Saylors were going to see their grandchild for the first time. He said they needed to be alone for a while with Bella, and I agreed with him.

When everyone had gotten the opportunity to see Bella, I told everyone I just had to go see her one more time before going back to bed. The day had been very exhausting, and I did need to rest. In fact, this day had been so strange that I couldn't remember if I had eaten anything. That sure worried me, because I did love my junk food and I was getting hungry. I hoped no one told my doctor that I was cheating and eating things that he told me not to. I smiled to myself and was glad that they couldn't read my mind.

The next couple of days were pretty hectic. My doctor had let me stay a few extra days in the hospital so I could be close to my baby. Bella was doing better, but I knew that I was going to be leaving for home. The doctor was going to release me first thing in the morning. I didn't want to leave, but I had to. I was sure little princess would be fine, but I just had the mommy instinct to stay with her until she was home from the hospital.

Early morning found me not wanting to go home and leave my baby. I had reconciled myself to the fact that I had to go until Bella was released. I only prayed that it would be soon, although the doctor had warned me that she might be in the hospital for a few weeks. It just depended on how well her lungs responded to the new medicine.

The unit nurse came into my room after everyone had their breakfast and morning medicines. She told me that I could go stay with Bella until the doctor signed my dismissal. I could only hope the doctor would be late today.

Jacob went to get my wheelchair. He was going with us to see the baby before I had to go home. We went into her room. Bella looked like an angel. She was sound asleep, and her little face was sort of scrunched. I think she was dreaming, because she would have a little smile come across her face. I had always been told that a baby her age couldn't smile, and if they did, it was just gas pains. I decided I would rather believe that Bella knew we were there and she was smiling at us.

Jacob and I both went over to her crib. He held onto my hand, as well as Bella's warm, tiny hand. She was so small. I wanted to cry, but I knew that I had to be strong for her. I didn't want her to sense that I was upset. The nurse called us on the intercom and said that the doctor had released me. I was supposed to return to my room so the nurse could help me to the dismissal office. Jacob told Bella goodbye, and then he waited by the door for me. He said I needed to be alone with her for a few minutes. I told my darling baby goodbye. I promised her that I would be back to see her every day. I returned to my room, and the attendant was waiting to take me to the front of the hospital, where Jacob would be waiting for me with his car. We left the hospital with heavy hearts and headed home, where I knew my family would be waiting for us.

When we pulled into the driveway, Jonathen ran out to meet us. He had all sorts of questions for me. The main thing that he wanted to know was, "Sissy, can Bell come home?" I would try to explain to him that she was really sick, but that she would be home very soon. He was satisfied with that answer, but he had a ton of other questions for me. He was just a baby himself, and he couldn't understand what was happening with "Bell." I guessed that was my brother's new nickname for his niece.

Mom and Aunt Sammy had been busy preparing for me to come home. My room was completely organized and set up for Bella to come home. They were almost as excited as I was.

While we were getting settled in, the doorbell rang. I was surprised that anyone would be coming to the house on a day like today. It was still very cold out, and the weather wasn't very good. It was still in the thirties with some snow. I heard a lot of people downstairs.

Who could that possibly be? I wondered.

It was the ladies from church. They had decided to bring over a surprise potluck dinner to welcome me home. Everyone was so grateful that the Lord had helped Bella. The ladies wanted to let me know they had been praying for us, and how thankful they were that I was doing well and home from the hospital. They offered to help Mom if she needed anything, but she just laughed and told them that Aunt Sammy had helped her organize the disaster in my old room in preparation for her first grandbaby. I could hear the joy and pride in her voice. I just smiled at her remark about my room.

The family room was filled with a lot of happy women. Each of them had a story to tell about their first baby. All of them had a few pointers for me. I appreciated all of their input because I knew I would be really nervous when Bell did get to come home. I had helped Mom sometimes when Jonathen was born—however, he wasn't my baby, so I wasn't as scared then. I knew Mom knew what she was doing when Jonathen was born. She had a little more experience than I would have with Bella. She learned how to care for Jonathen because she experimented on me. I tried not to laugh as that thought came to me. I didn't want Mom to know what I was thinking.

The days preceding Bella's homecoming were very trying. We all tried to stay busy. Going to the hospital to see her was my main concern. Some days, Dad would take me to see her. If he couldn't go, then I would go by myself. Other times, Jacob would take me when he was off work. When he was working, he would go to the prenatal unit and see Isabella. He would call me to notify me of any changes, or just to let me know she was doing well. Jacob was a big help to all of us.

The day finally arrived. My angel was coming home. The doctors were amazed at how well she was doing. Bella was taken off of the machines completely. She could breathe on her own now. It had only been six weeks since she was born, but it seemed like an eternity to me.

It was snowing and I didn't want my mother to step out in the cold air, so Jacob said he would take me to pick the baby up. I knew in my heart that Jacob wanted to be the one to bring her home. I could sense that he was almost as attached to her as I was. I was happy that he was there for her.

We got to the hospital and took the elevator up to Bella's floor. Jacob took my hand and gently kissed it. He was smiling from ear to ear. He didn't have to say anything.

We both were very aware of the responsibility that lay ahead of me. His smile reassured me that he would be there if I needed or wanted him to be. Of course I wanted him to be there, but I didn't want him to feel obligated. The elevator door opened, and both of us rushed to get off to see Bella. It was hard to tell which one of us was more anxious.

The nurse was waiting for us. She picked Bella up. "Beth, honey, here is your little angel."

She handed her over to me, and I was almost afraid to hold her. She was so tiny and fragile.

I looked into her beautiful little face. "Hi, Angel Baby."

She looked at me, and I honestly think she knew who I was. I promised her right then and there that I would always take care of her and love her. Bella squinted, and I will always believe she knew my voice.

The nurse gathered Bella's things and gave them to Jacob. As she handed them to him, she said, "Okay, Daddy, take your little girl home, and always take good care of her."

Jacob thanked her and said, "I sure will take good care of little Angel."

No one knew that Jacob wasn't the father, and there was no reason to tell them any different.

We got to our car and started to put the baby in her newborn car seat. Jacob and I could not figure it out—we had never had to do this. A young mother was sitting in her car next to ours and saw what we were trying to do.

She got out of her car and asked if we needed help. Both Jacob and I were embarrassed, but we did tell her that we would appreciate her help. The young woman instructed us about the proper way to fasten Bella in her seat. The baby sure didn't look very comfortable. She was so tiny that the car seat almost swallowed her. We thanked the lady for her much-needed help, and we headed home with the little princess angel.

Mom and Dad met us in the driveway just as soon as we got home. Jonathen wasn't with them, and I wondered why. We went into the family room.

"Beth, take a seat and please don't move," Mom said to me as soon as I walked through the door.

What did she mean? I thought that was a pretty harsh remark coming from my mother. Didn't she realize that I am a grown woman now, plus I'm a mother? I thought it was a little crazy, but I did as Mom told me to. It didn't take me very long to understand why she had said that to me.

I heard a lot of commotion coming from the hallway. I tried to strain my ear to see what it was. There was noise coming through the door.

It was my little brother. "Happy surprise to you, Sissy!" he shouted.

Mom and Dad were right behind him. They were holding a beautiful pink quilt. On the front of the quilt were stitched song lyrics: "JESUS LOVES ME THIS I KNOW, FOR THE BIBLE TELLS ME SO. LITTLE ONES TO HIM BELONG, THEY ARE WEAK, BUT HE IS STRONG."

I started to cry. My little brother ran over to me and tried to wipe the tears from my eyes. He just kept telling me not to cry. I told him I was happy as I pulled him to me and hugged him tightly. I looked at my parents and whispered, "I love you."

I surveyed every stitch on the quilt. I asked Mom how she had managed to do this without me knowing about it. She said she worked on it while I was at the hospital. The quilt was absolutely beautiful. I only wish that I had it before I brought Bella home; she would have been an angel wrapped in it. I understood why Mom had waited until I brought the baby home, though.

Jonathen had promised Mom that he would keep the secret and not tell me about what she was making for Bella. He didn't tell anyone, so Mom told him he could give it to Bella as a surprise when my baby came home. He was one happy, little boy. Now that I was a mother, I think I understood what a mother's love really was, and it made me love Jonathen even more.

There was so much excitement with the baby coming into our house, we hadn't unwrapped her for Jonathen to look at her. He was insisting that he hold her. I was very apprehensive at first, but he said he would hold her tight and wouldn't hurt her.

I had to chuckle just a little at his little way of begging me.

I told him to get into the chair, and I would help him hold her. Mom had already warned me that he was waiting to hold her, so she had showed me how to stand behind him and put my arms through his little arms. He would think that he was holding her by himself. We were wrong. He knew I was holding Bella with him.

He looked so sad and said, "Sissy, I won't hurt Bell. I want to play with her."

I realized then that I would have to make sure that someone was with Jonathen most of the time; otherwise, he just might try to get her out of her crib to play. I had a lot of help, so I knew we would manage fine with little brother.

The first couple of weeks after Bella came home were pretty awesome. Every day, someone would come to visit or drop a gift off for her. It seemed that all of our friends really were anxious to hold her. My mother was the most anxious to always be around her, especially when it came to rocking her to sleep. I had heard that rocking a baby to sleep would spoil them, but I didn't care if my mom rocked her. I would just have to deal with it if she ended up spoiled.

This one particular day, I called my brother into the room where Bella was. He came running up to the crib and wanted to get her out. I had him climb up on my bed. He stuck his little arms out to hold her. He had remembered how I had told him to be careful and hold her really tightly. It was so sweet to watch him.

It was like something special happened in my room. Jonathen was trying to talk to Bell. He told her she would be okay and that he would help take care of her so she would get better and be able to play with him. This was priceless to watch a child tell another child not to cry, and that he would take care of her. I only wish that my camera had been in my room at that moment, but I had left it downstairs in the family room.

Bella tried to focus her eyes on Jonathen, as if to say, "Okay. I'm listening to you, and I won't cry while you are holding me."

I know that sounds a little far-fetched, but we really don't know if babies and small children understand baby talk. Maybe they do. I'd like to think that they know more than we give them credit for.

Bella wasn't crying, but I heard sniffling just outside my door. I tiptoed over and quickly opened the door to see who was there. I guess I surprised them. There stood Mom, Dad and Aunt Sammy. They had heard what Jonathen was saying to the baby, and they just couldn't keep from crying. They were in a little huddle, hugging each other. I really did need my camera now. Each of them hugged and kissed Jonathen. He loved all of the attention.

My father just stood there for a few minutes, watching the baby. Then he swept Jonathen up in his arms and asked my little brother if he wanted to go to the workshop with him. My father told Jonathen how proud he was of the way he held Bell and talked to her. My brother was so proud of himself—you could see it in his big blue eyes. Mom told Dad to bundle Jonathen up really well before they went outside. She also gave Dad orders to bundle himself up as well. She smiled as they left the room, because she usually did not give my father any orders. I had to laugh at her.

Aunt Sammy and Mom took turns holding Bella. They were like new moms themselves. We talked for a few minutes before we had to put the baby to bed. Bella had fallen asleep. I was getting really tired myself. When Mom and Auntie left my room, I crawled into bed to take a nap while my baby was asleep.

Bella usually was a good baby and didn't get very fussy, but when she did, I sometimes couldn't get her to quit crying. My mother just had to take her from me, and almost instantly she would quit crying and go to sleep. I almost found myself getting a little jealous over my mom calming her down. Mom sensed that and explained to me that sometimes newborns know if a mom is nervous, and they react the same way. I believed my mother. I knew in my heart that Mom was right, and I didn't need to be jealous if she calmed the baby down.

Chapter Twenty-Four

Bella was a good baby most of the time. As I stated earlier, my mom could calm her down quicker than I could. It was strange, but I appreciated the fact that mom could do more with her than I could. She just had the magic touch, I guess.

One early morning, Bella was really fussy, and no one could get her to stop crying. My mom said that sometimes a baby will get out of their normal sleeping pattern, and that would make them be irritable. Mom said she thought Isabella would be fine, but maybe I should take her to the doctor for a check-up, just to make sure that she was okay.

I made an appointment and took Bella to the doctor. He did a thorough exam and told me that she was fine. He said that sometimes a newborn baby would get out of their usual routine and would be fussy.

How about that? I thought. *My mother told me the same thing that the doctor is saying to me. From now on, I will not be jealous of my mother. If she can do more than I can with her grandbaby, I will welcome her wisdom.*

The next week was going really well, and Bella had gotten back on her regular sleeping schedule. We were all happy for that, because all of us had been losing a lot of sleep, what with Bella's days and nights mixed up. Thank God for answered prayer. I knew that the whole family had been praying for the baby. She had been in control of all our wakening hours. We all needed to get some sleep at night, instead of catnaps when Bella was asleep.

Today was starting out great. I was busy cleaning our room and doing laundry for Bella, when a loud knock sounded on my bedroom door. Before I could answer, my father swung my bedroom door open. I could tell that something wasn't right. His voice was shaky and upset. He told me that I needed to come downstairs with him. I checked to make sure the baby was still asleep and followed my dad. I could see a lot of strange lights across the front windows, and I got scared. I asked my dad what was going on, and he told me that it was Mom. She was sick, and my father had dialed 9-1-1.

I asked Dad what was wrong with my mother, and he told me he thought it was the cancer. Mom was the one who had told my dad to call for the ambulance. She knew that something wasn't right, and she wanted to go to the hospital. For my mom to ask to go to the hospital made me know that this was serious. I told my dad that I would stay here with Jonathen. He reassured me that he would call me as soon as he got to the hospital.

The ambulance workers had already started to put my mom in the back of the ambulance before I had a chance to see her. I stood in the frigid air and watched as they drove away with Mom.

I hurried back into the house to check on Jonathen and Bella. Both of them were sound asleep. I was so worried about my Mom. I had the urge to go into her bedroom and pray. I knelt beside Mom's bed and asked God to please help her.

"This family needs her, and I especially need her now, dear Lord, to help me with my baby," I said to God.

I don't know how long I knelt there and prayed. I finally got off my knees and lay across my mom's bed. I put my hand under her pillow. It made me feel closer to her. I felt something under her pillow. I lifted the pillow and there was my mother's journal. It was open, but I didn't dare read it. I did notice the last entry, however, because the book was opened and I saw what was written there. I guess Mom was writing when she got sick this morning. The only words that were written were: Promise me, no matter what happens to me, promise me that you will learn to love again.

I wanted to think my mom was writing a poem; she had always been good with words. I told myself that I would just ask Mom what it meant. As soon as I had thought those words, I knew I couldn't ask Mom. She would know that I had read her journal, and I didn't want to lose her trust in me. Mom had taught me that a journal was a very private thing. It wasn't for everyone to read, unless you gave them permission to do so. I guess that's why I always kept my journal hidden in my bedroom chest.

The morning was slipping away fast, and I had not heard from my father. I knew Jacob would be getting ready to be at work, so I called him and told him what was happening with my mother. He said he would check on her just as soon as he got to the hospital. He promised he would call me as soon as he knew how she was doing. Jacob had been working a lot of hours and had not been able to visit the baby or me. He told me he was sorry, that he would see us just as soon as he could. Jacob said he would call Pastor Johnson and have the church praying for Mom.

I thanked him and told him I would be waiting to hear from him with good news about my mother.

I didn't hear from my father or Jacob for a couple of hours. I was so scared. The phone rang, and I ran to answer it. It was my father. I could tell by the sound of his voice that this wasn't good news.

I was frantic and pelted my father with questions. "What's the matter with Mom? Is she okay? Are you there, Daddy?"

My father was very quiet. He finally said to me that Mom was coming home.

"What do you mean, coming home? Is she well enough to come home?" I just didn't understand what was going on.

"Elizabeth, would you clean your mom's bedroom and put clean linens on her bed? We will be there in a couple of hours, and then you can talk to your mom. She can explain what's happening. Take care of Jonathen and the baby. Remember that your mother loves you, and so do I."

With that, there was a click. My father had hung up.

I could feel a deep hurt way down in my heart.

I just knew that something horrible was happening to our family. I was just so helpless to do anything except wait and pray. My only consolation was that God did love me, and no matter what happened, he would be close by. Thank God for the principles my mother and father had taught me. I always knew that God was in control of all things. Whatever occurred in our lives, it was in God's plan.

The next few hours seemed like an eternity to me. I tried to stay busy taking care of Bella's needs and keeping Jonathen occupied. I was worried because Jacob hadn't called me, and that was unusual.

It was now two o'clock, and I heard a noise outside. I went to the front door. It was Jacob, coming up the driveway. I did a double take. I didn't see anyone run as fast as Jacob did. He jumped out of his car just as my father pulled along beside him. Jacob had my mother with him. He opened my mom's door and reached inside to help her. I could see that Mom was having trouble standing on her own. My father saw she needed his help, so he came over and just swept her up in his arms. Mom was protesting, but all the time she was smiling and telling Dad to let her down. I could just tell that she did not want him to sit her down—she needed his strength, but she didn't want to acknowledge it in front of me. I knew my mom was trying to be strong for all of us.

I opened the front door, and Dad almost ran past me. He had to get mom out of the cold air.

I just stood there for a few moments, trying to get my thoughts straight. I heard Jacob ask me if I was alright. That was all it took for me to collapse into his arms. I begged Jacob to tell me what he knew about my mother.

"Is she okay? Why did they let her come home? Are you going to answer me?" I said.

Jacob was holding onto me tightly, but I could feel him loosen his grip and sort of pull back from me so he could look me in my face. He started to say something, but Bella started crying right then. I had almost forgotten about her and Jonathen being alone upstairs. I hurried up the steps as fast as my legs would go.

Jacob followed me to the bedroom. There was Jonathen, standing by Bella's bed, trying to keep her from crying. He was so good with her, even if he was still just a baby himself.

I asked Jacob to stay with them until I could go to the kitchen and get her a warm bottle. He said he would. I heard him as I walked out the door talking to the baby. He was telling Bella that he would do anything for my little girl.

I was almost ready to go into the room and hug him, but Jacob had no idea that I was eavesdropping on their conversation.

I had to pass Mom's room. Dad saw me and asked me if I could come there just for a minute.

"Your mom wants to talk to you," he said.

I peeked in their room. Mom was propped up on a couple of pillows. Dad had brushed her hair and helped her get into one of her soft nightgowns. I told them I was going to get the baby a bottle, but that I would be back shortly to join them.

Mom said she would love to feed her grandbaby, and asked me to bring Bella to her. I told her I would, and that I just knew Bella would want her MawMaw to feed her. Mom smiled. I hurried off to the kitchen. I would do anything to make my mother feel better.

I warmed the bottle. While it was heating up, I grabbed a cold glass of milk and cookies for Jonathen. He usually had to eat with his little baby Bell. I gave Jonathen's snack to Jacob, who said he would play with my little brother while I visited with my mother. I picked Bella up and swaddled her in a light blanket. Bottle in hand, I headed for mom's room.

I went over to Mom's bed and handed her Bella. My mom held her snugly and fed her the warm bottle. Bella wasn't going to sleep, so my mother started singing to her. Mom had a beautiful voice. She often sang in church. She was singing one of her favorite songs about heaven. My father and I were captivated by her song. It felt like she was singing it for us. I look back now and realize she was singing for us and trying to comfort us in her own way. We were supposed to be the ones comforting her, but that was my mom—she always thought of others before herself.

Jonathen, Jacob, and Aunt Sammy had slipped into the room. Jonathen had gotten himself a pillow, curled up at the foot of mom's bed, and fallen asleep. Dad carefully picked him up and carried him to his own bed. I guessed my father didn't want Jon to hear whatever Mom wanted to tell me.

Bella had gone to sleep, too. I told Mom I would put her to bed and come back to their room. As I went back to Mom's room, I saw my parents embracing. I didn't want to intrude on them, so I stopped outside their door. I hadn't noticed that one of Jonathen's little screaming fire trucks was by my feet. I stepped on it before I could move it. It started to wail like a real truck, siren and all.

"Beth, is that you?" Dad called.

I was almost embarrassed to go in, but I did. Dad told me to sit down on the bed, beside my mom. They were waiting on Jacob, who had gone downstairs to make a phone call to his boss.

My parents wanted know if both of the kids were asleep, and I told them they were. Jacob knocked and entered my parent's bedroom. He settled into Mom's rocking chair, next to where I was sitting on her bed. I knew that whatever Mom was going to tell me was going to be bad. I could feel it in my heart and soul.

Mom reached over and clasped my hand tightly. She looked at me with love and concern in her eyes.

"Beth, I am dying," she said gently. "That's why I just had to come home and be with my family for just a little while longer. Jesus is going to take me home to live with him."

I remember laying my head on my mother's chest as she wrapped her arms around me. She was trying to comfort me, but all I could say was, "I can't give you up, Mom. I need you, Dad needs you. Jonathen and our little angel need you, too. Jonathen needs his mommy, and Bella needs her MawMaw."

I was sobbing, but Mom didn't try to stop me. She knew that I had to cry and get my hurting heart settled. I looked around the room. Everyone was crying. We just could not lose my mother.

My crying soon turned into anger against the doctors and God. How could the doctors know for sure she was going to die? How could a loving God let my mom die? Did they not understand that I needed her? Could they not see that our lives were centered on my mom, around all of her strength and wisdom? I could not stop my emotions, and all sorts of unanswered questions were tumbling in my mind. My crying was interrupted by the strong voice of reason: my mother. She told me she understood that I was hurt and scared, but that Lord was going to help this family to get through this test and trial. She knew that I wasn't accepting what she was telling me.

"Beth, I'm going to die, but I will always be a part of you. I'm going to see you again. I am just going to be out of your sight. I promise you that we will be together again in heaven someday. I am just going to be living in a new home."

I just could not listen to this anymore. Even though my mother promised me that she would see all of us again in heaven, I was so numb that I just had to get out of the room. I ran outside, into the cold evening air. The temperature was still around thirty degrees. Dad called for me to come back, but I just had to be alone.

I stood there on the porch, shivering from the cold. Jacob had quietly followed me and was just standing there to see if I needed him. The wind had started blowing. I was freezing, but I was also numb. I could see my breath. I was so angry that I didn't even care if I froze to death. Life was so unfair to me, especially this past year.

Oh, God, don't you care? Don't you love me? Can you hear me, God?

I suppose I was asking a lot of crazy questions from God, but I realize now that God wasn't mad at me, and he sure wasn't punishing me. My crying halted when I heard Jacob whisper in my ear.

"Elizabeth, honey, it is going to be alright. I'm here with you. I promised you that I wouldn't leave your side, and I meant that."

I wanted to answer him, but knew I would get hysterical again if I did. Sometimes I had a hard time controlling my emotions. It had always been a problem for me. All of my life, I had been a very vocal, outspoken person. When I would get upset, I could not restrain my tears.

Jacob persuaded me to come back into the house. I agreed to go back to where the family was.

As we entered the family room, I heard loud sobbing coming from another room. I hurried to see where it was coming from, and to see who it was. There was my dad, leaning on my mom's rocking chair, crying uncontrollably. I walked over to him and put my arm around his trembling shoulders. My father put both of his arms around me, and we just clung to one other. Through his tears, he tried to tell me how much he loved my mom, and he knew that he would soon have to let her go. I felt so helpless. I wanted to comfort him and tell him things were going to be okay, but I knew that I was going to lose my mother. God was in control, and he was the only one who could keep my mom from dying. We just needed his strength to face the days ahead. I knew I had to be strong for my father and my little brother. Jonathen couldn't understand what was happening to our family. I had to be the one to be there for him, because my dad was too distraught to be strong.

I realized the next few days and weeks were going to be very difficult for all of us. I was so glad that Aunt Sammy was there with us. She had been such a great help with Jonathen and little Isabella. My mother required a lot of special care, and my aunt knew how to care for her better than I did. Aunt Sammy had helped take care of her husband and my grandparents when they were sick and needed special care.

My father wanted me and Aunt Sam to make Mom's room as cheerful as we could. We put mom's bed close to the window, so she could watch the little birds each morning as they came to sit on her windowsill.

One morning, I heard her talking to someone. I quietly stood outside her door to listen. She was talking to the small bluebird that I had often seen on my bedroom windowsill. Was this a sign from God? I don't know, but I did know that the little creature had been a joy to me at times, and now he was singing for my mother. I knew she was happy now. Even though she was in pain, she had a slight smile on her face.

Chapter Twenty-Five

Time has a way of helping to lighten the cares of this old world. Each day, as I watched my mother's condition grew worse, I tried to accept what was happening to her. Some days, I would sit and watch her sleep. On several occasions when I thought she was asleep, she was just talking to the Lord silently. That's what she told me when I would ask her if she was asleep. Her faith and courage seemed to be even stronger now than it had in the past.

I recall one evening, my mother wanted to talk to me alone. I propped her up on her pillows. Her breathing was becoming more difficult. I perched on the edge of Mom's bed. She took my hand into her frail one, and began talking to me. She was very weak, and I had to listen closely to hear what she was saying.

Between very shallow breaths, she promised me that she would always be with me. She asked me to promise her that I would continue to attend church and help my dad teach Jonathen about God. I swore that I would do my very best to care for Jonathen and Isabella.

My precious mother looked at me with all the love she could. Tearfully, she spoke.

"Elizabeth, I want you to promise me that you will let your heart love again. I know you're afraid to do that, but the Lord will help you to open your heart, so that you can be happy and content once again. I know that Jacob loves you. I can see it in his eyes when he looks at you. Please don't be stubborn and let true love pass you by."

With tearstained cheeks, she asked me again to make her that promise. I told Mom that love hurts too much, and she replied that true love is worth the pain. I hugged my mother and promised her that I would do my best to let my heart love again. I wanted to have the kind of love that my parents had demonstrated to me all of my life. Although I promised my mom what she wanted to hear, I wasn't sure if I was capable of keeping my promises.

The next few days were very painful for the entire family. Mom was slowly fading away. She had talked to my aunt. I'm not sure what they talked about, but I know it was something good.

Jonathen wanted to lay in bed with Mom, but sometimes it was very difficult to let him. My mother's pain had gotten a lot worse. If she cried, Jonathen would cry and tell her it was going to be alright. His little voice would quiver, and he would sing, "Jesus loves mommy, this I know, for the Bible tells me so." Mom would try to hold him, but she was just too weak.

The night Mom passed away will always be in my memory. Dad cradled his wife in his arms, expressing how much he loved her and that he would keep his promise he had made to her. Jacob and his mother had come to be with us. Pastor Johnson was with us also. We all gathered around her bed. Mrs. Turner sang my mother's favorite hymn, and we all joined hands and prayed. I watched my mother look up to heaven and smile. She took a deep breath, closed her eyes, and went to sleep.

There was a great peace in the room, despite that we all were crying. I let go of my mother's hand. I kissed her on the cheek and left the room so my father could say goodbye to her in private.

My dad came into the family room, his eyes swollen and red. He was trying to be strong, but it was very difficult for him to let Mom go. My aunt also went into Mom's room. I could hear her crying and telling her sister that she would do her best to see that Jonathen was taken care of.

She promised Mom that she was going to be going back to church and get things settled with God.

I heard her tell Mom, "James will be alright, Hannah. He will keep his promise to you and love again someday. We all promise that we will be together in heaven once again. Goodbye, my sweet sister. Go rest now, and please tell Mom and Dad hello for me. Don't forget to tell Henry that I still love him, and I will see him again also."

Aunt Sammy re-joined us with tears flowing down her cheeks. Pastor Johnson talked with us for some time. It was a great comfort just to hear him say that Mom was at perfect peace now and was in no more pain. Jacob had come to the window beside me, where I was staring out at the light snow that had begun to fall. He was such a strong man.

The next several days were going to be rough for us. Dad had to make arrangements for the funeral, and he wanted Jacob and me to help him. We knew what Mom wanted, so that wasn't very hard to decide. Mom had already told Dad what to do. He just needed us to lean on.

The next morning, we went to the funeral home to select a coffin for Mom. Dad chose a beautiful white and pink one for her. Pink was a good color for my mother. Mom was to be buried in the same cemetery, where her parents were buried.

After all of the arrangements were made, Dad and I went home to be close to Jonathen. He was very confused, and didn't want to eat or play with his toys. I heard him talking to Bell and telling her that his mommy was going to live in another place called heaven. It was sad to listen to him, but it was also comforting to hear him talk to his niece like a little man. Children are wiser than adults sometimes.

The day of Mom's funeral had arrived too quickly, but we all knew that we had to be strong for my mom's memory. We arrived at our church, and it was so crowded. I didn't realize that my mother knew so many people. The service was very moving. Jacob opened with prayer, and Pastor Johnson did the sermon. Jacob's mom did the special singing. It was beautiful when she sang mom's favorite song, "How Great Thou Art."

I don't think there was a dry eye in the church. They weren't crying for my mother, they were rejoicing, knowing that Mom was at rest and had met the great God who she loved and talked about every day of her life. I was glad my father was doing a lot better, just hearing Mom's friends talk about how she had influenced their lives. Several women from the ladies' group had wanted to speak at her funeral, and my dad said it would be good if they did. It was wonderful to know how my mother had helped so many people. I wasn't aware that she had done so much for her friends and her church. I guess I was just too involved with my own life, especially since I had graduated and left home. I was glad to be home again, where I know now that I had always belonged. I know that Mom was thrilled when I came home, even though I had a lot of hard times ahead of me. Mom said she would help me, and she did, right up until she took her last breath.

My thoughts dissolved when I heard the funeral director say, "This concludes the service."

Everyone made their way to their cars for the drive to the final resting place for Mom.

Chapter Twenty-Six

The next months found all of us making new adjustments in our lives. Jonathen was beginning to talk about how, when he grew up, he was going to go to school. He had learned his ABCs, and he could now count to twenty without missing a number. Bella had started smiling a lot and cooing when we would play with her. She was now healthy and had gotten over the problem she initially had with her lungs. She was such a joy to all of the family.

Jacob and I had gotten a lot closer. He loved Isabella and played with her every time he came to my home. We would talk a lot about Mom. I asked Jacob one day if he thought Mom would be able to know what was happening with the family. He couldn't answer that question, but he did say that if my mother was aware of what was going on with the family, she would be happy that all of us were coping with her passing. I was so glad to hear Jacob say this. I knew that no one knew for sure what went on in heaven, but there was no doubt in my mind that Mom was happy and at rest in heaven with Jesus.

I asked Jacob if he would take me to the cemetery. It had been a while since I'd visited my mom's grave. He said he would pick me up in the morning around eleven o'clock. My dad and aunt agreed to watch Jonathen and Isabella while I was gone.

Jacob arrived at precisely eleven the next morning. His car wouldn't start, so he had to drive his truck. I ran outside to meet him so he wouldn't have to get out of the truck. The cemetery wasn't too far from home. I told Dad I wouldn't be gone very long. Bella was still asleep. I knew Dad could handle her if she woke up before I got home.

The winter weather had left the road leading up to the entrance of the cemetery in terrible shape. Jacob had to keep dodging huge potholes. He hit one of them, and his glove compartment popped open. All of his papers flew out and went under my feet. I leaned down to pick them up. I noticed a small square package, wrapped in silver paper. I handed it to Jacob and inquired what it was.

Jacob pulled over to the side of the road, parked his truck, and turned to look at me. He explained to me that he had been waiting for the right time to talk and give the box to me.

"I guess the Lord is trying to tell me this is the right time, Beth. The box is for you. Go ahead, open it," he said, his big blue eyes scanning my every move.

I tore the silver paper off. There was a tiny black velvet box. I cautiously lifted the lid, and my eyes were fixated on the most beautiful diamond ring I had ever seen. I was stunned.

"I love you, Beth. Will you marry me?"

For a moment, I was mute. My heart pounded. I just knew that something special was happening between us. Jacob leaned over, took me in his arms, and told me again that he loved me. He kissed me and said he wanted me to be his wife and how much he loved my baby.

"I have loved you from the very first time I saw you. Please, Beth, tell me you will marry me," he murmured.

"Yes!" I exclaimed. "Yes, yes, Jacob! I love you, too, and I will marry you."

He pulled me closer to him. He stroked my hair and kissed me tenderly.

Jacob took the ring from the box and slid the ring on my finger. The sun was shining so bright on the diamond that it almost glowed. It was beautiful. I just stared at it. I couldn't think of anything to say, at that moment. Jacob kissed me again, and I returned his kiss. It seemed as if we were the only two people on earth. I had a feeling that if my mother could see what was happening here, she would be ecstatic. She loved Jacob.

Jacob and I walked hand-in-hand to my mom's grave. Her marker had a small vase on it, and I knelt down to remove the old flowers from it. I started to place my flowers in the vase, but I couldn't make the flowers stand up. There was something in the vase that was keeping the flowers from staying straight. I removed them and looked to see what was in the vase. I picked up a small folded piece of paper. I opened it and read these words that were written there.

I will love you forever, my love, the note read. It was signed by my father.

I could feel the tears on my cheeks. I gave the note to Jacob, and he placed it back in the vase after looking it over. He arranged the bouquet so it would stand up straight. We agreed that we would keep this as our secret, and not tell my dad we had read his note. I vowed to Jacob that I would love him just like my mom had loved my father. He made the same promise to me.

I couldn't wait to go home and tell Dad the news. I wanted to tell him I had accepted Jacob's proposal. I knew he would be happy. My father and Jacob had a great relationship.

Jacob and I had stayed a little longer at the cemetery than intended. The days were now quite short, so by the time we got home, the sun was fading behind the evening clouds. It was a beautiful sight.

We pulled into the driveway, and I could see my father standing on the front porch. He was looking into the heavens, as if he was seeing something there. The blazing colors of spring had settled over our house. It looked so peaceful. I called out to dad and asked him what he was doing. When we came to where he was standing, he told me that he was thinking about my mom.

"You know, Beth," he said, "it was on a day like today that I asked your mom to marry me."

I felt a cold chill go through my body. Jacob looked at me, and I guess we both were wondering if dad already knew.

I opened my mouth to inform my father that I had something to tell him, when Jonathen came running around the side of the house. He had a small yellow flower in his hand.

"Where did you get that, Jonathen?" I said.

"It was from Mommy's garden," Jonathen said. "It's for you, Sissy."

I stooped down, gave him a hug, and went up the porch stairs, where Dad was still watching the sky.

"Beth, what was it you were going to tell me?" my father inquired.

I told my dad about Jacob's proposal. He didn't seem a bit surprised. He told me that he already knew how much we loved each other, and that my mother knew it long before he did.

Mom seemed to know everything. God had blessed her with that knowledge.

Jacob thanked my father for his blessing. I kissed Jacob goodnight and told him to call me in the morning. He said he would call me early. He shook hands with my dad and left for home. We waved at him as he left the driveway. I was so happy that I had almost forgotten to go see Bella and tell Aunt Sammy the good news. I knew she would approve of our engagement. Jacob had stolen her heart, too.

I hugged my father again and told him goodnight. I helped him get Jonathen off to bed. I went into my bedroom, where my angel baby was already asleep. I got into my PJs and kissed Bella on her little pudgy cheek. I was still so excited, I could hardly think rationally.

I knelt down beside my bed and thanked God for all the good and bad times that he had brought me through this past year. I told him how much I loved Jacob. I thanked him for my angel baby, Isabella. I even asked him to tell my mother that I loved her, and to let her know how happy I was. My heart was so content that I had no problem falling asleep.

Sometime in the night, I had the same reoccurring dream. It was the same one that I had several times before. I saw myself crossing the same bridge, and I heard the same voice. The closer I got to the voice, the clearer the face of someone became. The person kept telling me to keep going. I didn't see the face as clearly as I wanted to, but I could see the side view of their body. There were two people standing beside me. The one was in a white flowing robe with pure white hair. The person did not speak to me, but I felt a sense of love and peace coming from him. I looked ahead to the voice that was calling to me. The woman's face finally became clear.

Standing in the distance was my beautiful mother. She had her arms open wide for me. There was another being next to her, who smiled at me. That's when I recognized her. It was Bella's angel, who had visited me in the hospital. I tried to reach out and touch them, but I couldn't get close enough. They both just seem to fade away out of my sight.

I woke up. The sun was beginning to rise, and I knew that the Lord had truly visited me that night. He was letting me know that he was still with me and would never leave me. No matter what happened in my life, I just had to keep going and trust him. My mother had told me this same thing before she died. Mom had promised me that if I would trust God, he would keep his promises to me. The Lord said in the Bible that he would never leave nor forsake me. I knew that his promises are real and true.

I got out of bed and walked over to Bella's crib. She was smiling up at me. I almost felt like she knew that I once again had a special visitor in the night. I picked her up and held her close to me. I told her how blessed she was and how much I loved her. She laid her curly head on my shoulder, as if to say, "I know, Mommy."

My thoughts were cut short when my little brother came running into the bedroom. He was hungry, and he wanted to play with Bell. I took him by the hand, and the three of us went downstairs to start another day. What would it have in store for us?

The warm spring air was beginning to get a lot warmer, and I wondered where spring had vanished to. It was almost summertime, and I had a lot of plans to make. Jacob and I had decided to have our wedding the following spring. We had so much to do to prepare for it, that we need some time to get ready. We wanted to save some money so we could get our own place.

Dad would need me to help with Jonathen, at least a little while longer. Jonathen was adjusting fairly well without Mom, but some days he would get irritated and cry for her. I was hoping that he would get a lot better as soon as he started kindergarten. He would be starting school the same year I get married. Things seemed to going in our favor as we made our plans for the future.

Mom had been gone for almost a year now. My father had not done anything with her personal possessions. He had asked me if I would take care of them. I had told him that I would sort through all of her things and dispose of them properly. I was not all too comfortable with this, but I knew that it had to be done before I left my father's home.

The day I decided to clean my mom's room and sort through her belongings was a hard day for me. I asked Dad to take Jonathen with him to the workshop. Aunt Sammy said she would take care of Isabella for me. I just needed to be alone with my mother's things.

I went to my parents' bedroom and closed the door. I actually held a conversation with Mom in my mind. Sometimes I would even ask her what I should do with a particular item. I guess it just made me feel better if I talked to her and asked her opinion. I know she didn't hear me, but I pretended she did.

I sorted her clothes in separate piles. Some of them I was going to give to charity, but most of them I would take to our church. We had several ladies that could wear her clothes, and I wanted someone who needed them to have them. I spent almost a day going through her things. The last thing I had to do was clean out her dresser drawer, which contained most of my mother's prized possessions. I could recall as a child, I would sneak into her room and play with her jewelry. She caught me on several occasions. She never got mad at me, but she did explain to me that I shouldn't bother other people's belongings. It was a good lesson that I never forgot.

I took one of the drawers out of the dresser and started to sort things out. I tried to keep things organized so that, with my father's help, I could divide her things the way that I wanted to.

Lying in the bottom of the drawer was my mother's journal. I hesitated to open it, when I noticed a piece of paper sticking out from one of the pages. It had my name written on it. I pulled the paper out. "Beth, read this after I am gone from you," the front page read.

What could this be? I wondered.

I hurriedly opened it. I was crying so hard that the words were a blur. My mother had left me something that I would always have.

I regained my composure and started reading what my mother had written for me.

Beth, I know you are still amazed after the angel visited you in the hospital, when Bella was born. I was curious to know what the angel's name meant after you told me her name was Isabella. I got out my Bible and read a lot of Scriptures, and I also went to the library and got a Hebrew dictionary. I found out what Isabella meant in the Jewish language. I was so excited. I wanted to tell you, but I just felt like I should leave you this information so you would have it to keep after I am gone away to heaven. The name Isabella means "God's promise." Isabella is also another form of the name Elizabeth. In the Bible, Isabella means "God's Oath." Can you believe that the Good Lord knew from the beginning that I would name you Elizabeth? Or how he would send a special angel named Isabella to visit you, and then you would name our little angel Isabella? How wonderful is that, my dear Beth? God has sent you an angel to take care of. He has promised that he would be with you both. When you read this, please know that I was happy when you told me that you were expecting. I didn't want it to be through rape, but I do thank God for you and our little Bella. I know God has a plan for your life. Please be wise in any decision that you make. I want you to be happy, and I don't want to influence your decisions concerning your future, but please pray about your future with Jacob. I loved Jacob, and I know he loves you. I must go now. It is getting late, and I am tired. I love you, Beth, and I promise you once again that in my spirit, I will always be near you. Help your dad with Jonathen. I pray that your father can someday find real happiness again, just like we had together. Love, Mom.

How could this be? My mother knew all along what I was going to name my baby. I remembered now that the same angel who visited me had also made a visit to her. I clutched the note to my chest and knew that I must treasure it, so that someday I could give it to my daughter. I felt like I had found a hidden treasure. I guess I really had found one.

I finished going through my mom's things and went downstairs to join my aunt and Bella. Bella was starting to grow a lot, and she loved to play with Aunt Sammy. They were crawling around in the floor when I came into the family room. My aunt looked at me real strange. Could she detect something magical had happened to me, or had my mother told her about the note and what it contained? I didn't tell Aunt Sam about my experience in Mom's bedroom, but I knew that someday I would show her the note. I got down on the floor with them and started making funny noises for Bella. She had learned to laugh out loud, and I loved to hear her squeaky little voice, as she giggled and played with me.

Jonathen ran into the room and jumped up and down, trying to hog all of my attention. He had been the baby a long time, and he still wanted all of us to play with him first. I pulled him down beside me and started to tickle his belly. He laughed and tried to tickle me. We had so much fun that day. I felt like I was in seventh heaven, if there is such a thing.

The phone rang, so I had to quit playing and go answer it. It was Jacob. He wanted to come over, and I told him that was fine. He would be here in about an hour, so I had to hurry and do my hair and get dressed. I couldn't wait to see him. I was so sure that I would just have to show him my "treasure note" from my mother.

When Jacob arrived, both of the babies had fallen asleep, so we had some time by ourselves. I let Jacob read the note, and he did enjoy the part where mom said she loved him. We talked about different things she had said, and somehow the conversation turned to the statement she had made about my father finding real happiness again. Jacob agreed with Mom, and he also told me that he was pretty sure that one of the ladies from church was interested in my dad. I was surprised because I hadn't seen them talking or anything, but Jacob had. I knew the woman, and I knew she was a good person. Her husband had been dead for about five years now. Could this be something in God's plans for my father? Only time and God knew that, and I was going to stay out of dad's business. I knew he was a wise man and would make right decisions for himself and Jonathen.

Everyone's future seemed to be getting a little brighter. Aunt Sammy had decided to stay here in Georgia. She had landed a great job at the local newspaper office. She was going to find her own place and move out of my father's house very soon.

Jacob and I were busy still making plans for our future together. We both knew that we were going to be happy and that God had put us together. God's promises are true and faithful, and we are looking ahead to see what the future holds for us.

Whatever it is, we will face it together with our little angel Bella, depending on the Lord for his divine guidance. The next chapter in our lives is just around the corner. I am anxious to see what lies there, as Jacob, Bella, and I go hand-in-hand into our own little world.

About the Author

Jann, is from a small town, just east of Cincinnati, Ohio. Jann has a southern heritage and her roots are also grounded in a strong Christian faith.

She has six siblings, three brothers and three sisters. The concept of this story came to her in a dream, inspired by the spirit of GOD.

This book tells the story that is sure to inspire its readers.

Jann is married and is involved in her local church, where her husband is the pastor. They have five children and one grandchild.

Jann has overcome many trials in her life. She was born with cystic fibrosis and was confined several times in the hospital. Her parents were told she would not live to go home. A miracle happened at the age of three and Jann was sent home healed of cystic fibrosis.

Jann accepted Christ in her early childhood. She hopes to inspire others with her story.

CPSIA information can be obtained
at www.ICGtesting.com
Printed in the USA
BVHW071322090919
557922BV00002B/107/P

9 781635 258820